THE MAN

WHO

COULDN'T

MISS

Also by David Handler

FEATURING STEWART HOAG

The Man Who Died Laughing
The Man Who Lived by Night
The Man Who Would Be F. Scott Fitzgerald
The Woman Who Fell from Grace
The Boy Who Never Grew Up
The Man Who Cancelled Himself
The Girl Who Ran Off with Daddy
The Man Who Loved Women to Death
The Girl with Kaleidoscope Eyes

FEATURING BERGER & MITRY

The Lavender Lane Lothario
The Coal Black Asphalt Tomb
The Snow White Christmas Cookie
The Blood Red Indian Summer
The Shimmering Blond Sister
The Sour Cherry Surprise
The Sweet Golden Parachute
The Burnt Orange Sunrise
The Bright Silver Star
The Hot Pink Farmhouse
The Cold Blue Blood

FEATURING BENJI GOLDEN

Phantom Angel • *Runaway Man*

FEATURING HUNT LIEBLING

Click to Play

FEATURING DANNY LEVINE

Kiddo • *Boss*

THE MAN

WHO

COULDN'T

MISS

A STEWART HOAG MYSTERY

DAVID HANDLER

wm

WILLIAM MORROW
An Imprint of HarperCollins*Publishers*

THE MAN WHO COULDN'T MISS. Copyright © 2018 by David Handler. All rights reserved. Printed in the United States of America. No part of this book may be used or reproduced in any manner whatsoever without written permission except in the case of brief quotations embodied in critical articles and reviews. For information, address HarperCollins Publishers, 195 Broadway, New York, NY 10007.

HarperCollins books may be purchased for educational, business, or sales promotional use. For information, please email the Special Markets Department at SPsales@harpercollins.com.

FIRST EDITION

Designed by Diahann Sturge

Library of Congress Cataloging-in-Publication Data

Names: Handler, David, 1952– author.
Title: The man who couldn't miss : a Stewart Hoag mystery / David Handler.
Description: First edition. | New York, NY : William Morrow Paperbacks, 2018. | Series: Stewart Hoag mysteries ; 10
Identifiers: LCCN 2018015440| ISBN 9780062412850 (trade paper) | ISBN 9780062412874 (ebook)
Subjects: LCSH: Hoag, Stewart (Fictitious character)—Fiction. | Ghostwriters—Fiction. | GSAFD: Mystery fiction.
Classification: LCC PS3558.A4637 M292 2018 | DDC 813/.54—dc23
LC record available at https://lccn.loc.gov/2018015440

ISBN 978-0-06-241285-0 (paperback)
ISBN 978-0-06-285114-7 (library edition hardcover)

18 19 20 21 22 RS/LSC 10 9 8 7 6 5 4 3 2 1

For Gunga Dan Mallory, who gave me an Act Three

Chapter One

His voice on the phone was booming and authoritative, especially for five thirty in the morning. "I'm trying to reach a Mr. Stewart Hoag."

"And you have."

"Sir, this is Sergeant Frank Tedone of the State Police's Organized Crime Investigative Task Force. I'm sorry to bother you at such an early hour."

"Not a problem. I was already up." I was up early every morning during that summer of 1993. Merilee's rooster, Old Saxophone Joe, started crowing well before five. And I'd finally, joyously found my voice again after the somewhat awkward decade-long crash landing since the *New York Times Sunday Book Review* had proclaimed me the "first major new literary voice of the 1980s." I was writing like an excited kid again, morning, noon and night. When the phone rang I'd already been pounding away for an hour on my 1958 solid steel Olympia portable out in the spartan guest cottage on my ex-wife's eighteen-acre farm in Lyme, Connecticut. My fingers could barely keep up with the words that were flying from my head as Lulu, my basset hound, lay under the writing table with her head on my foot, snoring like a lumberjack. Her sinus allergies have a tendency to act up when she spends time in the country.

Actually, Lulu wasn't super thrilled about life on Merilee's farm. She was afraid of the night creatures—coyotes, fishers, bobcats, gray foxes, raccoons and barn owls. She was afraid of the chickens out in their wire coop that was attached to the barn. She was afraid of the ducks in the duck pond. She was afraid of the duck pond itself. Can't swim. Only dog I've ever met who can't. Just sinks to the bottom *glug-glug-glug*. Frankly, Lulu would have been a lot happier scarfing up pickled herring in the air-conditioned lobby of the Algonquin Hotel. But wherever I go, Lulu goes. We're a team, like Flo & Eddie.

It may interest you New England architectural history buffs to know that Merilee's guest cottage had originally served as a private chapel back when a prosperous shipping magnate named Josiah Whitcomb built the nine-room farmhouse back in 1736. It may also interest you to know that I would much rather have been sleeping inside of that nine-room farmhouse with Merilee instead of sharing the former chapel's iron bed every night with Lulu and her snoring. But in the immortal words of Michael Jagger, you can't always get what you want. Besides, summering anywhere on the farm beat the hell out of sweating away in my steamy fifth-floor walk-up on West Ninety-Third Street.

"How may I help you, Sergeant?"

"Mr. Hoag, your name has come up in connection with a criminal investigation."

"*My* name? How so?"

"Are you acquainted with a Robert Romero? Robert John Romero?"

I searched my memory bank. My fallback second career as America's preeminent ghostwriter of celebrity memoirs had brought me into contact with numerous megastars and their hangers-on, quite a few of them murderers. But none named Romero. Robert John Romero. "Don't believe so, why?"

"He listed you as a personal reference on a job application he filled out last month at B & B Building Supply in East Fairburn. The address he put down for you is on Joshua Town Road in Lyme. Is that correct?"

"It is. Actually, it's my ex-wife's house."

"That would be Miss Nash?"

"Yes, it would. And yet you say he listed *me*?"

"That's correct. Were you ever contacted by the employer?"

"No, I wasn't. He gave them this phone number?"

"He did. Is there any significance to that?"

I didn't tell him that the line he'd reached me on was Merilee's unlisted business line. That there was absolutely no way someone I'd never heard of would have it. My many scrapes with the law had taught me not to volunteer anything. "Why are you looking for this guy?"

"B & B hired him as a favor to a mutual friend. Make that *former* mutual friend. Last week he repaid the favor by taking off with a truckload of custom Marvin windows worth more than fifty grand and never coming back. Romero has ties to organized crime in his background. That's why we've been assigned the case. We're looking for him hard. If anything comes to you, anything at all, please call me, okay?"

I assured the sergeant I would, jotted down his number and I went back to my writing, savoring the fresh morning air that was streaming in the windows and screen door. I'd always wanted to be a writer in residence on a historic farm in Connecticut—especially in Lyme, the bucolic Yankee Eden situated at the mouth of the Connecticut River on Long Island Sound, halfway between New York City and Boston. Lyme had a town hall, a Congregational church, a general store, a boatyard on Hamburg Cove and not much else, unless you count the cows and the chickens. Privacy was prized above all. Celebrities like Merilee Nash were left alone. Out here, she was just plain Merilee. And her place was plenty private. Her nearest neighbor on Joshua Town Road, Mr. MacGowan, lived nearly a mile away. In addition to the main house and guest cottage she also had a three-story carriage barn, apple and pear orchards, vegetable garden, and open pasturage that tumbled down to Whalebone Cove, where six acres of freshwater tidal marsh were home to one of the state's last remaining stands of wild rice, not to mention several rare marsh plants. Also great blue herons, long-billed marsh wrens, ospreys and the occasional bald eagle.

For me, the farm had never qualified as home. Merilee bought it after we divorced, when the judge awarded her our eight-room apartment on Central Park West and our red 1958 Jaguar XK150. I ended up with Lulu, my crappy old fifth-floor walk-up on West Ninety-Third Street and my second, decidedly less dignified career as a pen for hire. But Merilee, who is nothing but classy, was so thrilled that I was working on a novel again that she'd insisted I come stay with her. She was still rooting for me and, I hoped, rooting for us to get back together. I know I was.

Not that I'd seen very much of her for the past couple of weeks. She was busy rehearsing around the clock at the Sherbourne Playhouse, the tiny, dilapidated summer theater in nearby Sherbourne, where Merilee was directing and starring in a special one-night-only $1,000-per-seat benefit performance of Noël Coward's *Private Lives*. Her dream was to raise the $350,000 that was needed to rescue the legendary playhouse where the likes of Katharine Hepburn, Tallulah Bankhead, Marlon Brando, Montgomery Clift and Merilee herself had made their professional debuts. She was staging Coward's giddy four-character romantic farce with three equally famous classmates of hers from the Yale School of Drama, all of them fellow Oscar winners—Greg Farber, America's top hunk of a leading man, Dini Hawes, the slender strawberry blonde with the lilting North Carolina accent who was Greg's real-life wife, and Marty Miller, the chubby, balding human volcano who'd just won a Tony Award for his portrayal of Willy Loman in last season's brilliant Broadway revival of Arthur Miller's *Death of a Salesman*. Marty and Dini were playing the delicious lead roles of Elyot and Amanda that Coward had written for himself and Gertrude Lawrence. Merilee and Greg were playing Sybil and Victor. The tiny role of Louise, the frumpy maid, had been given to a gifted young Yale graduate named Sabrina Meyer.

All of the performers were donating their time and talent to try to save the fabled natural-shingled 1911 playhouse, which had originally been a community center back when Sherbourne was a brass mill town known for being the largest maker of ornate casket handles in America. These days, the mill was an abandoned red brick riverfront ruin and the playhouse was sliding off of its rotting foundation sills. It also needed a new roof, siding, plumbing, wiring and septic system. Sherbourne's building inspector intended to condemn the treasured little theater if Merilee and her friends couldn't come up with the bucks.

Merilee was throwing herself body and soul into trying. *Private Lives* marked her directorial debut. Directing had been a goal of hers for years and she was extremely excited. Also extremely on edge because a star-studded A-list theater crowd would be making the trip out from New York tomorrow night for the show, everyone from Meryl Streep to Elia Kazan. Even the great Kate Hepburn herself, who lived in a waterfront estate in the nearby Fenwick section of Old Saybrook, had plopped down $1,000 to attend.

The gala performance, which had been garnering huge media coverage, ranked as one of the summer's major cultural events—right up there alongside of the rollout of *Jurassic Park*, Steven Spielberg's $150 million computer-enhanced action adventure about a dinosaur theme park gone amok. The managing director of the Sherbourne Playhouse, Mimi Whitfield, was doing a great job of publicizing the hell out of it. If her name sounds familiar to you that's because Mimi was a *Sports Illustrated* Swimsuit Issue cover model back in the '70s. I think she came after Cheryl Tiegs and before Christie Brinkley. When her supermodel days were over, Mimi married and divorced a toad-faced commercial real estate baron. These days she was a forty-something Park Avenue socialite who summered near Sherbourne in the exclusive Point O'Woods beach colony and ran the playhouse.

Since Merilee was so busy with rehearsals, I had the farm to myself most of the time and could make as much noise as I wanted. Music is very important to me when I write. It helps me find what I'm searching for. I'd brought my turntable, speakers and a precious collection of vintage vinyl out to Lyme with me from the city—Patti Smith, Blondie, the Velvet Underground with Nico. But it turned out that absolutely nothing captured what I was trying to get down on paper like the Ramones' album *Rocket to Russia*, the louder the better. There was something about the opening chords of "Rockaway Beach" that took me right back to where I wanted to be, which was in the middle of my first wild, crazy love affair when I was a young, would-be writer in New York. *My* New York—the gritty, grimy, crime-ridden, graffiti- and garbage-strewn New York of the '70s. The New York of the Mudd Club, Max's, CBGB and the Chelsea Hotel, where the first great love of my life and I were having sex in her third-floor room on that historic night of October 12, 1978. I was there. I heard the cops and the EMT crew arrive. Heard the crazy commotion coming from room 100, where Sid Vicious, the spiky-haired bass player of the Sex Pistols, had plunged a seven-inch hunting knife into the stomach of his girlfriend Nancy Spungen. Allegedly, I should say. Sid was never convicted of her murder. He died of a drug overdose before he came to trial.

Every morning now I was up well before dawn writing about those wild days and nights. Every morning I was growing more and more convinced that the novel I was producing, *The Sweet Season of Madness*, was turning into something truly special. I'll freely admit it to you it was no *The Bridges of Madison County*, which was the publishing world's idea of a genuine blockbuster that summer. But it was raw and real and I hadn't written anything that felt this good in a long, long time. All of which is my way of saying that when Sergeant Frank Tedone of the Connecticut State Police's Organized Crime Task Force called me at five thirty on that particular summer morning, life was pretty damned sweet.

Which should have been my first clue that something was about to go sour.

The phone rang again. The unlisted business line again. Not ten minutes had passed since Sergeant Tedone had called. I assumed he was calling back to tell me it had all been some kind of crazy misunderstanding.

"That you, Hoagy?" The voice was hoarse and unfamiliar.

"And you are . . . ?"

"Name's Romero, bro."

"Do I know you?"

His harsh laugh quickly morphed into a wet cough. "Let's say I know you, okay, bro?"

"Not okay. What is it you want?"

"Not much. Some money is all."

"Didn't you just make off with a truckload of windows?"

"I already owed that money to somebody who was about to break my legs." He sounded as if he were calling from a highway rest stop. I could hear trucks lurching into gear, cars screaming past. "I need to get far away fast. Mexico, I'm figuring. Things are getting a little too hot around here. Twenty-five thou ought to do. But I need it tonight. It's gotta be tonight. I'll call you later with the where and the when. And no games, bro. No cops. Not if you value that happy home of yours. You do this for me and I'll be out of your hair forever."

"I didn't realize you were in my hair."

"Oh, yeah, I'm good and there."

"How so? Why would I pay you that kind of money? Who are you?"

"Ask the great big movie star."

"MERILEE, WHO IS Robert John Romero?"

By now it was eight and we were putting away our respective breakfasts in her huge farmhouse kitchen, complete with its gallantly hideous yellow and red linoleum floor and double work-sink of scarred white porcelain. The kitchen table was a washhouse table from the Shaker colony in Mount Lebanon, New York.

I was having a toasted baguette with homemade blackberry jam. Merilee was drinking a protein shake. For Lulu it was a half-tin of her 9Lives mackerel for cats. She has mighty strange eating habits and, trust me, the breath to prove it.

So gifted was Merilee at controlling her responses that her hand on the glass of her protein shake wavered only fractionally at the mention of Romero's name. I doubt that anyone would have even noticed it, but I'm not anyone.

She was officially forty now, yet never had looked lovelier. Merilee had never been conventionally pretty. Her jaw was too strong. Nose too long. Forehead too high. Plus she was nearly six feet tall in her bare feet, broad shouldered and big boned. Right now, she had on a tank top and workout pants. Her waist-length golden hair was tied up in a bun. Her heavily marked-up copy of *Private Lives* sat on the table before her.

"No one calls him Robert," she said after a long silence. "He's always been R.J."

"Fine. Now that we've got that cleared up, who is he?"

"Someone I knew back when I was in New Haven. So did Greg, Dini and Marty. We all did."

"He was at Yale with you?" The fact that his name rang no bells didn't necessarily mean anything. Plenty of people who come out of prestigious programs such as the Yale School of Drama don't make it. In fact, most don't.

"Yes, he was. And we . . . he and I went out for a while," she added, coloring slightly.

"Is that all you two did?"

"What's that supposed to mean?"

"Merilee, I don't own your past any more than you own mine. You have your secrets. I sure as hell have plenty of my own. But the Connecticut State Police are after this guy and he seems to think he has something on you. Something that I should give him money to keep quiet about."

"How much more does he want?"

"Twenty-five thousand. And you just said the word *more*. Have you been paying him off?"

Merilee nodded her head, swallowing. "He showed up here out of the blue one morning two weeks ago. That day you went into New York to get your teeth whitened."

"Cleaned and polished, not whitened. How many times must I tell you?"

"They look distinctly whiter."

"Because I have a summer tan. And you're straying. He showed up here . . ."

"Not more than ten minutes after you left. I swear, it was as if he'd been watching the house." She shot a glance out the windows at the woods beyond the duck pond before turning back to me. "I hadn't seen him in over fifteen years. He acted like it was last Tuesday. Flopped right down at this table, chattering nonstop, and waited for me to make him breakfast." Which explained how he'd come by her business phone number—it was printed on a card that was stuck to the refrigerator door. "So I gave him some ham and eggs. And then I gave him ten thousand dollars."

"Why would you do that?"

"In the hope that he'd go away. But I-I . . ." She faltered, her face etching with concern. "I've just made a mess of things instead."

"Not necessarily. And don't furrow your brow or you'll get lines."

Merilee got up, poured us more coffee and sat back down at the table, gazing out the window. "Plus I really, really don't need this right now. We go out on that stage tomorrow night live in front of the likes of Mike Nichols and Arthur Miller. Jackie O is going to be there. *Everyone* is going to be there." She heaved a sigh of profound regret. "And by the time the curtain falls my very short directing career will be over."

"Why do you say that?"

"Because we're simply not ready to go on. We need to rehearse all night tonight, and even that won't do the trick."

"What's wrong, Merilee?"

"Greg and Dini are what's wrong. Their energy and focus just aren't there. Greg's a solid leading man but when it comes to dry British humor he's outright terrible. Plus he still hasn't nailed down his accent. Sometimes he sounds like John Cleese playing Basil Fawlty. Other times he's channeling James Mason in *North by Northwest*. And that's not even the biggest problem."

"Which is . . . ?"

"No matter what I say to him he keeps missing his beat.
You can't fool around with Noël Coward's timing. Coward's
all about the rhythm. If you play him right, his words soar into
the clouds. If you play him wrong the words just lie there on
the stage floor like a sack of potatoes. Which is precisely where
we are right now. I'm incredibly grateful that Greg and Dini
have given me these two weeks. But they're just so distracted.
They've got their twin girls here with them along with Dini's
mother, Glenda. And the instant the curtain falls tomorrow
night a limo will be waiting to whisk them directly to JFK.
Greg is flying off to spend sixty days in Death Valley shooting the new Clint Eastwood western. Dini is heading down
to Savannah to costar in the new Julia Roberts for Jonathan
Demme. Both productions are waiting on them. All I hear
about day and night are the logistical details. How the twins
will be going to Savannah with Dini and Glenda while Steve
and Eydie, their golden retrievers, will be heading for the
desert with Greg and his personal assistant, Eugene. Except
Eugene and the dogs aren't here because the beach house that
Greg and Dini have been renting wouldn't allow dogs. Which
means that the limo will have to stop off at their apartment
on Riverside Drive to pick them up en route to JFK and so
on and . . ." Merilee shook her head wearily. "I'm not unsympathetic. They lead busy lives. Plus I think Dini is coming
down with the flu. But I *need* their full attention for the next
thirty-six hours or I will become a theatrical laughingstock."

"That'll never happen, Merilee. And you'll get their full
attention. They're professionals. How is Marty behaving?"

"Marty's, well, *Marty*. Late for rehearsals, hungover. And, for some reason, he always smells like curried mutton. But he's totally locked in and ready. And *he's* the one I was worried about."

Marty Miller, who listed his name in credits as Martin Jacob Miller so as to avoid confusion with Martin Milner of *Route 66* and *Adam-12* fame, had an on-again, off-again problem with drugs, alcohol and binge eating. He was also a relentless womanizer.

"It never occurred to me that Greg would be the one who'd drive me bonkers," she went on. "Who knows, maybe looking out across the footlights tomorrow night and seeing Kate Hepburn sitting there will wake him up. I don't seem to be able to. I guess I'm just not cut out to be a director."

"I don't believe that for one second. You're Merilee Nash. You're good at everything you do."

"Bless you for that, darling." Her gaze fell on the latest issue of *People* magazine, which lay on the kitchen table. The cover story was all about Hollywood's hottest, unlikeliest new lovebirds—Ted Danson and Whoopi Goldberg. "Do you think they're for real?"

"Of course they are. They're on the cover of *People*. We were on the cover of *People* and we were for real, weren't we?"

"You know we were."

"What I don't know is why you gave R. J. Romero ten thousand dollars and why he now expects me to give him twenty-five thousand more. Merilee, what's this all about?"

Her face tightened. "Brace yourself. You're not going to like it."

"I already don't like it."

She raised her chin at me, hands folded before her on the

table. "Out of all of us at Yale, R.J. was the one who had *it*," she began quietly. "He was incredibly handsome, with so much raw animal intensity that when he walked out onstage you couldn't take your eyes off of him. He grew up in the Federal Hill section of Providence with small-time wiseguys and hustlers. He was authentically street. Greg had zero charisma compared to R.J., who had total contempt for Greg. Still does. He thinks the only reason Greg has become such a big star is that he knows how to suck up to the right people. Greg's a nice guy. He gets along well with people. That was R.J.'s big problem at Yale. He argued with everyone. It was always about staying 'authentic' to his Federal Hill roots. Dini was hot for him right away. It was mutual. They paired off long before she got involved with Greg. After she and R.J. broke up, she lived with Marty for a semester. But it turned out they weren't a good match, so then she moved on to Greg."

"Sounds as if she worked her way through the whole class."

Merilee's lips broke into a smile. "It wasn't like that. Dini was a romantic. She still is."

"And R.J.?"

"Honestly, I thought he'd be the next De Niro. We all did. Every woman in the drama school got weak in the knees around him. And every man hated him. You wouldn't believe the envy."

"Yeah, I would."

"Me, I wanted to tame him. I couldn't, of course. He was unreliable, unfaithful, stoned half of the time and in way over his head when it came to gambling. He'd bet money he didn't have on long shots that never came in. He always owed some rough character money, which he'd pay back by borrowing it from me. He never paid me back, but I didn't care. I was madly in love with him. He was so talented and beautiful and . . ." She broke off, her jaw clenching. "Now I'm about to tell you something that I've never told anyone. Not a living soul. One night, a faculty member threw a party for everyone at her place out in Stony Creek. R.J. had borrowed his cousin Richie's Porsche so we could go. It was a wonderful evening. We all laughed a lot, drank a lot of wine. It was very late by the time he and I started back to New Haven, and I quickly realized he was in no condition to drive. He'd snorted a ton of coke in the bathroom, which I hadn't been aware of until he started flying down those narrow, twisting country roads in the pitch-black, going faster and faster. I begged him to pull over and let me drive. He just laughed and went even faster—until we went screeching around a bend and he . . . we *hit* a man, Hoagy. A fellow who was out walking his dog along the shoulder of the road. I-I'll never forget the sound that it . . ." She broke off, shuddering at the memory. "R.J. cursed and floored it out of there. I screamed at him to go back. He wouldn't. He was coked to the gills and it turned out he hadn't exactly borrowed his cousin Richie's Porsche. He'd stolen it. I remember I kept screaming at him to stop the car. He finally pulled over, called me a 'crazy whore' and shoved me out of the car in the middle of nowhere. I walked the rest of the way home to my apartment, weeping. Ten miles at least. My feet bled."

"Did you call nine-one-one?"

Merilee closed her eyes before she slowly shook her head. "I intended to, I swear. I-I even dialed the number from the first pay phone I came to. Only, I panicked and hung up. Next morning, it was on the local news that a prominent professor at the School of Architecture had been the victim of a late-night hit-and-run driver. A neighbor heard it happen and called the police."

"Did the man survive?"

"He did not," she replied, her green eyes filling with tears. "R.J. killed him. *We* killed him."

"You weren't driving."

"I was there. I knew who was responsible. I could have given his family some comfort. Seen that justice was done. But I didn't. I was too afraid of what would happen to me. So I kept quiet. And I've stayed quiet all of these years. Never told anyone."

"You could have told me."

"No, I couldn't. I was too ashamed. I was also hoping it was behind me. That *R.J.* was behind me."

"What happened to him?"

"He started getting work off-Broadway right away, but kept blowing it. Didn't know his lines. Fought with his directors. He got himself fired from three or four shows. Still, he was so gifted that Marty Scorsese gave him a plum role in *Raging Bull*. Yet he managed to get himself fired from that, too. Drugs were involved, apparently, and I heard he actually *punched* Marty, who's the size of a flea. After that, he was done. R. J. Romero destroyed a can't-miss career, Hoagy. Single greatest waste of talent I've ever seen. The last I heard, he'd drifted back to the world of small-time Federal Hill hoods that he came from."

"Except now he's back in your life."

"And still betting the house on impossible long shots. Would you believe he asked me if I'd let him read for *Private*

Lives? I said, there's no role for you. Besides, the man hasn't been within ten miles of a workshop in God knows how long. Plus he's strung out on heroin and looks *awful*."

"I'm surprised you can even concentrate on *Private Lives* right now."

"It's the only thing keeping me sane. That and having you and Lulu here."

"Has he been hanging around rehearsals?"

"There's a gazebo on the town green right near the playhouse. I've spotted him there. He just sits there, watching and waiting."

"Do your cast mates know about this?"

"No," she said sharply. "He hasn't had the nerve to speak to any of them. And I doubt they'd recognize him if they saw him. I barely did."

"Why has he shown up now after all these years?"

"Because he's desperate. Because he thinks I'm the last bargaining chip he has left. He said if I didn't pay him the ten thousand dollars he'd tell the police that *I* was driving the Porsche that night."

"They'd never believe him."

"Doesn't matter. He'll run straight to the media and the story will be all over *Entertainment Tonight* by nightfall. Any charge against someone like me, no matter how frivolous, leaves its mark. And this isn't frivolous. A man died." She took a deep breath, letting it out raggedly. "My reputation will be ruined."

"I wonder why he used my name as a reference on that job application."

"So you'd ask me about him and stir up trouble. Along with

all of the rest of his delusions, I'm quite convinced he's hoping to win me back."

"He told me he wants to escape to Mexico."

"R.J. says lots of things. Half the time, he even believes them. But they're never true. He'll just keep coming back to us for more money until the police catch him. And when they do, I have no doubt he'll throw me to the wolves." She reached over and grabbed my hand, gripping it tightly. "Hoagy, what am I going to do?"

"For starters, I'm coming to rehearsals with you this morning. That'll let him know that I'm keeping an eye on you." I heard a low growl from under the table. "*We're* keeping an eye on you. I'm also going to arrange to have lunch with Bruce Landau." My high-powered New York City lawyer was summering nearby on the shoreline in Guilfoyle.

"What can Bruce do?"

"He has good contacts. He knows people."

"What about your novel?"

"My novel can wait." I squeezed her hand. "You should have told me about this before, Merilee."

"I was taking care of it. Or I thought I was." She detested clingy females. Was so stubborn about hiding her vulnerabilities that it was almost a sickness. "Besides, it was my own private shame."

"I wouldn't call it your own private shame any longer."

"Why, what would you . . . ?"

"I'd call it blackmail."

Chapter Two

I'm highly superstitious when it comes to a new manuscript. There's only one copy, much of it scribbled by hand in the margins or on the back of its smudged pages, some of which I've cut up with scissors so I can move certain paragraphs from one page to another and then piece them back together again with Scotch tape. If the manuscript were to disappear, then whatever I've written so far would be gone forever and I'd never be able to re-create it. I live in constant fear of this happening. My crappy old brownstone on West Ninety-Third Street is a total firetrap. The building hasn't been rewired since Truman was in the White House. The ancient oil-burning furnace in the cellar frequently sends billows of acrid-smelling exhaust up the stairwell. I never leave the apartment for a lengthy period of time without gathering up the manuscript and storing it in the vegetable bin of the refrigerator. You probably think I'm joking but I'm not. I'm also not alone in this. I can think of at least half a dozen very famous authors in New York City whose manuscripts-in-progress smell faintly of rotting onions.

I'm telling you this because as I was getting ready to leave

for the Sherbourne Playhouse I glanced around at the chapel
and realized that I didn't feel safe leaving *The Sweet Season of
Madness* sitting there on the writing table. I considered sliding
it underneath the mattress but what good would that do me if
the chapel caught fire? After careful consideration I ended up
tucking it inside the freezer chest in Merilee's mudroom alongside a leg of venison that her elderly neighbor Mr. MacGowan
had given her during hunting season.

Merilee had already taken off for the theater in the Jag by
the time R.J. called me back with the when and where for the
money drop—nine o'clock tonight at the old cast iron gate to
Sherbourne's abandoned brass mill. After I got off the phone
with him I set up a lunch date with my lawyer, Bruce Landau,
showered, stropped grandfather's razor, shaved, powdered my
neck with Floris No. 89 talc and dressed in the new white linen
suit from Strickland & Sons, a pale blue shirt, polka-dot bow
tie, perforated spectator balmorals and my snap brim fedora.

For wheels I had use of the powder blue 1950 Ford Woody
wagon that Merilee had bought from the estate of her dear, de-
parted nonagenarian Lyme friend Margaret, an aviatrix who'd
been a test pilot during World War I. Solid as a tank, heavy and
quiet. And the Woody wasn't bad either. Had forty-two thousand miles on it, no rust, its original wood and five brand-new
wide whites. Merilee also kept an old tan Land Rover around
that she used for lugging stuff to the dump, but it shook like
crazy if you tried to push it past fifty on the highway. So I took
the Woody, with Lulu curled up next to me.

Sherbourne was nestled along the bank of the Sherbourne
River between Lyme and New Haven. Many of the old factory
towns in Connecticut, towns that had once produced everything

from wall clocks to buttons to bullets, had become decaying eye-
sores. But the attractive ones near the shoreline, like Sherbourne,
had managed to survive as quaint weekend getaways for New
Yorkers. The three-story Victorian Sherbourne Inn, which over-
looked the lush town green with its ornate gazebo, had once been
the home of the brass mill's owner. The town had a smattering
of bars, restaurants and art galleries. And it had the Sherbourne
Playhouse, which was steeped in so much theatrical history that
there was no way that Merilee and her friends were going to let
it be torn down.

A crew was beginning to raise a huge tent on the green for
the champagne bash that was scheduled to take place two hours
before the curtain rose tomorrow evening. Inside this tent the
three hundred or so New York City stage and society luminaries who were attending the one and only benefit performance
of *Private Lives* would have a chance to chatter and soak up
flattering coverage from *Entertainment Tonight, Inside Edition*,
the New York newspapers and local New York and Connecticut
TV stations. Trucks were lined up everywhere delivering tables
and chairs and lighting and portable generators.

Mimi Whitfield was supervising the entire operation. When
it came to event planning Merilee said that Mimi was a wonder.
Back in her modeling heyday Mimi had driven a Mustang con-
vertible in a famous TV commercial in which she'd laughed so
deliciously while the wind blew through her mane of lustrous
blond hair that she'd become an American icon. She still had
the mane of blond hair, sky blue eyes and great cheekbones. And
for a woman who was two or three years north of forty she still
looked plenty desirable in a blue silk tank top and tight jeans,
even if she was now sporting a nonsexy pager on her Hermès

belt. I knew Mimi from back when Merilee and I would run into her at Elaine's, where Lulu enjoyed the distinction of being the only dog in New York City who had her own water bowl. In those days Mimi was dating one of the Yankees' starting pitchers. I knew her to be a climber. It wasn't long before she traded in her pitcher for the toad-faced real estate baron who was now her ex-husband.

She took a break from barking orders at the tent crew to give me her great big cover girl smile. "Say a prayer for me, Hoagy, if you have any pull with the man upstairs."

"I haven't, I'm afraid. Any reason in particular?"

"The weatherman's predicting a fifty percent chance of thunderstorms and gale-force winds tomorrow evening. If it rains during our performance I'll have a total disaster on my hands. Our roof is so completely shot that the actors will get drenched standing right there onstage. So will the audience. The dressing rooms will flood—also swarm with the rats that live in the basement under the theater." I heard a low, unhappy moan and felt Lulu trembling at my feet. She's terrified of rats. "And if it gets windy enough the tent will break loose from its stakes and go flying across the town green. It can't rain. It just can't."

"Then it won't. It just won't. Not to worry, Mimi. The evening's going to be a smashing success."

Another delivery truck pulled up outside of the theater. Mimi's pager promptly beeped. She hustled off to attend to it.

"It's *LULU*!" I heard two little girls cry out from behind me.

Lulu let out another low, unhappy moan as Greg and Dini's seven-year-old twin girls, Durango and Cheyenne, came dashing across the green toward us, looking like miniature Disney pirates in their red bandanna head scarves, sleeveless white T-shirts and blue denim cutoffs. Durango and Cheyenne were thin, snub-nosed, strawberry blondes just like their mom. The twins were eerily identical. I'm talking Diane Arbus identical. The only way to tell them apart was that Durango had recently lost a front tooth. They both adored Lulu. Fell right to their knees on the grass, tugging on her ears, patting her and making a huge fuss.

"Hey, Lulu!"

"We missed you, Lulu!"

Lulu suffered the indignity of their attention with stoic good grace. She was accustomed to kids going gaga over her. Goes with the territory if you're a basset hound. Though she did extract payback by letting out a huge yawn.

Durango made a face. "Eew. Hoagy, how come her breath is so bad?"

"She has rather unusual eating habits."

"What does she eat, boogers?"

"Girls, don't you make a nuisance of yourselves," Dini's mother, Glenda, ordered them fiercely, absolutely determined that her privileged granddaughters not behave like spoiled brats. She was making her way across the grass toward us at a considerably slower pace, puffing in the warm morning air. Glenda, a North Carolina widow in her sixties, was short and heavy. She wore her white hair parted in the middle and cropped at the chin. Or I should say chins. I could make out at least three before they melted into a puddle at the open collar of her short-sleeved magenta print blouse, which she wore with nonmatching magenta slacks and bone-colored walking shoes. Her bare arms jiggled.

"Nice to see you again, Mrs. Hawes," I said, tipping my fedora.

"I sure do wish you'd call me Glenda, Mr. Hoag."

"In that case make it Hoagy."

"As in Carmichael?"

"As in the cheesesteak."

Her blue eyes narrowed at me suspiciously. "Are you one of those New York City smart alecks that I hear about down in Siler City?"

"I'm afraid so."

"I've never much cared for smart alecks."

"Then it's my mission to change your mind."

Glenda sighed fretfully. "I sure do wish we were all finished here and on our way to Savannah."

"Why, is something wrong?"

"Dini's running a fever and feels all achy and tired. Mimi knows a Doctor Orr here in town. He was kind enough to examine her last evening. Thinks she may have picked up a virus that's been going around."

"There's a virus going around?"

"Hoagy, I was a school nurse in Chatham County for twenty-seven years. Trust me, there's always a virus going around. What worries me is that she might have contracted that Lyme disease of yours from a tick bite when we were walking in the woods last week," she said accusingly, as if I were personally responsible for it. "The doctor didn't find the bull's-eye rash you hear about, but he said you don't always get them. He took a blood sample and said he'd put her on antibiotics if she gets any worse. For now, she's just supposed to get some rest." Glenda let out a humorless laugh. "I guess he's never met an actress before. That girl works fifteen hours a day. Greg does, too. I wish those two would take some time off to enjoy their success. But they're not giving themselves so much as a day off in between jobs."

"When you're in demand there's no such thing as time off."

"Merilee takes time off now and then, doesn't she?"

"Merilee's rather unusual that way. She also avoids L.A. as much as humanly possible."

Glenda shook a chubby finger at me. "You two ought to get married again and have yourself some kids. A man's not a real man unless he has a wife and children. Listen to what I'm telling you. I know a few things."

"Yes, I'm sure you do," I said, sighing inwardly. This would be one of the downsides of being one-half of a famous couple. People with whom you are barely acquainted feel they know you intimately and are entitled to offer unsolicited personal advice and criticism. Especially criticism.

I excused myself and moseyed off. Lulu ambled along next to me, grateful to be rid of the bothersome twins. I worked my way past a row of trucks toward the red brick carriage barn that was across a courtyard from the playhouse. The barn was where the sets were built and the props stored. The crew chief, an aging, silver-ponytailed hippie named Cyril Cooper—better known as Coop—was calling out orders to his crew of high school volunteers who were toting paint cans, drop cloths and props across the courtyard to the stage. I looked to see if anyone was paying close attention to what was going on. Possibly a trucker who was standing around doing nothing. I spotted no one. Nor did I see anyone checking out the action through the windows of the proudly tattered Backstage Tavern, which was directly across the narrow street from the playhouse's stage door.

I did, however, attract the attention of one of the crew members who was lugging paint cans—a round rubber ball of a young woman in a tank top and shorts whose long, shiny black hair was held in place with a headband. "My God, you're Stewart Hoag," she said, staring at me wide-eyed.

"That's the rumor. And you are . . . ?"

"Nona. Nona Peachy. I'm a drama major at Brown. Home for the summer with the fam and thought I'd pitch in. I just love this old playhouse. My dad, Doug, appeared here a couple of times when he was a young performer. He desperately wanted to be an actor. He and my mom lived in a basement apartment in Greenwich Village when I was little, and he was in a couple of off-Broadway shows, but when my mom got pregnant with my little brother he gave it all up to become a venture capitalist. Don't ask me what that is."

"Wasn't planning to."

"Now I'm the one who has the dream." Nona's eyes gleamed as she gazed at the ramshackle playhouse. "I'll cry my head off if they tear this place down, I swear," she said. Then off she went to join the others.

Me, I did a full lap around the town green. Checked out every shop window and parked car as well as the terrace and lush, manicured rose gardens of the Sherbourne Inn. I saw no one. If R. J. Romero was watching the theater he was pretty damned good at being invisible.

I returned to the theater and went in the stage entrance. The tiny playhouse had almost no backstage area. Just a few steps after I'd walked in the door my face was practically flush up against the backside of the stage set's backdrop. I also ran into a pair of narrow, cast iron spiral staircases. One led downstairs to the dressing rooms, the other up to a catwalk in the rafters where the lighting man operated. Flanking the stage, in the wings, were the lighting and sound consoles, which looked as if they'd been installed by a young Tom Edison. A service corridor ran along the outside wall of the building to the front of the house. A door opened into the lobby, where Mimi's office was located.

There was a small desk by the stage door where Dini's husband, Greg Farber, was having a heated discussion on the phone with Eugene, his personal assistant, who was dog-sitting the family's golden retrievers at their apartment on Riverside Drive.

"Eugene, you can't let Steve off of his leash, remember? He's super protective of Eydie and gets aggressive . . . Hey, now, don't freak out. It's okay. No one got hurt." This was Greg being soothing and kind. He was very good at being soothing and kind. "Listen, I have to go into rehearsal now. I'll check in later, okay?" He hung up, flashing a grin at me. "Greetings, Hoagster."

"Back at you. Trouble on the home front?"

"Steve got loose in Riverside Park and almost made a snack of someone's Chihuahua," Greg answered, standing there in a white oxford cloth button-down shirt and jeans. He had a big square head, neatly combed sandy hair, granite jaw and broad shoulders. The screen made him look tall. He wasn't. He was three inches shy of six feet tall, which made him six inches shorter than I am. He had an open, honest face and a reassuring demeanor. On-screen, he came across as a man whom the audience was sure would always do the right thing, no matter whether he was playing the president of the United States or a saddle tramp. In my opinion, he was not nearly as gifted as his classmate Marty Miller. But he was very, very solid at playing the Good Guy. Solid enough to win an Oscar a few years back for *The Tall T*, a remake of a 1950s Elmore Leonard western that had originally starred Randolph Scott, an actor who'd known a thing or two himself about a reassuring demeanor.

"So how goes the writing thing?" he asked me as he gave Lulu a pat.

"Shockingly well. I'm working on something I really like."

"I'm so happy to hear that, man. Can't wait to read it."

Greg and I became drinking buddies when he and Merilee were shooting a movie together in Maine. This was back during my season in the sun, before everything fell apart. He and I drank single malt together, took long walks in the woods and told each other stuff we didn't tell anyone else. I told him I had no idea for a second novel and was convinced that my career as a novelist was over, which thus far had proven to be eerily prophetic. He told me that he woke up every morning consumed by the terrifying certainty that he was a total fraud.

"I'm super excited myself," he informed me. "At this very moment Mr. Clint fucking Eastwood is hanging around in Death Valley waiting for *me* so that the cameras can start rolling. Hey, did you hear how I got the gig?"

"I did not."

"I walk into his Malpaso office on the Warner's lot, okay? He's sitting there behind his desk with that Dirty Harry deadpan on his face. Stands up, sticks out his hand and says, 'Hi, I'm Clint.' I punch him in the jaw and knock him flat. He gets up, rubs his jaw and says, 'Okay, you're hired.'"

Dini joined us now, looking pale, wilted and not at all well. Dini Hawes was barely five feet tall, extremely slender and partial to vintage clothing and accessories, the zanier the better. Today she wore an oversize Hawaiian shirt with a pair of extremely loud madras shorts. Nestled in her strawberry blond hair was a pair of pink cat's-eye sunglasses from the Fabulous Fifties. Dini had slightly pop-eyed blue eyes, a bunny rabbit nose and a fetching little twist to her mouth. No one was better at playing offbeat southern crazies than she was, but she also excelled at gutsy crusading reporters and public defenders. She could also be very funny if the role called for it. "Hey, Hoagy," she said in that soft, Siler City accent of hers.

"Hey, back at you, Dini."

"Did you get through to Eugene?" she asked Greg.

"Steve got in a fight," he answered curtly. "Dogs get in fights. It was nothing."

"Hon, if he can't control Steve and Eydie then that's *not* nothing."

There was an edge to both of their voices. No wonder Merilee was having a problem with them—they weren't getting along. I wondered if it was the sensory overload of working together plus having the twins and her mom around or if something more was going on. Then again, maybe they were just scared shitless about walking out on that stage tomorrow night in front of Broadway royalty.

"There were no photographers around. The dog's owner

isn't talking about suing us. So just let it go, okay? Everything's under control."

"Your mom told me you're running a fever," I said to Dini. "You okay?"

"I'm fine. Just some bitty bug. I wish she'd stop talking about it."

"Any idea where your illustrious director is?" I asked.

"In her posh dressing room," Dini answered. "*Our* posh dressing room. All of the actresses in the cast have to share."

"Hey, at least you don't have to share a dressing room with Marty," Greg pointed out. "His B.O. makes me gag, I swear."

"Is he here yet?" Dini asked him.

"Of course not. Late as usual."

I took the spiral staircase down to the dressing rooms, which were in the basement underneath the stage. There was a narrow corridor dimly lit by one bare lightbulb that made an alarming sizzling noise. It smelled damp and moldy, possibly because of the numerous puddles of water in the low spots in the concrete floor. The doors to the actors' and actresses' dressing rooms were adjacent to each other on one side of the corridor. Directly across the corridor from the dressing rooms were the doors to the His and Hers bathrooms.

The actresses' dressing room was a full step down from the corridor. It was also flooded, which I gathered was a regular state of affairs. The makeshift flooring of planks stretched across cinder blocks kind of gave it away. A sump pump was running, which made it sound as if a motorbike were idling in there, yet at least two inches of water remained on the basement floor beneath the planks. The bottom three or four inches of the dressing room's particleboard walls were rotted out because of repeated water damage, which meant—insofar as rats were concerned—that nothing separated the dressing room from the basement under the theater. Which explained why Lulu cowered between my feet, trembling, as I stood there in the doorway. She could hear them scurrying around. There were two tiny dressing tables and mirrors. In lieu of a wardrobe rack there were hooks on the walls for the performers' costumes, which were on hangers inside of protective plastic garment bags because the exposed overhead pipes dripped.

Merilee sat at one of the dressing tables in a denim shirt and khaki shorts scribbling notes on her copy of *Private Lives*.

"My God, Merilee, this place is a total dump."

"Nonsense. It reminds me of the old days when I used to play the Keith Orpheum circuit."

"Merilee Gilbert Nash, you never played the Keith Orpheum circuit."

"I know, but I love saying it."

"Seriously, I'm surprised it hasn't been condemned."

"It *has* been, remember? That's why we're trying to raise this money." She gazed up at me. "You really didn't have to come here today."

"No, I really did."

"I don't suppose you've seen Marty, have you?"

"Afraid not."

"I'd better have someone call the inn to rouse him."

I heard footsteps behind me, turned and found myself face-to-face in the dressing room doorway with Sabrina Meyer, the young actress who was playing Louise, the maid. She was strikingly beautiful—tall, slender and olive-complexioned, with slanted, smoldering brown eyes and a head of cascading golden ringlets. The perfume she was wearing smelled like vanilla.

"Sabrina, say hello to Hoagy," Merilee said. "Officially known as Stewart Hoag."

"*The* Stewart Hoag?" Sabrina dumped her shoulder bag on one of the dressing tables. "It's an honor to meet you. I'm such a fan of your book. My modern lit class read it when I was an undergrad in New Jersey."

New Jersey, for those of you west of the Rockies, is Ivy-speak for Princeton. "Was it a large class?"

"A small seminar. Why?"

"Just calculating my royalties."

She let out a delicious laugh. "Brilliant *and* funny." Which prompted Lulu to bare her teeth at her. "Why is your dog . . . ?"

"She's very protective of me."

"Do you need protecting?"

"Twenty-four hours a day," I said as Merilee watched us spar, one eyebrow arched mockingly.

"Are you sticking around for rehearsal?" Sabrina asked me.

"If the director doesn't mind."

"The director would be thrilled," Merilee assured me.

"Then I'll see you upstairs in five," Sabrina said, heading out the door.

"*If* Marty ever shows up," Merilee called after her. To me she said, "So are you planning to?"

"Planning to what?"

"Sleep with her?"

"How would I know? I've just met her. Besides, she's not my type."

"You have a type?"

"Oh, most definitely. Tall, strapping blondes with high fore-heads and a strong territorial streak."

"Was I being territorial?"

"Little bit."

"I apologize. Honestly, darling, you're a free agent. If you really, truly want to 'hit' that, go right ahead."

"Thank you, I will. How is she in the show?"

"Terrific. Hollywood will be snatching her up. The only thing that might hold her back is she's extremely fragile. Has a history of self-medicating."

"Self-medicating as in . . . ?"

"Heroin. She did a stint at McLean Hospital in Massachu-setts last year. But she's clean right now. Alert and eager, as I believe you can attest to."

Dini came in now and flopped down wearily at her dressing table, her face flushed.

"How are you feeling?" Merilee's brow was furrowed with concern.

"*God*, I wish people would stop asking me that."

"You don't have to bite my head off, Dini."

Dini reached over and patted her hand. "Sorry. It's not easy having my mother here. She keeps hovering and clucking. For-give me?"

"Of course."

"I wanted to ask you about my attitude at the opening of act two. I'm still not sure I understand where Amanda's coming from."

"Let's have a look," Merilee said, leafing through the play.

I left them to it. Went back up the spiral staircase with Lulu just in time to see a chubby, balding, supremely disheveled

Marty Miller stagger through the stage door, reeking of tequila, cigarette smoke and, yes, curried mutton. His rumpled polo shirt and baggy seersucker shorts looked as if he'd slept in them—facedown on the floor of his room. He wore rubber flip-flops in lieu of shoes, which was highly unfortunate because the smell of his bare feet was strong enough to make my eyes water. Hungover, disheveled and unwashed qualified as normal for Marty, a self-destructive loner who took such terrible care of himself that he looked ten years older than his classmates.

"Good morning, Marty," I said as he squinted at me, his gaze slightly out of focus. "Are you aware that your right hand is bleeding?" It was a soft, pudgy hand, and he had quite a gash on the back of it. "What happened?"

He studied the hand with bewildered detachment, as if it were someone else's. "I . . . don't remember."

"I'll fetch the first aid kit from Mimi's office," Glenda said briskly as she stood there with Durango and Cheyenne, who were whispering to each other and giggling. Mimi's office was up front off of the lobby. "Come with me, Marty. We'll wash that in her bathroom. The ones downstairs are filthy."

"Yes, matron," he intoned, holding his hands out like a convict being led off to a jail cell. "Actually, I'm growing quite fond of the palatial digs that Greg and I share in the bowels of this playhouse. Girls, did you know that this playhouse has bowels?"

"Does not," Durango said, giggling.

"Does, too," he assured her. "All theaters have bowels."

"Do not," Cheyenne shot back, giggling.

"I hardly think this is an appropriate topic of conversation, Marty," Glenda said reproachfully as they headed up the corridor to the lobby with the girls tagging along.

"Yes, matron," he intoned once again. "I humbly apologize, matron."

Greg was still parked at the small desk by the stage door. Sabrina was seated outside on a bench under a sycamore tree in the courtyard studying her lines.

"Does Marty ever bathe or change his clothes?" I asked him.

"Not as far as I can tell," Greg said. "I blame it on Dini. He had a huge thing for her back when we were at Yale and I swear he's been on a personal hygiene strike ever since they broke up. He's still sweet on her. I guarantee you he'll be on her in a flash if we ever split up."

"Are you planning to split up?"

"Hell, no. I'm the happiest I've ever been. The past few days have been a bit bumpy, but you know how that goes. You've been married."

I nodded. "And my marriage went kablooey."

"Well, ours isn't. It just hasn't been easy squeezing this show in between our shooting schedules."

"Merilee really appreciates you doing it."

"We're happy to, man. We both made our stage debuts here, same as Merilee did. It's just that . . ." He trailed off, shaking his head. "Two weeks of rehearsal isn't nearly enough time to master Coward. Performing his work is like playing chamber music. The tempo and interplay have to be pitch-perfect. Every hesitation, no matter how slight, is huge. The genius of the man is that he makes it look so damned easy. It's not. It's intricate and incredibly complicated."

"Speaking of complicated, you haven't seen R. J. Romero hanging around here, have you?"

Greg looked at me in astonishment. "*R. J. Romero?* Wow,

there's a blast from the past. Why would that bastard be around?"

"He's been calling Merilee lately, bugging her for money. He even wanted to know if there was a part for him in *Private Lives*."

"As who, Louise the maid?" Greg shook his head in disgust. "Everyone in our class thought he was such hot shit. I thought he was a fraud."

"I understand he wasn't a huge fan of yours either."

"We weren't exactly pals, if that's what you mean. I'm real sorry to hear he's started hassling Merilee. Anything I can do?"

"Just let me know if you see him around. And please don't mention this to the others. I don't want him to become a distraction."

"Absolutely." He gazed out the open stage door at the courtyard, where Sabrina was still studying her lines. "I thought the guy was human trash. Lying, cheating scum. Didn't matter. The girls loved him. Dini had a huge thing for him. So did Merilee. The guys, we all hated his guts. Marty probably still does. R.J. used to call him Porky Pig. He used to call me Tom Brokaw because he thought I was such a droning stiff. I'd say the two of us have done pretty damned well for ourselves considering how fat and untalented we are. What's *he* done?"

"Become a petty criminal. Not so petty, actually."

"And I can tell you why. Because he's trash." Greg gazed at me, smiling. "I've missed talking to you, man. When I get back from Death Valley we ought to go out for beers."

I blinked at him in shock. *Beers?* "Absolutely," I responded in dumbfounded amazement. *Beers?* "Let's do that."

"SHALL WE PICK up where we left off in act one?" Merilee said brightly as the cast stood gathered on the playhouse's stage. Per Coward's stage directions, the set depicted the terrace of a hotel in the south of France. There were two French windows at the back opening onto two separate suites. The terrace space was divided by a line of small trees in tubs. Awnings shaded the windows. "Our newlyweds, Elyot and Sibyl, have just gone back inside their honeymoon suite from the terrace," she continued, glancing down at her copy of the play. "There's a slight pause and now Victor enters from the other suite . . ."

And with that Victor (Greg) emerged onstage, followed a moment later by Amanda (Dini), his new bride, and the run-through began. This being Coward the dialogue was deliciously biting, witty and wise. This being Coward the situation was also fraught with farcical possibilities. After all, Amanda has no idea that Elyot, who just happens to have been her first husband, is honeymooning in the suite right next door. Elyot is equally in the dark about Amanda's presence there.

I sat a few rows back with Mimi and Sabrina, who wouldn't appear until act two. It was a tiny theater—318 seats, to be exact, which made it less than half the size of a small Broadway house. Glenda and the twins had returned to their rented beach house. The twins thought rehearsals were stupid.

As Dini and Greg played their scene together, I was quickly aware that Merilee hadn't been exaggerating when she told me the show was in trouble. Despite being under the weather, Dini was delightful as the cynical, sharp-tongued Amanda. But Greg, well, totally sucked. It wasn't just his dreadful accent, which I thought sounded like Tony Curtis doing Cary Grant in *Some Like It Hot*. His timing was way off. Dini kept gamely trying to pull him along, but I could see the desperation in her eyes. Every finely honed theatrical instinct that she possessed was telling her that total disaster was looming.

The cast took a short coffee break when the scene ended. I made my way into the wings to whisper goodbye to Merilee. "See you later?"

She shook her head. "We'll be rehearsing all night," she whispered gloomily. "What am I doing wrong? Why can't I get through to him?"

"Greg's a pro. He'll come through for you."

"Do you really think so?"

"Absolutely."

Her green eyes shined at me. She was on the verge of tears. "Hoagy . . . ?"

"Yes, Merilee?"

"You're a terrible liar."

Chapter Three

Bruce Landau was summering nearby at his beach house in the ultraposh shorefront village of Guilfoyle, where he kept his thirty-six-foot Pearson 365 moored at the ultrasnooty Guilfoyle Yacht Club. Guilfoyle had a historic town green, complete with a Revolutionary War Memorial, that made Sherbourne's town green look like a sad little weed patch. It had a steepled white Congregational Church from the 1700s. Galleries that sold all sorts of ugly, obscenely expensive art. Shops that sold all sorts of ugly, obscenely expensive antiques. And it had The Nook, a dark, narrow diner with booths of well-worn wood.

I nosed the Woody into one of the diagonal parking spaces out front and strolled in, my eyes getting used to the dark. From the radio in the kitchen I could hear R.E.M.'s "Everybody Hurts," which was that month's officially designated whiny song. I couldn't go anywhere without hearing Michael Stipe mewling.

Bruce hollered to me from a booth in the back, turning high-class heads left and right. He wasn't much for couth. But you wouldn't want to go up against him in court. The man was three parts pit bull and one part wild boar. He'd arrived straight from the yacht club, it appeared. His Izod shirt and tan shorts had varnish and paint stains all over them.

We both ordered BLTs. Lulu opted for a tuna melt, hold the toast, and kept a safe distance from Bruce. He sprays a lot when he eats.

Bruce took a gulp of his iced coffee and jumped right in. "Speaking as your attorney, my feeling is that Merilee has very little to worry about from this yutz. Should she have reported the accident at the time? Yes. Did she behave irresponsibly? Yes. But his uncorroborated testimony won't be enough to prompt any district prosecutor to file charges against her. Or buy him any kind of deal."

"Even if he claims that she was driving the car?"

Our sandwiches arrived. We dove in.

"Strictly his word against hers," he advised me between huge, open mouthfuls. "And we're talking about a desperate sleazeball here. Trouble is, we both know it's the media fallout that'll kill us. No way we want it out there that Merilee Nash was ever mixed up in something like this."

"How do we contain it, Bruce?"

"I've reached out to a fixer named Pete Tedone who happens to owe me a favor. Pete was a deputy superintendent of the Connecticut State Police until his sweet darling wife got caught shoplifting several valuable items from the Gucci store on Fifth Avenue in New York City. He was right there by her side the whole time and had no idea what she was up to, or so he claimed when store security landed on her. I managed to get the charges dropped. Pete took early retirement and went private, but he's still got great contacts. His cousin Frank is on the Organized Crime Task Force. He's the guy who phoned you this morning. Trust me, if Pete can't make this go away no one can." Bruce glanced past me to the front door, waving his arm in the air. "And here he is, right on time."

Pete Tedone was a chesty fireplug in his late forties with a shaved head and a twenty-inch neck. The cheap, shiny black suit that he had on was just a bit too snug in the shoulders. He sat across from me next to Bruce and asked our waitress for a root beer milk shake, which immediately intrigued me. I'd never heard of any such thing.

"Okay, gents, here's what we know . . ." He opened a file folder on the table. Inside there were incident statements, arrest reports, clippings. He arrayed them before us very neatly, all corners squared. "As to the alleged hit-and-run in Stony Creek, the details that Miss Nash provided correspond with the police reports from 1976. A Yale architectural historian named Frank Lawson was indeed fatally struck late one night while he was out walking his dog. The family posted a reward for information. No one ever came forward. Case remains classified as an unsolved vehicular homicide." Tedone's root beer shake arrived in a tall fountain glass. He took a thirsty gulp, wiped some tan-colored foam from his mustache, and moved on to the next document. "As to why Mr. Romero has chosen now to show up in her life again, the answer could be that until four months ago he was serving a nickel at Enfield Correctional for breaking and entering. His third fall, not for nothing. The man's already gone down for receiving stolen property and for felony-weight coke possession. He has a wife and two kids in Providence, but I doubt he's spent more than six months under the same roof with them in the past ten years. The man can't stay out of trouble. He did manage to land that job at B & B Building Supply, but it wasn't long before he was stealing stuff from the yard and peddling it at construction sites. As soon as they got wise to him he took off with a load of Marvin windows and they never saw him or their truck again."

"Is he hooked up with a crew?" Bruce asked.

"Used to be loosely affiliated with a mob family in Providence," Tedone replied. "But I hear they kissed him goodbye years ago. Word is he owed bookies and loan sharks money left and right, then snorted up the coke he was supposed to be peddling to pay them back. He's lucky they didn't ice him, but they always cut him slack because they thought he was going to be a big movie star someday." He put the papers back in the folder and closed it. "If you want my sense of things, Hoagy, you shouldn't get within five miles of this guy—because when he gets busted, and he will, you'll need plausible deniability. Don't talk to him on the phone. Don't meet with him. And for damned sure don't give him so much as one shiny quarter."

"He's already been to the house. Merilee gave him ten thousand dollars."

Tedone grimaced. "Buddy, you may have a problem."

"Tell me something I don't already know."

"Let's explore our options." Bruce stabbed the table with a blunt finger. "Scenario one, Hoagy agrees to the payoff at the time and location of Romero's choosing. We tip off Pete's cousin Frank, the Task Force reels him in and—"

"And he drags Merilee down with him," I said. "That can't happen."

Tedone leaned over the table toward me, lowering his voice. "There are ways to make sure it doesn't."

"You can't keep his lawyer away from the TV cameras."

"It'll never get that far. You arrange the meet like Bruce just said. We tip off the Task Force, only I'm the one who shows up, not you. Romero's a miserable bum without a friend left in the world. I'll make it abundantly clear to him that should he ever say word one about Merilee Nash to anyone, including his lawyer, he will not survive his first night in custody."

"Why, what'll happen to him?"

"He'll die while resisting arrest," Tedone said offhandedly, as if making such a thing happen was no more difficult than ordering a pizza with three toppings instead of two. Apparently, for him it wasn't. This was what made him a fixer. "There'll be a thorough investigation of the circumstances surrounding his unfortunate death, but the officers involved will be fully exonerated. At which time you'll be asked to make a suitable contribution to a fund for the survivors of the troopers in this state who've been killed on the job."

The very same $25,000 that Romero was demanding, I guessed. Except this way I could write it off as a charitable donation. The tax deductible hit. What would they think of next?

Across from me, Bruce's face was blank. He wasn't saying yes. He wasn't saying no.

I looked down at Lulu under the table. Lulu was looking back up at me.

"Let's be very clear about something," I said. "That's not how I want to handle this."

Tedone shrugged his bulging shoulders. "No disrespect, but you don't have a lot of wiggle room. If you want this guy out of your ex's life this is how it's done. Believe me, no one will be sorry to see him go. And there's absolutely no way it'll ever get back to you."

"What about that job application with my name on it?"

"It'll disappear."

Bruce cleared his throat. "Hoagy, if it's any help, Merilee never has to know about this."

"Yes, she does. I'd never conceal something like this from her. She once cared about the guy. Still does, for all I know. Thanks but no thanks. I'll handle it in my own way."

"You'll pay him the money, won't you?" Tedone shook his shaved head at me. "That's a fool's play. Also way too risky. This guy's got nothing left to lose. He could shoot you dead. Or bop you on the head and hold you for a million dollars' ransom."

Lulu let out a low moan.

Tedone frowned. "What's her problem?"

"She feels I'm worth at least two million."

He peered at me doubtfully, as if it had just dawned on him that I wasn't like other people. "I don't agree with your decision, but if you've made up your mind then I have to respect it. Only, I'm watching your back from now on."

"No."

"Trust me, you'll never even know I'm there."

"No."

"Be sensible," Bruce implored me. "You've got to have backup."

"Lulu's all the backup I've ever needed."

"Do you own a gun?" Tedone wanted to know.

"Merilee keeps a .38 at the farm. She got it last winter when there was an outbreak of rabid raccoons."

"Pack it," he urged me. "Fully loaded."

"Not a chance."

"Why the hell not?"

"Guns go off."

Tedone drained the last of his root beer milk shake, sighing with exasperation. "You've asked me for my professional advice. You want to ignore it, fine. But take it from me, my friend. Your whole world is about to blow up in your face."

"It won't be the first time."

I HAD SOME arrangements to make in Old Lyme, Lyme's shoreline neighbor, before I headed back to the farm. Two stops at the shopping center. My first was at the local branch of New England Savings, or at least it had been New England Savings until it recently got itself devoured by an outfit called Citizens Bank. Banks were gobbling each other up like crazy lately. It was, the TV commercials kept promising, the dawn of a whole new era of consumer choice. I could barely contain my excitement. As it happened, a shiny new green and white CITIZENS BANK sign was going up over the door right as I walked in. I wondered if it was an evil omen to walk underneath a bank's new sign. I asked the workmen who were bolting it into place, but they weren't particularly helpful. Or friendly, come to think of it.

After my stop at the bank I went over to Gull's Way, the bustling travel agency where four middle-aged ladies worked the phones morning, noon and night making airline, hotel and cruise reservations for local residents. When I was done there I succumbed to my curiosity and steered the Woody across the Connecticut River to Walt's Market in Old Saybrook for a gallon of Salem Valley Farms vanilla ice cream and a six-pack of zippy, old-fashioned Stewart's root beer in glass bottles. Then I crossed the river again and headed back into the lush green hills of Lyme. Lulu rode shotgun with her front paws on the armrest and her large black nose stuck out the open window, enjoying the exotic scents wafting from the dairy farms. When I reached Hamburg Cove I turned off at Joshua Town Road, a narrow country lane that twisted its way for miles through ancient forests and historic farms edged by fieldstone walls, until I arrived at the end of the road, where there was a large sign on a wooden post that said PRIVATE. Also a paddock gate that Merilee usually left open.

After a half mile of rutted dirt driveway I pulled up next to the barn and got out. Lulu and I were immediately greeted by Old Saxophone Joe, crowing his fool head off as always. I went in the kitchen to put the ice cream in the freezer and the root beer in the refrigerator. As soon as I opened the refrigerator door Lulu parked herself in front of it. She wanted an anchovy. She likes them straight out of the fridge. The oil clings to them better. I gave her one, then got the Waring blender out and made myself a root beer shake, sampling it carefully.

I found it to be altogether delicious. A definite keeper. Pete Tedone knew his fountain drinks. After I'd drained every last chilled drop I headed out to the chapel.

The phone was ringing as I walked through the chapel door. The home phone line.

"God, it's so good to hear your voice," Merilee said morosely.

"Is it really going that badly?"

"I swear, Hoagy, it's beginning to feel like talent night at Camp Minnetonka. I'm hiding in Mimi's office with the shades drawn. If there's too much light I can see my career passing right before my eyes. How can I offer this lifeless dreck to Paul Newman and Joanne Woodward tomorrow night? We simply haven't got it—with the exception of Marty, which is rather bizarre considering that he's the one who's a completely screwed-up human being."

"The stage is his refuge."

"And Sabrina is spot-on."

"This is a major showcase for her."

"But Dini and Greg are *somewhere else*. I'm becoming convinced that Dini's ten times sicker than she's letting on. And Greg, I swear, just doesn't *get* British humor. Truly, I don't know what to do with him. But enough about this awful mess. Let's talk about my other awful mess. Was Bruce of any help?"

"Plenty. You have nothing to worry about criminally."

"But what if R.J. goes to the media?"

"Bruce said he'll take care of it."

"Are you being honest with me? You sound funny."

"Funny ha-ha?"

"Funny as in you're holding out on me. Bruce isn't going to hire someone to beat him up or something, is he?"

"Of course not. That isn't his style."

Merilee fell silent for a moment. "This has unearthed emotions that I've kept buried for a long, long time, Hoagy. I'm not feeling particularly proud of myself right now."

"You were young and frightened. You made a mistake. We all do. God knows I have."

"But that poor man *died*."

"You weren't driving. It wasn't your fault."

"So why does it feel like it was?"

"Just try to let it go, okay? We're handling it, and you've got *Private Lives* to deal with."

"I've scheduled another run-through for six o'clock. We'll keep at it all night until we get it right."

"And you will."

She sighed wearily. "I wish I shared your confidence. I doubt I'll make it home. I'll just take a room at the inn and catch a couple of hours of sleep. Give Lulu a hug for me, will you?"

I changed into a frayed black T-shirt, work jeans and my old Chippewa boots. Went in the wire chicken coop to say hey to the girls. Came away with a basket filled with nine fresh brown eggs. Then I paid a visit to the garden and harvested some arugula, romaine lettuce, parsley, chervil and chives. Did some weeding, too. Lulu kept me company by rolling around on her back in the tall, cool grass with her tongue lolling out of the side of her mouth. I sat back on my heels and watched a red-tailed hawk circle over Whalebone Cove and wondered why life couldn't be this uncomplicated and pleasurable all of the time. Then I shook myself and carried my bounty inside to the kitchen.

I was washing the greens when the phone rang. The business line.

Same hoarse, raspy voice, although this time he sounded as if he were calling from the pay phone in a barroom. I could hear the clinking of ice in glasses, raucous laughter. "You got my money, smart guy?"

"I paid a visit to the bank."

"Good. Know where the old brass mill in Sherbourne used to be?"

"The ruins on the riverbank? Yes, I do."

"Meet me at what's left of the front gate at nine o'clock. Come alone, or we'll have ourselves a problem."

"I'm afraid I can't do that. I have a four-legged partner."

"Leave him at home."

"He is a she. And I can't. She gets lonesome and howls."

"Whatever," he grumbled, hanging up on me.

It was nearly six. I put down a fresh can of 9Lives for Lulu. Made myself an omelet out of three freshly laid eggs topped with just-picked herbs and a salad of the arugula and romaine. I ate at the kitchen table, sipping a glass of chilled Sancerre. By the time I'd washed the dishes it was time to go. I grabbed the envelope I'd prepared, climbed into the Woody with Lulu and took off, still dressed in my frayed black T-shirt, work jeans and Chippewas.

Not all of Sherbourne was quaintly picturesque. On the outskirts of the village, on the eastern banks of the Sherbourne River, lay the crumbling red brick ruins of the long-shuttered brass mill. The riverfront there was a fetid, toxic waste dump of sludgy black water, broken glass and garbage. Some enterprising young artists were hoping to renovate the old mill for studio space. But for now it was a place where local kids went to get their buzz on. Dealers were busted there periodically for peddling weed.

There were no streetlights. No one was around. All was darkness and ominous quiet. I parked the Woody a quarter mile away and hoofed it, flashlight in hand, manila envelope tucked under my arm. Lulu marched stoutly along by my side, large black nose to the ground, snuffling.

As we neared the ravaged brick pillars that had once supported the mill's twelve-foot cast iron front gate she let out a low warning growl.

R.J. was already there waiting for us. In my flashlight's beam he looked like a creature that was meant to live in the dark—all jawbones, snaggly, rotting teeth and wild, bulging eyes. He was gaunt and pale and a sheen of oily sweat clung to his forehead. He wore a tank top, cutoffs and sneakers without socks. The butt of a handgun stuck out of the waistband of his cutoffs.

Behind him I noticed a couple of blankets, a duffel bag and some empty peppermint schnapps bottles. He was hiding out here from the law. Not to mention whoever he owed that money to.

"That's funny," he said in his raspy voice. "You're taller than I thought you'd be."

"That's funny, you're not."

Next to me, Lulu settled into a low, watchful crouch.

"But you done good, bro." He shined his own light on the envelope under my arm. "Didn't call the cops."

"How do you know I didn't?"

"Because you smart guys know how to roll. You take what you want, then you protect what's yours. That's how it works, right?" He had dry mouth. Kept licking his lips. "It should be me up there."

"Up where?"

"On the big screen. I got more acting talent in my little finger than Tom Cruise has in his whole body."

"As it happens, quite a few of us can say that."

"I just wouldn't kiss up to them is all. And they don't like that."

"*They* being . . . ?"

"Directors. Not a one of them ever gave me a fair shot. Just kept telling me what to do, where to go."

"Yeah, that's why they call them directors."

"The smug bastards," he said bitterly. "They treated all of the others like their precious little princes and princesses. Pampered them, stroked them." R.J. fished a rumpled pack of Kools from his back pocket and lit one, his hands shaking. "But not me, never me. I had the looks. I had the chops. I had it all. So how come they didn't give *me* a chance, huh?"

I didn't answer him. He wasn't expecting me to. Wasn't talking to me.

Lulu got up now and circled around behind him, a low growl coming from her throat. She has a pretty menacing growl for someone with no legs.

R.J. watched her, amused. "What's Dumbo up to?"

"She doesn't like to be called that."

"Like I give a fuck." He flicked his cigarette off into the darkness. It hit the pavement with a shower of sparks. "Give it here," he said, meaning the money.

I handed him the envelope. He ripped it open greedily, shining his light inside. "What's *this*?"

"You said you wanted to get away to Mexico. I took you at your word. That's a first-class ticket from JFK to Mexico City. Direct flight, no layovers. And an Amtrak ticket from the Old Saybrook station to Grand Central, where you can catch a bus out to the airport. Also five thousand dollars to get you started. Five thou will go a long way down there. I trust that your passport's up-to-date?"

"I told you to bring me *twenty-five* thou!"

"I know what you told me but I don't take direction well. I suppose we're a lot alike in that regard."

R.J. gaped at me in disbelief. "Bro, what in the hell are you doing?"

"Giving you a chance to make a fresh start. It's a good deal. The best you're going to get. I'd take it if I were you."

"What are you, tripping? I am in deep to some very cruel dudes. I *need* that twenty-five thou!"

"And I need to floss daily. Doesn't mean it's going to happen."

Behind him, Lulu moved in closer, her growl now a full-fledged snarl.

"Tell her to cut that out," he warned me, his eyes narrowing.

"I can try, but she's very independent minded. All of the women in my life are."

"You are not showing me respect," he said, biting the words off angrily. "You think I can be bought off with chump change and a plane ticket?"

"You're the one who brought up Mexico. I've made every effort to accommodate you. And, like I said, it's the best deal you're going to get. Believe me, the other one that's on the table is a whole lot worse."

He tore up the plane ticket and scattered the pieces in the air. Likewise the train ticket. The money he pocketed, breathing heavily in and out. "Okay, here it is. I'll give you one more chance, but only because I got no other choice."

"One more chance for what?"

"I need twenty-five thou more."

"You're not going to get it."

"And you're not listening to me. Shut up and *listen* to me, will ya? You got twenty-four hours. Bring it to me tomorrow night, same time, same place. Right here. And you'd better have it. If you don't then I will make your life a living hell. Are you hearing me?"

"I'm afraid not. Is there a point to this?"

He glared at me savagely, his wild eyes bulging, his rotting gray teeth bared. "Be here tomorrow night with that money. All of it. Or you'll be sorry you ever met me."

"I'm already sorry I met you. Come on, Lulu, let's go. The air around here stinks."

I started back toward the Woody, Lulu on my heel.

"You were warned!" R.J. called after me. "Remember that, smart guy!"

We got in the Woody and I drove away. I needed to get the stench of the decaying old mill and R. J. Romero's sweaty desperation out of my nostrils. I steered down to Guilfoyle's town beach and walked along the water's edge with Lulu for a couple of miles, soaking up the clean, fresh breeze that was coming off of the Sound. We weren't alone out there. Couples were walking hand in hand, talking softly and laughing. Main Street over by The Nook was crowded with parked cars. The local revival house was showing *The Loneliness of the Long Distance Runner* with Tom Courtenay and Michael Redgrave, which is an okay movie if you're into brilliant. I found an empty stool at The Nook's counter, which gave me another chance to hear Michael Stipe mewl "Everybody Hurts" on the kitchen radio. Had a cup of coffee and one of The Nook's famous apple cider doughnuts. Lulu settled for a bowl of water before she stretched out under me and dozed, tuckered from our beach walk. Then we headed home.

Narrow, twisting Joshua Town Road wasn't easy to drive late at night. There were no streetlights or porch lights. I'm talking total darkness. It was hard to go more than twenty miles per hour. And that was on a nice, balmy summer night. You ought to try it in the sleet sometime. It took me nearly an hour to make it from The Nook back to Merilee's farm at the end of the road beyond the PRIVATE sign. She'd installed an electric eye that tripped floodlights to illuminate the courtyard between the house, chapel and barn. Otherwise it would have been impossible to find your way around.

I pulled in and shut off the Woody's engine. Right away, I noticed that something was wrong.

It was quiet. Too quiet.

Old Saxophone Joe wasn't crowing.

Lulu got between my feet. She was shaking.

It didn't take me very long to find his body and all of the feathers and blood. He'd been beheaded. His head was affixed to the barn door with a hatchet. Blood had oozed from it down the barn door into the dirt.

"It's okay, girl," I assured Lulu, swallowing my revulsion. "We're okay."

I had zero doubt that it was R.J. who'd been here and done this. I stood there, looking around at the darkness beyond the floodlights, feeling very exposed and vulnerable. The farm had no security system. Just neighbors. And the nearest one, Mr. MacGowan, lived a mile away. As I stood there, Lulu trembling between my feet, I tried to remember if I'd passed anyone heading up Joshua Road just now. I hadn't. I took a closer look at the blood on the ground under Joe's head. It was congealing. So it had been a while since he'd come and gone.

Assuming he'd gone.

The farmhouse door was locked and the lock hadn't been tampered with. He hadn't tried to get in. Not that way anyhow. I walked all of the way around the place, flashlight in hand, to see if he'd broken any windows. He hadn't. I unlocked the door, went inside and searched the place, turning on lights everywhere I went until the whole house was ablaze. He hadn't stolen anything. Paintings, antiques, Merilee's jewelry, her great-grandmother's silver. Nothing was missing. Or at least it didn't appear to be.

He'd simply wanted to send a message. And he had.

And, in case you're wondering, the answer is: Yes, I did check the mudroom freezer chest. My manuscript was still in there with the venison leg.

I was fetching a shovel, broom and an old burlap gunny-sack from the barn when I heard a car coming up the drive-way. Lulu began to bark furiously.

It was a silver Ford Crown Victoria sedan. Pete Tedone got out, wearing the same shiny black suit he'd had on at lunch, and looked around at the place admiringly before he strode toward us. Lulu stopped barking and greeted him, her tail thumping.

He bent down and patted her before he straightened back up, looked at Old Saxophone Joe's head hatcheted to the barn door and said, "Wow, you're even dumber than I thought."

"How so?"

"You tried to make a deal with him. This guy's in no position to make a deal. He owes twenty-five thou to somebody who will kill him if he doesn't pay up. What good does a plane ticket do him? He won't live long enough to make it to the airport."

"Back up a second. You followed me to the travel agency?"

"Let's say I've been monitoring your activities. That's what Bruce hired me to do. He's worried about you. And, no offense, I can see why he is."

"Were you at the old brass mill, too?"

"Quite some eyesore, isn't it? The town ought to tear it down."

"I had no idea you were there. You're good at your job."

"That's why I get paid the big bucks, although I must say that you sensitive artistic types give me a real pain, you know? If it were up to me I'd have blown Romero's head off right there, thrown his body in the river and all of your troubles would be over. Instead, you still owe him that money, Miss Nash's reputation is still hanging by a thread and now you've got yourself one headless rooster. You want some help dealing with that?"

"I'm good, thanks."

"Have a lot of experience burying decapitated roosters, do you?"

"Can't say I do, but I'll be fine."

He took off his suit jacket, laid it on the hood of his car and rolled up his shirtsleeves. "Come on, pal. I'll give you a hand."

Tedone held the gunnysack open while I stuffed Old Saxophone Joe's remains inside. I used the broom to sweep up as many feathers as I could. Then I yanked the hatchet from the barn door and deposited Joe's head in the sack. Tedone cinched it shut and we carried it into the woods behind the house. He held the flashlight while I dug a hole three feet deep in the moist soil, dropped the sack in and covered it over with dirt. I piled a fieldstone cairn on top to mark the spot. Lulu took in the entire operation with mournful watchfulness.

When we got back to the barn I filled a bucket from the work sink and took a scrub brush and cleanser to the barn door. Then I cleaned and oiled the hatchet while Tedone washed up.

After I'd washed up I said, "Buy you a cold root beer?"

"I wouldn't say no."

I went inside and returned with two glass bottles of the Stewart's that I'd bought at Walt's Market.

Pete Tedone took a long drink, letting out a grateful sigh. "This is the good stuff."

"Nothing but the best at this pop stand."

He drank down some more. "So have you changed your mind?"

"About what?"

"About that proposition I laid out to you this afternoon. The one that involves putting a certain sum of money toward a charitable cause."

"No, I haven't changed my mind."

"You're dealing with a very, very low class of person here," he said, draining his root beer. "I'd advise you to reconsider."

"I'm afraid not. Can I buy you another round?"

"No, thanks. I want to go home, take a shower and snuggle with my wife. I love my wife. That's why I'm burying headless roosters in the woods instead of sitting behind a big desk in Middletown pulling down a fat salary and benefits. Because we do whatever we have to do for the women we love."

"Yes, we do."

He tossed his jacket in the car and got in. "I'm not unsympathetic to your situation, you know," he said through his open window. "If you bump Romero off you'd never be able to tell her, and you can't live with that. I get it." He looked around admiringly again. "Beautiful farm she's got here. I've seen places like this in magazines but I've never actually been to one." Then he turned to me and said, "He won't be back tonight. Get yourself a good night's sleep."

Pete Tedone started up his Crown Victoria and worked it back down the long drive to Joshua Town Road. I went inside the house, poured myself a large Macallan and drank it while I turned off all of the lights and locked up. Then I went out to the chapel, showered, got into bed and lay there in the dark with Lulu, listening to the night creatures and the crickets while Lulu whimpered softly. She was upset about Old Saxophone Joe. I did my best to console her but she really isn't cut out for the stark realities of farm life. Street muggings she understands. Chopping a rooster's head off she doesn't. I can't say that I do, either.

I turned on my bedside lamp and reached for a collection of essays by E. B. White, who is someone I reread every few years just to remind myself what good writing is.

That was when the phone rang. The business line.

"Hey, smart guy." Same raspy voice and wet cough. Same sarcastic familiarity. "Get my message?"

"That was totally unnecessary."

"I warned you not to mess with me."

"You're a sick human being, Romero. You need help."

"I need my money. Just wanted to make it perfectly clear to you that I'm not kidding around."

"All right, I'll get you your damned money."

"Tomorrow night, right? Same time, same place."

"Tomorrow night's the performance of *Private Lives*. There'll be an after-curtain party. We'll have to make it a bit later."

"How *much* later?"

"Let's say eleven o'clock."

"That works for me." He fell silent. "I have your word?"

"You have my word."

"Good, because I'm hiding out from some very dangerous guys. That makes me a dangerous guy. I'd sure hate it if you disappointed me again."

"I won't. But just to be clear about something . . ."

"Yeah, what is it?"

"This is not going to end well for you."

He let out a harsh, wet laugh. "It doesn't end well for anyone. You're supposed to be smart. Haven't you figured that out yet?"

Chapter Four

I noticed two things right away when I awoke shortly before dawn. Old Saxophone Joe wasn't crowing and a warm drizzle was falling. According to the radio weatherman the forecast now called for a 70 percent chance of "severe" thunderstorms and "dangerously" high winds by that evening. Not exactly a good omen for the gala benefit performance of *Private Lives* in the roof-challenged Sherbourne Playhouse.

I hadn't slept well at all. Too much on my mind, none of it good. Plus Lulu simply wouldn't stop whimpering about Joe. She was sad, and trust me when I tell you that there's nothing sadder than a sad basset hound.

I put the coffee on, hungering to get the Ramones on my turntable, crank the volume up to eleven, and dive headfirst back into my novel. But I couldn't focus. Not after the insanity of yesterday and what was sure to be even more insanity today. That unwanted intruder known as Real Life, the bane of every novelist's existence, had taken charge. I would get zero work done today on *The Sweet Season of Madness*, and I knew it.

So I got busy packing a garment bag instead. My tux. Starched pleated white shirt. Bow tie. Studs and cuff links.

Black patent leather shoes. If you live long enough, and I sincerely hope that you do, you'll discover that there are very, very few people who can carry off wearing a tux with effortless grace. There's Fred Astaire. There's Marlene Dietrich. There's me. I wasn't sure if anyone else would be wearing one tonight, but I wasn't about to pass up the opportunity. When I'd finished packing I showered, shaved and dressed in the featherweight glen plaid worsted wool suit, a lavender shirt, powder blue knit tie, white bucks and fedora. I readied the guest cottage for the coming storm by closing and latching all of the windows and locking the door. I went in the house and collected Lulu's bowls, some canned food and her anchovy jar. Stowed them in the antique doctor's bag that I use as her travel kit and stashed it in the Woody with my garment bag. Then I closed and latched all of the windows in the house and stowed the deck furniture in the barn. The chickens could take care of themselves. Their wire coop had a little door into the barn that they could use when they needed to.

I took one last look around, suddenly realizing that in the event of a power outage, which happened frequently in Lyme when it got stormy, that the venison leg in the mudroom freezer chest might thaw and drown my manuscript. Seized by sheer panic at the mere thought of it, I moved the pages from the freezer to the bread box in the kitchen.

Then I locked the house, got in the Woody with Lulu and moved on out, easing down the long, bumpy driveway until I hit Joshua Town Road. After a half mile or so I pulled in at Mr. MacGowan's weathered farmhouse, where he was sitting on his covered porch in a pair of overalls puffing on his pipe and reading that morning's New London *Day*. Angus MacGowan was a barrel-chested widower in his seventies whose family had been farming in Lyme since the 1600s. He was an abrupt, cranky Yankee but incredibly kind once he decided someone was okay. And Merilee was definitely his idea of okay. He was her go-to expert when it came to anything that had to do with livestock. The man knew pretty much everything there was to know. Not that he worked very hard at farming anymore. In fact, farming had never actually been his sole means of support. He'd taught math at the high school for forty years.

"Morning, Hoagy," he called out cheerfully. Lulu waddled straight to him for a pat on the head. "Get you a cup of coffee?"

"I've got to be running, thanks."

He peered at me, one eye squinted shut. "Yet you look to me like a fella with trouble on his mind."

"Old Saxophone Joe passed away last night."

"Sorry to hear that. Did he take sick?"

"He got attacked."

Mr. MacGowan nodded knowingly. "Fox, most likely."

"I wondered if you might have an extra rooster I could buy off of you."

"Afraid not," he said, rustling the pages of his newspaper.

"Okay. Just thought I'd ask."

"Let me rephrase that. I have an extra rooster I can let you have but I won't accept money for it."

I smiled at him. "Thank you, Mr. MacGowan."

"Actually, you'll be doing me a favor. I've got me a pair that tussle day and night. Be good to get one of them out of here. You being a city fella, I should warn you it's not easy to bring a new rooster into a coop. Those hens can get awful nasty. You'll need a take-charge type. Me, I'd say Quasimodo's the man for the job. Want me to bring him by later and introduce him to the girls?"

"I'm afraid I'll be gone all day. We both will."

"Not to worry. I'll take care of it. Happy to." He peered at me again. "You've still got more on your mind."

"I'd appreciate it if you wouldn't say anything about this to Merilee. Unless she asks, that is. She may notice that Quasimodo doesn't look or sound like Old Saxophone Joe. Then again, she may not."

"You'd rather she didn't know he got himself eaten, is that it? Say no more. I understand."

"Thanks, Mr. MacGowan. You're a good neighbor."

"You folks had yourselves a busy night last night, didn't you? Cars coming and going."

"Busier than we like. Did you happen to see them?"

"Nope, just heard 'em. I was in bed reading my new Tom Clancy. Now *he* can tell a story. One of 'em drove by here around ten o'clock in a real beater that needs a new muffler. Hung around for a half hour or so before it took off. Then you came home in the Woody. I'd recognize the purr of that engine in my sleep. Then another car came along not long after you. Newer engine." He fanned himself with his newspaper. "Feel that tropical air moving up from the Gulf of Mexico? Heck, you can practically smell it. Going to pour tonight. Count on it." He fanned himself some more before he said, "I'll see to Quasimodo. Don't you worry about a thing."

"Thank you, Mr. MacGowan. We won't be home tonight until very late. And we're not expecting any company."

"Say no more. I hear anybody heading up your way—like, say, somebody who needs a new muffler—I'll call the resident trooper." He studied me curiously. "Merilee got herself one of those celebrity stalkers or something?"

"Or something."

THE SHERBOURNE INN, the yellow, three-story Victorian mansion that anchored the town green, was famous for its English-style rose garden. A full-time staff of gardeners kept everything pruned and tidy. The boxwood hedges were so neatly squared off they looked as if they'd been razor cut. Not a weed was to be found anywhere. It was all just a bit too twee for me. I prefer controlled chaos. But most people seemed to love the inn's garden. Some of them even chose to get married there.

The mansion's hardwood-paneled first floor had been converted into a formal dining room and an informal taproom where they had Guinness on draft and cooked up a not terrible bacon cheeseburger. There was a screened-in wraparound terrace overlooking the rose garden where breakfast was served.

Marty Miller was seated out there at a table by himself poring over his marked-up copy of *Private Lives*. He had on a different colored polo shirt than yesterday's but he still gave off that same pungent scent of curried mutton. And he was still wearing flip-flops, sad to say. His bare feet smelled like Camembert that had been left out in the sun for too long. He was unshaven and what little he had in the way of blond hair was uncombed. Hadn't changed the bandage that Glenda had put on his soft, pudgy hand yesterday. It looked dirty, crusty and a bit revolting, actually. On the table before him was a plate of corned beef hash topped with four poached eggs. Also a side order of sausages.

"Glad you stopped by, Hoagy," he said, brightening as he glanced up at me. "I hate to eat alone."

"Is that why you ordered enough food for two?"

"No, that's because I'm a *P-I-G* pig. Millie, will you please get over here, you gorgeous creature?"

Our young, fresh-faced waitress bustled over in her gingham uniform to fill my coffee cup. She was a sturdily built milkmaid type with apple cheeks and bright blue eyes who was clearly awed by the presence of such a big movie star.

"Get my friend whatever he wants and put it on my tab," Marty said, winking at me. "The playhouse is paying for it."

I ordered the corned beef hash with two poached eggs. "And a small plate of smoked salmon for my friend, please." Meaning Lulu, who'd started to curl up under our table until she got a whiff of Marty's feet and relocated herself over by the screen door to the garden.

"Sure thing," Millie said, bustling off.

"I hear they are talking *deluge* tonight," Marty said to me as he went to work on his breakfast. He ate pretty much as you'd expect—by lowering his head to the plate and shoveling the food in like a snowplow. "Something tells me we'll be up there onstage clutching umbrellas. Meanwhile, our full house of heavy hitters will be sitting there in fancy dress getting totally drenched. Coward would be chortling his head off. Too bad the old boy's not around to see it."

"Marty, I was wondering if we could talk about your days at Yale. You and Dini, Dini and R. J. Romero . . ."

He tensed ever so slightly. "Why do you want to dredge up that old shit?"

"I truly don't. It's surfaced on its own."

"I see . . ." He shoved half of a sausage into his mouth, chewing on it. "Actually, I lied. I don't see. That's what is known as a space holder. Something to say when you have nothing to say. It's, um, not a very pleasant story, Hoagy. You'd better sit down."

"I am sitting down."

"Son of a bitch, you are."

Millie brought me my breakfast, topped off my coffee and delivered a small plate of smoked salmon to Lulu, beaming at her. Lulu dove in gratefully.

"Where would you like me to start?" Marty asked with a complete absence of enthusiasm.

I went to work on my hash, which tasted even better than it looked. "How about with Dini and R.J.?"

He shrugged his soft, pudgy shoulders. "They paired off right away. And broke up just as fast. The bastard tore her heart out."

"How did he manage to do that?"

"Stole some jewelry from her. Her grandmother's cameo brooch, to be exact, which was of great sentimental value. Worth a pretty penny, too. Naturally, he swore he knew nothing about it. But she knew he took it. The guy was a compulsive gambler. Owed lots of people money. People who were even more unsavory than he was. Anyway, when she pressured him about it he slapped her right across the face, the no-good bastard."

"I take it you weren't a fan."

"He was scum. A small-time hood who was laboring under the delusion that he was going to be the next Bobby De Niro. I confronted him about it. I said, 'See here, Romero, did you strike Dini Hawes?' I was very chivalrous in those days. Watched one too many Errol Flynn movies. In response he produced a five-inch folding knife from his back pocket, held the blade against my throat and said, 'Back off, Porky, or I'll cut you.' Then he told me what a stupid 'twat' Dini was. That's what he called her. A 'twat.' That sweet, beautiful girl, her heart filled with so much goodness and love . . ." Marty's face reddened. "I was crazy about her, as you may have surmised. How could I not be? I was a chubby oaf from West Islip. Never a good student. Never good at sports. Never good at anything. Mostly, I was just filled with a burning desire to be someone else."

"A born actor, in other words."

"Exactly. And, to me, Dini was such an exotically fascinating creature. She wore these weird antique dresses and petticoats that had belonged to her grandmother. I swear, she was like someone straight out of Tennessee Williams. But she was also so supportive and kind. Kept telling me how talented I was. Dini believed in me when I barely believed in myself. I was incredibly insecure. Didn't belong to any of the cliques. And I sure as hell didn't look like Robert Redford. I finally worked up the nerve to pursue her after she and R.J. broke up, and we ended up moving in together."

"What did she see in him?"

"In R.J.? Danger. Edge. He was a bad boy. All nice girls love bad boys."

"Was he talented?"

"Yes, but with an asterisk. He could only play one character—himself. He wouldn't shed his own skin and try to tackle, say, Shakespeare. He didn't know how. Didn't understand the words and wasn't interested in learning what they meant. Good actors are smart. Good actors are inquisitive. R.J. was a poseur—the kind who other actors can see right through. The teachers at Yale tried to push him, but he didn't want to put in the work. Just wanted to show up. Acting is a lot more than just showing up. It's digging into each and every word the playwright has written and trying to figure out how to bring those words to life in ways that are unexpected, revealing and, above all, emotionally honest." Marty stuffed another hunk of sausage in his mouth. "That digging, that *journey*, doesn't necessarily take you to a happy place. In fact, the destination can be so painful it eats you alive. But that's the job."

"And you do it damned well."

Marty lowered his eyes uncomfortably. "That's nice of you to say."

"I saw your Willy Loman. I was so blown away I could barely get out of my seat. No one's ever played him so *human*."

"Lee Cobb's the template. He played Willy angry. No huge fucking surprise there. Lee Cobb played everybody angry. If they'd cast him as Elwood P. Dowd in *Harvey* he would have been yelling at his imaginary six-foot rabbit. When they revived *Salesman* in '84 with Dustin he played Willy as a befuddled nebbish, which I didn't . . ." Marty trailed off, gazing out at the rose garden as he searched for the words. "I never saw Willy that way. I saw him as a man like my pop."

"What does your dad do?"

"Did. He's gone." He turned back to me, a pained look on his face. "He sold cars for a Chevy dealer in Huntington. He was always under pressure from the sales manager to meet his quota, earn his bonuses. But if a customer didn't think he could afford to buy a certain car Pop wouldn't try to talk him into it. He was a decent human being, which made him a lousy sales-man. He knew it, too, and hated it about himself. The man was consumed by self-loathing. One evening, after everyone had left, he went in the service department and hooked up a hose to the tailpipe of a car that was in having some work done. The sales manager found him dead in the front seat after my mom called him three times to say Pop hadn't come home. He *always* came home. I was thirteen when he died. She raised me on her own after that."

"You were born to play Willy, weren't you?"

Marty peered at me suspiciously. "Why do I suddenly feel like we're working on my memoir?"

"Sorry. Second-occupational hazard."

He let out a booming laugh that came all of the way up from his diaphragm just in case I'd forgotten he was a stage-trained actor, which I hadn't. "Maybe so. I sure wasn't born to play Elyot in *Private Lives*, but I'm having a hell of a lot of fun. How can you not have fun with Noël Coward? My God, his command of the language, his insights into people. And I'll let you in on a little secret. Merilee Nash can direct. She knows how to get across what she wants, but she also knows how to listen. I can see her doing more of this in the future."

"She'd like to. She's afraid she won't be able to get good roles in another few years, being of the female persuasion. She's always telling me that a leading man is allowed to be fifty but a leading lady isn't."

"She's not wrong. I will say this, he was one handsome son of a bitch."

"Are we talking about R.J.?"

Marty nodded. "You took one look at him and you knew that Hollywood would be calling. He used to complain that the teachers at Yale never gave him a fair shake because they resented him for his looks. It was a respect thing. He thought they didn't treat him with respect."

"Was he right?"

Marty puffed out his cheeks. "He was and he wasn't. They definitely resented performers who didn't 'need' the program. The ones who were headed right to the top simply because they won the lottery at birth. But a ton of the blame fell on him. He wouldn't learn his lines. Figured they'd just let him improvise, like he was James Dean in *Rebel Without a Cause*. We were doing Euripides, for crissakes." Marty sat back and lit a Lucky Strike, dragging on it deeply. "Plus he had these sleazeball friends who'd stop by to watch us rehearse. Street corner punks from his old neighborhood who thought they were at a party. Campus security had to be called a couple of times."

"Have you seen R.J. since those days?"

"Haven't seen him in, God, it must be twelve years. I was in a Mamet play at Circle in the Square. He came in to read for a small part. Hadn't prepared for it and was stoned off of his ass. When they asked him to leave, he told Mamet—*the* David Mamet—that he was a fake tough guy who was full of shit. A couple of stagehands threw him out."

"Sure you haven't seen him recently? Like, say, hanging around here?"

Marty's eyes widened with surprise. "The playhouse, you mean? No way. Or I should say not that I know of. I'm not positive I'd recognize him now. He partied plenty hard."

I finished my breakfast, wiping my mouth with my napkin. "He and Merilee were hot and heavy for a while, too, I understand. Any idea why they broke up?"

"Because he was no good, like I said."

"Was there a major blowup?"

"You mean did he smack her around like Dini? Not that I'm

aware of. The bad boy infatuation wore off, that's all. She got fed up with him and moved on."

So she'd given it to me straight. Her classmates didn't know the truth about the night that R.J. "borrowed" his cousin Richie's Porsche. She hadn't told a soul. Unless, that is, Marty was sitting right there across the table lying to me, which was certainly a possibility. Actors lie for a living.

"You want to know what I think?" He pulled on his cigarette, his eyes narrowing. "I think that for women like Dini and Merilee—sensitive, caring women who have good hearts—R. J. Romero is a phase they go through. It's like that phase in high school when guys like you and me think we're going to become normal, well-adjusted members of society, remember?"

"Sure do. I thought I was going to be a lawyer. Possibly even a Supreme Court justice. I even started wearing permanent press Sansabelt slacks to school."

Over by the screen door, Lulu raised her head and coughed, which is what she does because she doesn't know how to laugh.

"But I quickly returned to my senses and the genuine, crazy me took over again," I assured Marty.

"Did you burn the slacks?"

"Tried to, but they were flame retardant."

Marty let out a laugh. "Me, I decided I was destined for a career on Wall Street. Bought myself a pair of Florsheim cordovan wing tip shoes."

"Did you ever wear them?"

"Twice. They made me feel like Bozo the Clown. I stuck them in the back of my closet and there went a promising career in high finance. To this day, I still don't understand what an arbitrageur does."

"Trust me, you're better off not knowing."

Our waitress returned to fetch Lulu's thoroughly cleaned plate and to ask us if she could get us anything else. Marty treated her to a big smile and said we were just fine, thanks. Off she went, wiggling her generous hips provocatively.

"How long were you and Dini together?"

Marty's face fell. "She ended it after a semester," he said, stubbing out his Lucky in a Sherbourne Inn ashtray. "Told me we weren't a good match. She was right, of course. Wackiness aside, she was a traditional small-town southern girl who needed a calm, emotionally grounded adult male—not some wild man like me who's racked by demons. Still, it surprised me when she and Greg started getting it on."

"Were you and Greg friends?"

"We got along okay. He was a nice guy. Still is. We were just real different, that's all. He was quiet and conservative. Grew up working in his dad's sporting goods store in Tacoma. Liked to hunt and fish. Dini was so bohemian and eccentric that I couldn't imagine that Greg was her type. But he was exactly her type. And they've been happy together ever since, so far as I can tell."

"You still have a soft spot for her, don't you?"

"Is it that obvious?"

"Only to me. I happen to lug around a great big torch myself."

"Merilee? I don't blame you. She's the McCoy, as my pop used to say."

"She told me that R.J. considered Greg a total stiff."

"R.J. was dead wrong about him. Greg Farber can carry an entire fifty-million-dollar film on his back. Very few actors are capable of doing that. R.J. just resented him because Greg knew how to get along with people. He was respectful and considerate. He was also a professional, by which I mean he was willing to learn his lines and work hard. R.J. wasn't."

The waitress returned with our check. Marty signed it with a flourish, winking at her. She blushed as she went back inside, her hips continuing to wiggle.

He glanced at his watch. "We've got a full dress rehearsal at noon. Costumes, sets, lighting, the works. Merilee wants to make absolutely sure we've got our wardrobe and set changes down cold so we don't inflict forty-minute intermissions on our audience."

"And do you have them down cold?"

"Hell no. We're still flying blind. Chances are that one of us will tumble headfirst over Amanda's sofa in the middle of a scene. That's part of the thrill of attending a one-shot performance like this as far as the audience is concerned. Did you hear that Jackie O's coming? Word is she saw Tallulah Bankhead perform here when she was a kid." Marty glanced at his watch again. "That'll take us up to midafternoon. I'll probably come back here for a nap before showtime. Could use a bit of diversion, too." He waggled his eyebrows at me. "Do you think Millie's too young for me?"

"That all depends. Who's Millie?"

"Our waitress."

"I think she's still in high school, Marty."

"Does that mean no?"

Chapter Five

By the time Lulu and I made our way across the village green the bright summer sun had burned through the morning clouds and it was swelteringly hot out. Mimi, looking fabulous in tight jeans and an even tighter tank top, was out on the lawn dealing with two men from Sherbourne Roofing, whose truck was parked next to the stage entrance. The younger of the two had climbed an extension ladder that was propped against the side of the playhouse and was moving around very, very gingerly on the section of roof directly over the stage.

"No can do, Nick!" he called out.

"Why is he saying that?" Mimi asked Nick as I approached them. "What does he mean?"

"The beams are rotted out over the middle of the structure," Nick explained patiently. "If we try to walk across the roof we'll fall right through."

"How about a crane? Can you bring in a crane?"

"I'm not sure I can rent one on such short notice." Nick was trying really hard not to stare at Mimi's breasts snugged inside her tank top, which were still a sight to behold even though it had been sixteen years since she—*they*—had graced the cover of *Sports Illustrated*. "Even if I could we've still got the weight issue, as in the structure can't hold any. Best we can do is fling a couple of blue tarps over the stage and anchor 'em in place with a few bricks and boards."

"Wouldn't plywood be more effective?" she asked.

"Plywood's too heavy. Might crash right on through and kill one of your stars. You wouldn't want that to happen, would you?"

Mimi's nostrils flared. He was patronizing her. "There have been times when I would have," she answered tartly. "But this isn't one of them."

Nick tilted his Sherbourne Roofing cap back on his head, gazing up at his man on the roof. "Latest forecast I heard for this evening is an eighty percent chance of severe thunderstorms with wind gusts up to sixty miles per hour. That kind of wind will blow our tarps right off. For that matter, it could blow the whole roof off. Those old cedar shingles up there are so rotted out that the nails are barely holding them in place. Picture driving a nail into a piece of sopping wet toast. That's what my man's looking at." He glanced over at the big tent. "And I wouldn't place any bets on that thing staying put either."

"Is there a point to this?" Mimi demanded irritably.

"If it was me I'd postpone your event until tomorrow."

"Not possible. Two of my stars will be leaving town as soon as the curtain falls. Besides, hundreds of *very* prominent individuals have cleared their busy schedules to drive out here from New York City. It's got to be tonight."

"I wish I could help you, but I can't replace those rotted beams *and* reroof her in six hours. It's a two-, three-day job for a half-dozen men. Besides which, we're still talking about a building that's sliding off of its foundation sills. This playhouse should have been torn down five years ago."

"It's *not* going to be torn down!" Mimi said heatedly. "That's what tonight is all about. We're *trying* to save it."

"I understand," he responded, though clearly he didn't. Roofers are noted for their achy knees, not their sentimentality. "All we can do is tarp the stage area and say a prayer."

"What about the roof over the audience?" I asked him.

"We can tarp the whole danged building if that's what you want. But I'm telling you right now, if those tarps blow off, your *very* prominent individuals will get good and wet."

"So they'll get good and wet," Mimi said. "That'll make it a night to remember. Wouldn't you say so, Hoagy?"

"Yes, I would."

"Okay, whatever you want." Clearly, Nick didn't approve of the whole enterprise. "Should we get started?"

"Please," she said to him.

He trudged off toward the extension ladder to talk to his man on the roof.

"This may be it, Hoagy," Mimi said, watching him walk away.

"May be what?"

"The day I completely lose my mind."

"Not to worry, I'll help you find it. I have a ton of experience in that particular department."

Her pager beeped. She glanced at it and excused herself, striding briskly off toward the set warehouse, her fists pumping with determination.

Me, I went in the stage door and down the spiral staircase to the dressing rooms. It still smelled moldy and sour down there even though several box fans and sump pumps were going. And Lulu still had that same guarded look on her face that she gets whenever she's in the presence of r-a-t-s.

I found Merilee in the ladies' dressing room with Dini and Sabrina. All three were busy putting the finishing touches on their circa-1930 period costumes. Merilee wore a slinky pale yellow chiffon dress and saucy little hat. She was seated at the mirror darkening her eyebrows. Dini wore a knockoff of a little black Elsa Schiaparelli flapper-style dress and was fiddling with a gleaming black wig. Sabrina, whose wig was gray, was buttoning her dowdy maid's uniform.

Merilee eyed me in the mirror. "What do you think, darling?"

"I think it's you. All you need is a flask of hooch tucked in your garter. How are you feeling?" I asked Dini, who looked shaky and deathly pale.

"I'll be fine," she replied, her voice sounding quavery.

"Did you hear back from that doctor?"

"Not yet, but I'm sure it's nothing."

"I bet you have Lyme disease," Sabrina offered helpfully. "They have ticks all over the damned place around here. I can't wait to get back to the city."

"I'll conserve my energy during rehearsal and take a nap before the curtain," said Dini, who looked so sick it was hard to imagine she'd make it. But I'd seen Merilee crawl out of bed with a fever of 104 and light up a Broadway stage numerous times. It's what performers are born to do. The show must go on. Dini Hawes appeared frail and delicate but, trust me, she was constructed out of the same chromium steel as Michael Jordan.

I heard a commotion in the corridor behind me. Lulu was frisking with the twins, playfully whooping as they chased after her calling out, "Luluuuu . . . !"

"Mimi was just outside talking to a roofer about what to do if it pours tonight," I informed Merilee.

"What did he suggest?"

"He's going to tarp it, but he can't place too much weight on the tarps or the entire roof will collapse. He seems quite convinced of that. So if it gets really windy the tarps will blow off and everyone's going to get soaked."

"Darling, I wonder if you would do me a somewhat unusual favor."

"Do I have to wear a dress?"

"No."

"Then fire away."

"I want you to hit every Walmart you can find and buy up all of the umbrellas they have in stock."

"Say no more. I'm on it."

"We'll also need plastic buckets. Dozens of them. If the roof leaks it's going to drip in the aisles, the lobby, everywhere."

"Consider it done."

"If you can find us two hundred umbrellas I'll marry you."

"Does this constitute a proposal? You'd better be careful. I have two witnesses."

One of those witnesses, Dini, nearly crumpled to her knees when she stood up from her dressing table. She had to grab onto it to steady herself.

"Are you *sure* you can do this?" Merilee asked her, greatly concerned.

"I'm fine," Dini assured her.

"You're *not* fine," fumed Glenda, who'd arrived in the doorway just in time to witness her daughter nearly collapse. "I'm calling Doctor Orr to find out if he has the results of your blood work back yet."

"Mom, *I'm* his patient, not you, remember?" Dini pointed out wearily.

"I can still find out if he has them," she said stubbornly.

"Whatever." Dini sighed, her small hands trembling slightly.

On my way out I checked on Greg and Marty in their dressing room. Both actors had slicked back their hair with brilliantine. Greg was decked out in a vintage double-breasted white suit, Marty in a checked sports jacket and pleated cream-colored slacks. Something about their costumes reeked of summer stock to me. Possibly it was the overpowering smell of mothballs.

Greg sat before his dressing table mirror fiddling with a fake mustache. "What do you think?" he asked me.

"I think it looks like a pair of dead cockroaches."

"I was going to say dung beetles," Marty put in.

Greg studied himself in the mirror, turning his head this way and that. Off went the mustache.

"Dini seems to be feeling worse," I said to him.

"I know, poor thing. They'll knock it out with antibiotics, whatever it is. I just hope the twins don't catch it."

"What about you?"

"Me? I never get sick. I have the constitution of a horse."

"And the comic timing to match," Marty said.

"You'll pay for that," Greg shot back, grinning at him.

Sabrina joined me in the doorway in her frumpy maid's costume. "You guys look awesome," she observed, gulping. "I just hope I can hold up my end. I must confess that I'm starting to panic. There'll be a houseful of really great actors out there tonight."

"There are really great actors here already," I reminded her. "You've been working alongside of them for two weeks and doing fine. Trust me, you've got nothing to worry about."

Her dark, slanted eyes gleamed at me. "I didn't know you were sweet. On top of being brilliant, I mean."

"Sabrina, you really need to work at getting over your shyness with men," Marty advised her.

She ignored him. "I'm free for the next half hour. Would you like to get a coffee?"

"I'd love to, but I have that vital errand to run, remember?"

THERE WERE THREE, count 'em, three Walmarts skirting the shoreline within a thirty-minute drive of the Sherbourne Playhouse.

The first one I arrived at, in Clinton, was the standard cheerless, windowless, dimly lit gulag of a warehouse. Whenever I walk inside of a Walmart I'm convinced that we didn't win the cold war. There were surveillance cameras everywhere. Racks of cheap, utilitarian merchandise that had been manufactured in a giant sweatshop in some impoverished land halfway across the globe. The employees were so slack-jawed and dead-eyed that I swore they'd been lobotomized. And then there was the smell of those sweaty hot dogs that had been going round and round on the rotating electric grill in the snack bar for the past seven or eight hours. I wondered what continent those hot dogs originated from. I wondered what was in them. Actually, no, I didn't.

Lulu was highly allergic to the place. I think it was the dye that they used in those stacks of stiff, nondesigner jeans. All I know is she started sneezing the second we passed through the automated doors.

After I'd asked three clerks and hoofed it a half mile I found a box of twenty-four black travel umbrellas hidden among the camping and fishing gear. They were the sort that slide open and shut. I slid one open. It wasn't sturdy enough to handle a mild gust on Sixth Avenue, but we weren't expecting any gusts inside of the Sherbourne Playhouse. Or at least I certainly hoped we weren't. I asked a clerk if they had any more in the back. He obliged me with humanoid politeness and returned ten minutes later with another box, which gave me forty-eight. Not a bad start. Next I trekked to the housewares department and filled a grocery cart with twenty plastic buckets in assorted sizes and colors.

From there it was a half mile back to the cash registers to wait in line, which gave me a chance to catch up on the latest supermarket tabloid news. There was plenty of dirt about Burt and Loni's impending divorce if you wanted to read about that, which I didn't. Also the shocking revelations about new first lady Hillary Clinton's top-secret love affair with a man whom a highly reputable scientist believed was an extraterrestrial. I didn't pull that off of the rack either. Not when I could read about those captivating young lovebirds Lorena and John Wayne Bobbitt. It seems that Lorena had caught her husband cheating on her. On the night of June 23, while John was asleep in their bed, Lorena had proceeded to cut John's penis off with a kitchen knife, jump in her car and drive away with it. Somewhere near their Manassas, Virginia, home she'd thrown it out her open car window into an empty field, then suffered, um, misgivings and phoned the police. A thorough search of the field was undertaken and John and his severed penis were surgically reunited at the hospital a few hours later. He soon announced it was good as new—*all* systems go—and was now cheerfully squiring porn stars and nude models around L.A. by the dozen while Lorena languished in a Virginia jail cell awaiting trial, unaware that she had single-handedly contributed a major new verb—*to bobbitt*—to the rich tapestry of our language.

Back out into the icky, sticky summer air we went, the blacktop of the five-acre parking lot radiating the searing afternoon heat as I pushed the grocery cart back to the Woody. I unlocked the tailgate and stowed my purchases, closed the tailgate, turned and discovered that R. J. Romero was standing less than a foot behind me, grinning at me. His sweaty, gleaming face had a faintly jaundiced tinge to it in the bright sunlight. His rotting teeth looked grayish. He wore a striped T-shirt that looked as if he'd scored it off of Beaver Cleaver, blue jean cutoffs and sneakers without socks.

Lulu immediately growled at him.

"Your dog still doesn't like me," he observed, continuing to grin at me.

"That's because she has good taste."

He threw back his head and laughed.

I wondered if Pete Tedone was parked somewhere nearby keeping an eye on me and, if so, whether he would decide to step in. "So is this just two good-looking guys bumping into each other by chance or are you tailing me?"

R.J. didn't respond, just kept on showing me his gray teeth. His breath smelled like one of those aged, overworked storm drains in Times Square.

"Okay, I'll try a different approach. Is there something I can do for you?"

"Just wanted to make sure you're going to keep our date tonight."

"I said I'd be there. I'll be there. Now how about you get the hell out of my way?"

"Don't push me, smart guy. Bad things happen to people who push me. Or have you already forgotten about that chicken of yours?"

"It was a rooster, you moron."

"I don't like to be called a moron."

"Really? I should think you'd be used to it by now."

R.J. glared at me menacingly, his head cocked slightly to one side. "Same thing could happen to your little dog here, you know."

"No, it couldn't."

"Why's that?"

"Because I'd kill you first."

"You and who else?"

"Wow, I haven't heard that one since the fourth grade. You need to upgrade your threats a bit, if you don't mind some professional advice. You might also want to think about getting your teeth cleaned. I have an excellent dentist in New York if you ever want his name. Oh, and one other thing—don't ever come near that farm again."

"Why, what'll happen?"

"See above re: I'll kill you. And now this conversation is over. Unless there's something else you wanted to say."

"Nope." R.J. dug his rumpled pack of Kools from the back pocket of his cutoffs and lit one with a butane lighter, dragging on it deeply. "Just be sure you're there. Same spot. Eleven o'clock." And with that he went sauntering off across the parking lot like a cocky, overaged member of the Jets from *West Side Story*. Once an actor, always an actor.

I watched him to see if he got into a car, the one that Mr. MacGowan had told me needed a new muffler. But he just kept on going until he went inside of Walmart. Possibly he had a hankering for a hot dog.

I unlocked the door to the Woody, got in and rolled down the windows. Lulu put her head in my lap, whimpering.

"Don't you worry, girl. I won't let him hurt you. He's just a punk. I've got your back. Scout's honor."

AS I STARTED back toward Sherbourne with my mammoth haul of umbrellas and plastic buckets I could see huge, billowing dark clouds forming over Long Island Sound. Thunder rumbled off in the distance. The wind would gust suddenly and then, just as suddenly, the oppressively humid air would become totally still again. Yet there was an unsettling, ominous quality to the stillness.

When I arrived back at the playhouse four roofers were up on extension ladders doing the best they could to fling blue tarps over the old theater and secure them in place with boards. The tent crew was reinforcing the stakes that held the big wedding tent in place. Cases of champagne were being unloaded from a liquor distributor's van. A couple of local Connecticut

TV news crews were grabbing some B-reel footage for the five o'clock news.

I found a lobby door that was unlocked. The lobby walls were lined with posters of popular recent productions, which, due to the miniature dressing quarters, trended toward such popular acting duets as A. R. Gurney's *Love Letters* and D. L. Coburn's *The Gin Game*. Five elderly ladies—the playhouse's volunteer ushers—were whispering excitedly about who would see to which aisles tonight. As I began to dump the umbrellas and buckets outside of Mimi's office I heard those fabulous voices inside the theater and realized that I'd made it back in time to catch the last few minutes of the dress rehearsal. I slipped inside with Lulu, grabbed a seat in the back row and watched Coward's triumphant finale. Victor's indignant fury. Elyot's insulting hilarity. Sibyl shrieking like a madwoman. Amanda as maddeningly cool as can be. Poor Victor and Sibyl, it seems, have finally come to realize that they've just gotten themselves married to two divinely crazy people who are suited to be married only to each other.

I hadn't known what to expect after their intensive all-night rehearsal, but what I was watching sure as hell wasn't talent night at Camp Minnetonka. It was an ensemble of four world-class actors performing Noël fucking Coward together. Okay, so maybe the master's uniquely giddy dryness didn't come naturally to Greg. But he pulled it off like the pro that he was. And his accent had grown to become unobtrusively Niven-esque. Merilee had directed them to play it fast and straight. No mugging. I thought they were terrific, even though they had to compete with the shouts of the roofers and the *thunks* of their extension ladders. But performers are trained to ignore such distractions. And when the curtain came down I applauded them from the back row just as Mimi, Glenda and the twins did from down in front.

As the curtain rose back up I strolled down the aisle to the stage, where the four of them and Sabrina were quietly talking over their performance. The crew was removing the furniture so as to prepare the terrace set for act one.

"I kept jumping the gun," Dini was confessing to Merilee. "I came in too soon on your lines."

"You were great," Merilee assured her. "When we have a full house you'll feel the moment. But you look so flushed. Are you running a fever?"

"I'm fine," Dini insisted.

"You are *not* fine," Glenda said sternly from the front row. "Sit down over here so I can take your temperature."

Dini rolled her eyes. "Mother . . ."

"Don't argue with me," Glenda commanded her.

Dini joined her reluctantly, still in full costume and makeup. Glenda pulled a digital thermometer from her purse and stuck it under her famous daughter's tongue.

"You were awesome, Mom!" Cheyenne exclaimed brightly.

"Totally awesome!" Durango chimed in.

"What was I, chopped liver?" Marty asked them teasingly.

"You were sorta okay," Durango teased him back.

The thermometer beeped three times.

Glenda removed it from her daughter's mouth, squinting. "My dear, you're running a temperature of a hundred and two point eight. You need to get into bed right away if you want to have the slightest chance of going on tonight. Quite honestly, I'm not sure you're up to it."

"I will not miss this show just because of some stupid fever," Dini stated with a trouper's unwavering confidence.

"We'll discuss that later. Right now, I want you home in bed. And call Doctor Orr to find out about your blood tests."

"Mother, he said he'd call as soon as he had them."

"Fine, then *I'll* call him."

"We've already had this conversation!" Dini lashed out angrily. "*I'm* the patient, not you. So back off, will you? You're suffocating me!"

Glenda's lower lip began to tremble. "Well, you don't have to bite my head off."

Dini immediately let out a sigh of regret. "I'm sorry." She patted her mother's hand. "Forgive me."

"Your beach house is a half-hour drive away," Mimi pointed out. "That's a lost hour to and fro. Why don't I book you a room at the Sherbourne Inn? It's nice and quiet, and you can use that extra hour to get some sleep."

"That's where you'll find me," Marty said, heading for the dressing rooms to get out of his costume.

"Good idea, Mimi," Greg said. "I can take the girls home."

Mimi went backstage to call the inn.

"Will we have time for a swim, Daddy?" Cheyenne asked.

"Maybe a quick one. But then you have to get dressed. The sleeveless blue dresses?" he asked Dini.

Dini nodded. "And they each have a little knit sweater that goes with it. And bring their hooded rain slickers."

"Shall I come with you and dress them?" Glenda asked him.

"Not necessary," Greg assured her. "Daddy can handle it. Why don't you just relax in the rose garden over there while Dini's napping? And now, if you'll excuse me, I'm going to get out of this monkey suit."

Merilee studied me nervously as Greg headed offstage. "What did you think? Be brutally honest."

"I think it's fabulous."

"You really think it's good?"

"I believe the word I used was *fabulous*."

"Darling, I know you're trying to be supportive but I really need honest feedback right now."

"Merilee, have you ever known me to heap praise on anything when I didn't mean it?"

She frowned. "Well, no . . ."

"You did great. Attending tonight's performance will be a genuine privilege. I must report that there are some truly scary black clouds forming over Long Island Sound. On the plus side, my shopping excursion was a major success. I've bought up every cheapo umbrella between here and Timbuktu."

Mimi returned and said, "Success, Dini. I've wangled you a small third-floor room for the afternoon."

"Thank you." Dini was slumped wearily in her front row seat. She touched her index finger to her lips and tapped each of her girls on the forehead with it. "I'll see you sweeties soon," she said as Greg reappeared wearing a Mets T-shirt and plaid shorts, his face scrubbed clean of makeup. "Do what Daddy tells you, okay?"

"Yes, Mommy."

"Okay, Mommy."

"Feel better, sweetheart," Greg said to Dini gently. When he bent down to kiss her on the cheek she seemed to shudder. Maybe it was her fever. Then again, maybe not. "Let's go, munchkins."

He and the girls left. Merilee took Dini firmly by the arm and led her downstairs to the dressing rooms. After they'd cleaned off their makeup and changed into shorts they came back upstairs. Dini wore a flaming orange CHULA VISTA LANES bowling shirt with the name GLORIA stitched across her left breast. Merilee had on a frayed pink Izod shirt of mine that she'd rescued from the rag drawer back when we were still married.

Glenda took charge of walking her daughter across the green to the inn. I fetched the garment bag with my evening wear in it from the Woody and then Merilee and I trailed along after them in the sweltering heat, Lulu ambling proudly along ahead of us. She loves to walk with us when we're together, and so seldom gets the chance anymore. Those black scary clouds over Long Island Sound looked even blacker and scarier. They also seemed to be drifting northward over the Sound toward the Connecticut shoreline, even though the sky directly overhead remained a hazy, milky blue.

The dark coolness of the Sherbourne Inn's lobby was welcome. Sabrina sat by herself at a table in the dark wood bar with a glass of iced tea working on the *New York Times* crossword puzzle and wearing a pair of horn-rimmed glasses that said nerdy grad student more than glam actress. Glenda was placing a call from the phone at the front desk. Calling Doctor Orr to report on Dini's fever, I imagined. And no doubt trying to find out if he had the results of her blood test, too.

"Want something cold to drink?" I asked Merilee.

"What I want is to stretch out in my room for a while with you and Lulu."

"I believe we can accommodate you."

We went up the mansion's grand, curving staircase to her room on the second floor. It was a nice room, if your idea of nice is a four-poster bed, claret-colored velvet drapes and the pervasive scent of potpourri. I unzipped my garment bag and hung my tux from the shower railing.

Merilee kicked off her sandals and flopped down on the bed with a grateful groan. Lulu circled around the bed, whimpering helplessly. It was too high for her to climb up onto on her own. I gave her a hoist and she immediately stretched out next to her mommy with her head on her tummy. I took off my suit jacket and shoes and joined them there with Lulu between us making happy *argle-bargle* noises. It was the most contented I'd seen her in a long time.

"This is nice," Merilee murmured contentedly.

"Nice."

"But you'd better tell me about what's happening with R.J."

"Do yourself a huge favor. Don't waste any of your energy thinking about that loser. Just focus on tonight's performance. I'm taking care of it."

"*How* are you taking care of it?"

"By giving him what he wants. Bruce Landau figures the bum will end up back in jail or dead before long anyway. Best to just pay him off."

"So when are you . . . ?"

"Tonight at eleven, after the party."

"Have you got the money?"

"I'm all set."

"Why must it be *you* who makes the delivery?"

"Because that's how he wants it, and for now he's running the show."

"You know the .38 that Mr. MacGowan got me last winter when those rabid raccoons were around? It's in the glove box of the Jag, fully loaded."

"What's it doing in there?"

"I thought you might want it."

"I don't."

"Still, maybe you should take it."

"No."

She studied me with her piercing green eyes. "Hoagy, there's something you're not telling me. What is it?"

"Not a thing."

"You're lying."

"Am not."

"Are. Your left eyebrow is twitching. That's what makes you such a terrible poker player."

"I happen to be an excellent poker player. And let's not talk about this anymore, okay? R.J.'s a subject for four A.M. in the kitchen over bacon and eggs after you're all done accepting hugs and congratulations from the likes of Kate Hepburn and three hundred other nobodies."

"Has it occurred to you that those nobodies may get soaked to the skin in their seats?"

"It'll be an evening they'll never forget. They'll say to themselves, 'Do you remember that stormy night back in the summer of '93 when we schlepped out to Sherbourne to see Merilee Nash, Greg Farber, Dini Hawes and Marty Miller put on *Private Lives* and the rain came down so hard inside of the old playhouse that the four of them had to cling to umbrellas that none other than Stewart Hoag bought at Walmart?' Trust me, Merilee, this is the stuff of theatrical legend."

"Now you're just trying to cheer me up," she grumbled. "And it's working."

We lay there in silence, Lulu snoring contentedly now. Directly overhead, I began to hear the steady rhythmic squeak of bedsprings emanating from the third-floor room above Merilee's. Marty and his sturdy teenaged waitress having at it, I imagined.

"Hoagy, about these past few weeks . . ."

"What about them?"

"You working away so passionately on your novel. Me doing my thing here at the playhouse. The two of us talking about our days over dinner, enjoying each other's company. I keep wondering why we're not together."

"Because you kicked me out and divorced me, as you know perfectly well."

"I don't know anything perfectly well. Not when it comes to us." She leveled her gaze at me. "I wasn't very understanding, was I?"

"On the contrary, you were very understanding. You spent two whole years letting me snort coke, humiliate you and make a total jackass out of myself before you dumped me."

"I've been meaning to tell you something . . ."

"What is it?"

"You're not that jackass anymore. You haven't been for quite a while. And, my lord, you've really changed since you started writing this book. You've got a spring in your step. Your eyes are bright. I want to understand something about you. Will it always be like this?"

"Like what?"

"All highs and lows. No middle ground."

"I truly don't know. If I did, then I wouldn't be much of a writer. I have to walk the high wire without a net. That's where the good stuff comes from. It's not particularly healthy, or sane, but it's the only way I know how to feel truly alive. You're an incredibly gifted actress. You take the same sorts of risks yourself. That's what tonight is, isn't it? Tell me, would you be happy settled in for a nice, safe multiseason run on *Melrose Place*?"

"God, no."

I took her hand and gave it a squeeze. "But you're right. I do feel better about myself now that I'm writing again."

"Is it good?"

"Yes."

"You haven't sounded this confident in a long time."

"I haven't felt this confident."

"When will you let me read it?"

"Soon. A year, maybe."

She let out a laugh. "Only in your business does a year qualify as soon."

"Are you sure you don't want to take a nap?"

"Positive. This is what I need. Tell me, have you been missing the city?"

"Not particularly. Why?"

"I thought perhaps you were seeing someone there."

"There's no one, Merilee."

"I think you could have Sabrina if you want her."

"Not interested. How about you? Is there—?"

She kissed me. It's always been that way with her. She'll just suddenly kiss me midsentence. It wasn't a slurpy, let's get naked kind of a kiss. Just a tender, lingering one. Still, we hadn't kissed that way in years. It was . . . not unpleasant.

"What brought that on?" I asked when she pulled away, her eyes sparkling at me.

"I was just wondering if you're my Elyot and I'm your Amanda. If we really, truly belong together or if I'm just caught up in the plot of *Private Lives*. That does happen. I do know that about myself."

"As do I, and I for one am still glad you turned down the Glenn Close role in *Fatal Attraction*." I gazed into her eyes, getting totally lost in them. "I'll make a deal with you. If you're still wondering about it, say, two weeks from today, I'll take you out to the Monkey Farm Cafe. We'll drink Pabst Blue Ribbon and dance to the jukebox until we drop, then ride home to the farm with the top down and I'll tear your clothes off. How does that sound?"

"That all depends. Are you going to *do* anything after you tear them off or will you just fall asleep on the bed with your mouth open while I'm standing there in my birthday suit?"

"Not to worry, I'll drink strong coffee all day. An entire pot."

Thunder rumbled off in the distance. The afternoon sky was darkening.

Merilee glanced at the windows, her brow creasing. "Dini's genuinely sick. Do you suppose she has pneumonia or something?"

"If she had pneumonia the doctor would have already put her on antibiotics."

"I'm afraid she's going to collapse in the middle of our performance."

"What will you do if that happens?"

"Sabrina has understudied her part. She'll take over."

"Who'll play Louise the maid?"

"One of the prop girls learned Louise's lines. A college kid."

"Nona Peachy?"

"Why, yes. How do you know her?"

"She introduced herself. Wants to be an actress, as you may
have gathered. Her father, Doug, was an actor before he traded
in his dream for a white picket fence. Did some off-Broadway.
Ever work with him?"

She frowned. "Doug Peachy? I don't think so. Why?"

"Just curious." I gazed over at her. "You haven't left anything to chance, have you?"

"First lesson you learn in the theater, darling. Be prepared
for anything."

There was a flash of lightning outside of the window now,
followed several seconds later by a rumble of thunder.

"Hoagy, do you think I can actually pull this off?" Merilee
asked me with a slight crack in her voice.

"Are you getting the jitters?"

"My teeth are practically chattering."

"Of course you're going to pull it off. You're Merilee Nash.
The best of the best. Trust me, this is going to be a great night.
And it's all because of you."

"Can I kiss you again?"

"You can kiss me until the cows come home."

"What time do the cows come home?"

"Haven't the faintest idea. I'll ask Mr. MacGowan."

She kissed me tenderly before she said, "I may take a little nap after all. Will you stay?"

"I'll stay."

She dropped right off, breathing softly and slowly. Actors are famous for being able to do that. It's how they maintain their energy level during those long, grueling days and nights when they're on location shoots. Me, I lay there thinking about my meeting tonight at eleven at the ruins of the brass mill with the drugged-out sleaze who had the power to totally ruin her life.

Me, I didn't sleep.

Chapter Six

The precurtain champagne bash was an absolute trip. The big tent billowed in the wind, lightning crackled, thunder boomed and the rain came pounding down on us while an accomplished jazz trio from New Haven played heavenly highlights from the Cole Porter and George Gershwin songbooks, which are as heavenly as heavenly gets.

The weather hadn't scared off one single person. That's how much the Sherbourne Playhouse meant to the New York theatrical world. Limos and town cars surrounded the town green for blocks in every direction. Broadway's top director, Mike Nichols, was there with his wife Diane Sawyer. Meryl Streep and Sigourney Weaver were there. So were Neil Simon, Arthur Miller, Elia Kazan and Stephen Sondheim, each of them accompanied by assorted wives or partners. Jackie O, wearing an eerily serene smile on her eerily lacquered face, arrived with her tall, dark and handsome son, John, who I still say should have just become the next Tom Selleck instead of trying to be an assistant Manhattan D.A. The incomparable husband-wife acting duo of Hume Cronyn and Jessica Tandy showed up. So did that pretty fair husband-wife acting team of Paul Newman and Joanne Woodward. Newman was sixty-eight that year, and I just want to say if I ever live to be that old I want to look as good as he did.

Knowledgeable Broadway critics such as Frank Rich from the *New York Times* and Howard Kissel from the *Daily News* made the trip out. So did celebrity critics such as Rex Reed, pretend critics such as Dennis Cunningham from Channel 2 News, and gossip columnists such as Liz Smith and Cindy Adams. Camera crews from *Entertainment Tonight* and *Inside Edition* cruised the tent, as did paparazzi by the dozen. Big-time magazine editors such as Tina Brown of the *New Yorker* and Anna Wintour of *Vogue* had shown up. So had the likes of Gore Vidal, Dominick Dunne and George Plimpton, who still hadn't forgiven me for having sex on his pool table during a Brazilian poetry reading back in my bad boy days. Connecticut governor Lowell Weicker and his wife, Claudia, were there to provide the state's seal of approval.

And, as I've discovered is always the case at such an event, a notable celebrity was there whose presence made absolutely no sense whatsoever. In this case it was Long Island's own Gentleman Gerry Cooney, the former Great White Hope of the heavyweight boxing world, whose career in the ring had ended three years earlier when George Foreman knocked him cold in the second round. Gerry looked trim, fit and very suave in a tux, though not as suave as I did.

Everyone was dressed to the nines. Everyone, that is, except for Kate Hepburn, who showed up just a bit later than everyone else, decked out in a hooded yellow rain slicker, gingham shirt, torn jeans and an ancient pair of Keds sneakers. "By gum, this is a perfect night to see Noël Coward!" she cried out valiantly in that quavering voice of hers, her eyes positively gleaming with excitement. There was no getting around it—fifty-four years after she'd starred on Broadway as Tracy Lord in *The Philadelphia Story* Kate Hepburn, age eighty-six, was still yare. And still in a class all by herself. Everyone rushed to greet her as the tent billowed and the thunder boomed and the rain poured down.

I had to hand it to Mimi. If there was one thing the former supermodel knew how to do it was pull off a high-profile bash. There was an endless supply of Dom Perignon, waiters everywhere with trays of caviar and chilled shrimp, which thrilled Lulu to no end. There was laughter and genuine excitement in the lightning-charged air.

Which isn't to say that Mimi, who looked fabulous in a sleeveless silver cocktail dress, seemed to be having much fun herself. She looked so incredibly tense that I grabbed her and whisked her around the dance floor while the trio was playing Gershwin's "They Can't Take That Away from Me."

"You've done a fabulous job," I assured her.

"Do you really think so?" she wondered, her tall, lean body as taut as an ironing board. "I can't afford to fail at this level, you know. *Everyone* finds out."

One of the volunteer ushers ducked inside the tent and announced that the curtain would rise in fifteen minutes, which set off an immediate buzz of anticipation. The assembled luminaries began making their way out of the tent. Many of them paused to help themselves to a complimentary umbrella for the quick dash across the lawn in the pouring rain. Others said the hell with it and just dashed. The musicians and waiters remained behind. The plan was for everyone to return to the tent and resume the party after the curtain—joined by the triumphant cast members.

Inside the little playhouse I could hear the rain pelting down on the roof, but the blue tarps seemed to be holding. The aisles and seats were dry as the high-spirited audience members got settled in with the assistance of the volunteer ushers. So far, so good—although the rain *was* expected to continue for at least two more hours, by which time I expected the Oscar-winning cast members would need snorkels and fins to get down to their dressing rooms.

But first, they had a show to put on.

Lulu and I watched from the back of the house as the lights went down and the curtain rose, the better to take it all in. Merilee, as Sibyl, was the first of Coward's honeymooners to appear onstage. Merilee immediately got a huge roar of applause from the audience as she stepped out onto the French hotel terrace. Not only because it was she who'd put this production together but also because she was bravely standing there, holding an umbrella against the rain that was pelting down on her. The tarp over the stage hadn't held, evidently. As Merilee stood there, regarding the view from the hotel terrace, Marty soon joined her under an umbrella of his own and got a rousing ovation himself. And so they began. I don't know if the two of them got a lift from the packed house of celebrities or if it was the added challenge of playing the scene while standing in the rain, but they totally nailed it. Marty was dry, wickedly droll and his timing was impeccable. His Elyot was the perfect counterbalance to Merilee's splendidly simpering Sibyl. But that was Marty, curried mutton scent and all.

The stage lights did flicker a couple of times when the

wind really gusted—which made more than a few audience members gasp—but Merilee and Marty paid no attention and, mercifully, the power stayed on.

Soon, the two of them retreated back into their hotel room and, lo and behold, Amanda and Victor emerged onto the neighboring terrace, which called for another ovation for Greg and Dini. It was obvious to me that Dini was still feeling wobbly. She had to clutch her umbrella in both hands to hold it aloft. But Dini Hawes was a trouper to her core. Her voice was strong, her timing razor sharp. I'd heard from Mimi that Doctor Orr had made a black bag house call to the inn that afternoon. I wondered if he'd given her a B12 shot. Greg did his best to help her through it by keeping his arm around her. Since he and Dini were husband and wife in so-called real life Greg was able to turn it into a totally natural, romantic gesture. Somehow, he also *became* Victor in a way that he hadn't been before.

Honestly, the four of them were so wonderful that after a few minutes I forgot all about the rain that was pouring down on the stage. Besides, the rain wasn't that outrageous a distraction while they were standing there on the terrace in act one. They were supposed to be outside. It was raining. So what? The real challenge would be how they coped with act two inside of Amanda's Paris flat. There was always a chance the rain would stop by then but the intensifying downpours gave little hope of that.

As Coward's two couples realize with a mix of shock and horror that they're honeymooning in neighboring hotel suites the curtain slowly fell on act one. There was an immediate roar of applause from the packed playhouse. A few of the assembled luminaries left their seats to have a cigarette in the lobby or use the restroom but most of them stayed put, which Merilee taught me many years back is a very, very good omen. Behind the curtain, the stagehands went into high gear moving furniture and props around during the intermission so as to transform the hotel terrace into Amanda's flat.

Mind you, it turned out to be a much longer intermission than anyone had anticipated. And they didn't have to bother to account for why it was raining inside of Amanda's flat. Because, as it happened, there *was* no act two. The show could not go on—and not because of the weather.

But because one of the play's four stars didn't survive the intermission.

IT WAS MARTY who found the body.

Lulu and I weren't far away when he did. We'd gone backstage at the act break. I've always enjoyed watching the hubbub of the stagehands changing sets. Coop was all-business as he bossed his crew of able young volunteers through the process of converting the hotel terrace into Amanda's Paris flat. Up went one backdrop, down came another and, presto, we were indoors looking out a pair of windows at the rooftops of Paris. The sofa, easy chairs and end tables were carried to their marks on the stage floor. Props were placed here and there. True, the rain had not stopped falling on the stage. But Coop cleverly rigged a painter's drop cloth over the sofa as a decorative canopy, which not only gave the flat a bohemian atelier look but would also serve to keep the actors who were on the sofa dry. Actors who had to move around onstage would simply have to carry an umbrella. The audience wouldn't mind. In fact, I felt certain they would get a big kick out of it.

Sabrina sat in the wings on a folding chair in her frumpy maid costume and full makeup, watching them work. "I took in act one from here," she informed me. "I thought it would help me get a feel for the pace. It's going well, don't you think?"

"Very well," I said, noticing that she was trembling slightly. This was her professional stage debut, after all, and that's no small thing—especially considering how many theatrical giants had made their own debuts on this very stage, including the one who sat out in the house right now wearing Keds. "You'll be fabulous. And you look terrific in that costume."

"Thank you," she said, clamping her plump lower lip firmly between her teeth. "We decided it made sense for me to change into full costume before act one because there isn't enough room for all three of us in the dressing room at once. Plus Dini gets really locked in and doesn't like to break her concentration. The twins wanted to go down and visit her but she made them stay in their seats. Mimi's watching them."

"Where's Glenda?"

"She went down to check on how Dini's feeling. No way Dini can tell *her* what to do. God, Glenda's *so* bossy. I hate Glenda. Don't you hate Glenda?"

"I don't hate her, but I'm glad she's not my mother."

Mimi joined us there in the wings in her shimmering silver cocktail dress, the twins in tow. Both girls were pouty and glum in their sleeveless blue dresses.

"How come we can't see Mommy?" Cheyenne asked Sabrina.

"Because she's trying to stay in character." Sabrina smiled at her. "You'll understand when you become actors."

"I don't *want* to be an actor," Durango said. "I want to be a fire jumper."

"That's a pretty dangerous job," I pointed out.

"I'm not afraid," she said, crossing her arms before her defiantly.

"Sabrina, could you watch the girls for a sec?" Mimi's voice had an edge of urgency. "I need to call my plumber to see if he can find us a few more sump pumps *really* fast."

"No prob. We'll watch them swirl the furniture around. It's like magic."

I joined Mimi as she darted toward the stage door phone. The door to the courtyard was open despite the windblown torrents because the tropical air was so steamy it was practically suffocating back there.

"It's getting *really* nasty downstairs," Mimi informed me grimly as she reached for the phone. "I've never seen the water this deep."

I started down the spiral staircase toward the dressing rooms to check out the flood conditions for myself. Lulu was with me until she came to a sudden halt halfway down. She could hear the rats scrabbling for higher ground.

"Come on, don't be such a wuss," I said to her. "You're bigger than they are. Most of them, anyhow."

The dimly lit basement corridor was now a rushing river. The crew had set planks atop cinder blocks just like in the dressing rooms so that it was possible to step your way along. But the water was so deep that it was starting to slosh over the planks. The extremely loud sump pumps were running during intermission but they didn't seem to be accomplishing a whole lot.

Mimi came down the staircase a moment after me. "Sweet Jesus, it's like being belowdecks on the *Titanic*."

"Any luck on those extra sump pumps?"

"He said he'd see if he could find any. He didn't sound very optimistic."

I sloshed my way down the corridor toward the dressing room, Mimi sloshing right along behind me. "You'll ruin your sandals," I warned her.

"Good, that'll give me an excuse to buy a new pair."

We arrived just in time to witness a sight I would gladly have missed—Marty barreling out of the men's dressing room wearing a pair of billowing powder blue boxer shorts, heavy brogans, argyle socks and nothing else, his innumerable fat rolls jiggling as he charged straight across the hall into the tiny men's bathroom. It was a rock-solid certainty that the great Martin Jacob Miller would suffer an uncontrollable case of the shits before and after act one of every performance of every show in which he appeared. The man was famous for it. He slammed the door shut behind him and let out a loud groan, followed by a succession of simply awful bowel eruptions.

Lulu moaned unhappily. Last night it was headless Old Saxophone Joe. Tonight it was rats and Marty's poop.

Greg was in the men's dressing room changing into a tweed suit that must have been hot as hell to put on.

I caught his eye through the open doorway and gave him a thumbs-up. "Going great!" I called out.

"Absolutely terrific, Greg!" Mimi chimed in.

He beamed at us gratefully. "Thanks. Feels really, really awesome."

Mimi and I found Merilee and Dini changing costumes in their dressing room, or trying to. It wasn't easy with the water rising over the planks. Or with plus-size Glenda crowded in there with them demanding to know how her ashen-faced daughter was feeling. Not great, apparently. Dini's eyes widened suddenly, and she clamped a hand over her mouth, darting across the hall to the ladies' room to vomit.

Lulu let out another moan. This was definitely turning into her worst twenty-four hours ever.

"Dini will be fine," Merilee assured Glenda airily. "She just gets a nervous stomach sometimes."

"She's *not* nervous," argued Glenda, who was wearing a pastel pink polyester pantsuit and her bone-colored walking shoes for the occasion. "She's *ill*. She mustn't go back out on that stage."

Merilee steered Glenda toward the door. "She'll be fine. Now if you'll please excuse me I have *very* little time to finish changing."

"Why, yes, of course." Glenda moved out into the corridor, the water splish-splashing over her shoes and the cuffs of her pants. But she wasn't going anywhere. She intended to check on her daughter the instant that Dini emerged from the ladies' room.

"I'm definitely in the way, too," Mimi said, sloshing her way toward the spiral staircase. "I'm heading back up."

"Likewise," I said, following her. Lulu joined me eagerly.

"How is it playing so far?" Merilee called out to me.

I returned to the dressing room doorway as Mimi went upstairs. Merilee had changed into her act two costume, a pair of burgundy silk lounging pajamas. Her own. Or I should say mine. She stole them from me years ago because they looked better on her than they did on me.

"Close the door for a sec," she said to me.

Lulu and I joined her in there. I closed the door.

"Is it satisfactory so far?" she asked me, her eyes searching my face.

"No, can't say that it is. Great is more like it. But are you okay down here in this flood?"

"What, this?" She let out a snort. "Back in my Keith Orpheum days I had to stand in water up to my thighs when I played *Charley's Aunt* in Altoona."

"Merilee, you've never been in *Charley's Aunt*. Or Altoona."

"Have so." She grinned at me, her eyes bright with excitement. She was a theater creature. She thrived on this kind of chaos.

As I opened the door to leave, Dini emerged from the ladies' room looking gray and limp.

Glenda was parked right there waiting for her. "How are you feeling, dear?"

"Mother, *please* go upstairs, will you?" Dini said with exaggerated patience. "I have to change."

"Forgive me for caring," Glenda said, stung, as she went up the spiral staircase in a huff.

That was my cue to leave, too. "It's terrific, Dini."

"Thank you, Hoagy," she said softly.

As I started for the staircase with Lulu the men's room door flew open and Marty came back out in his boxers, huffing and puffing. "Hey, Hoagy, do you think it's safe to flush the toilet?"

"Is that your way of saying you haven't?"

"I'm afraid the septic system might be flooded, which means the toilet will overflow and we'll be standing here with everything I've eaten for the past two days floating by. You've got to figure the system's overflowing, right?"

"It's not something I really choose to give much thought to."

"Well, stay out of that men's room, if you want my advice."

"I wasn't planning to go in there, but thanks for the tip."

Marty went across the hall into the men's dressing room as Lulu and I sloshed back toward the staircase. We hadn't gone more than a few feet before he roared, "Hoagy, I need a hand *now*!"

I dashed in there and found Greg lying facedown on the concrete floor between the planks in at least six inches of water. The back of his head was a bloodied mess, as if someone had bashed him repeatedly with a hard object of some kind.

I immediately shoved a plank aside and waded down into the water. Marty did the same. Between the two of us, we were able to pick Greg up and lay him out, facedown, on a plank in his sopping wet tweed suit. He wasn't conscious.

Marty held his ear to Greg's nostrils, listening carefully. Or trying to over the roar of the sump pumps. "I don't think he's breathing," he said in a grief-stricken voice. "I've taken a lifeguard training course. Should I . . . ?"

"Go for it."

Marty turned Greg's head to one side and pressed firmly against his back with both hands, the plank creaking as Marty applied the pressure steadily. Water came streaming out of Greg's mouth. A lot of water, which meant it was coming from his lungs. But Marty's exertions didn't make Greg cough the rest of the water out. Or cough at all. Or so much as stir. Greg just lay there.

I knelt and took a good look into his eyes. They were open wide and glazed over. I know what dead looks like.

Greg Farber was dead.

By now I realized that Merilee and Dini were standing in the doorway, gaping in horror.

"Merilee, you'd better call the police," I said.

She went rushing off. Dini remained frozen in the doorway, her eyes wide with fright. Until, that is, she suddenly let out a shriek and fainted.

I caught her before she fell and hoisted her into my arms. She was light as a feather. "Don't touch anything," I said to Marty, who was still on his knees in the floodwaters, his eyes filling with tears. Lulu, I noticed, had started sniffing her way carefully around, snuffling and snorting. "Just grab your clothes and get out of here, okay? This is a crime scene."

"Right," Marty responded grimly.

I carried Dini up the spiral staircase to the stage door area and laid her gently on the floor. Took off my tuxedo jacket, rolled it up and placed it under her head as a pillow. Merilee was on the stage door phone with the police. Mimi was standing next to her weeping, the tears streaming down her face. Glenda was with them—until she caught sight of me tending to Dini and came racing over.

"She's fainted," I said. "Shock, I think."

"We'd better find her some blankets," Glenda said, immediately turning brisk and professional.

"There are some in my office," Mimi said, swiping at her eyes.

"You'd better call Doctor Orr, too," I said.

"And I'll need that first aid kit," Glenda said, following Mimi up the service corridor toward her office off of the lobby.

Merilee stood next to me, gripping my hand tightly. Hers was like ice. "Greg is . . . *dead*?"

I nodded. "Someone bashed him in the head a whole bunch of times, knocked him out and then he drowned. Or at least that's how it looks."

Glenda returned quickly, accompanied by Sabrina and the twins. Sabrina was toting an armload of blankets. Glenda had Mimi's first aid kit.

"Is Mommy okay?" Durango wondered fretfully.

"She's fine, honey," Glenda said. "Just had a little shock, that's all."

"What kind of a shock?" Cheyenne asked.

Glenda didn't want to answer her. No one did.

While Sabrina swaddled Dini in blankets Glenda found some ammonia ampules in the first aid kit, broke one open and waved it under Dini's nose.

Dini stirred, shuddering, and opened her eyes. She let out a gasp and cried out, "No, no, *no* . . . where's Greg?"

"It's okay, Dini." Glenda cradled her in her arms like a little girl. "Shhh, you're okay. It's okay."

"Where are my babies?"

"We're right here, Mommy," Cheyenne said.

Dini put her arms around the twins and squeezed them tight, tears running down her cheeks.

"Mommy, what's wrong?" Durango asked.

"Where's Daddy?" Cheyenne asked.

Somehow, Dini managed a reassuring smile. "We'll talk

about it when we're alone, okay? There are too many people around right now."

"Why would anyone *do* such a thing?" Merilee's green eyes were wide with disbelief. "And *how*? We were right next door. I didn't hear a thing, did you?"

I shook my head. "Not with those sump pumps going. Did you, Dini?"

"No." Dini's voice was a whisper. "But I was in the ladies' room being sick."

And Marty had been in the men's room coping with his problematic bowel. Just moments earlier, Mimi and I had seen Greg changing into his tweed suit. We'd exchanged a few brief, cheerful words. He'd been alone in the dressing room at the time. Or so it had appeared. Possibly, someone else had been in there with him. Someone who we couldn't see from the corridor. I had no idea. I only knew that someone, somehow, had managed to slip in there, bash Greg in the head and slip away while he lay facedown on that flooded basement floor. Or make that *not* slip away, because the odds were excellent that Greg's killer was still right there with us. It had to be someone who had access to the dressing rooms, didn't it? That meant a fellow cast member. Or Glenda. Or Mimi. Or possibly one of the stage crew. Unless, that is, we were talking about the wildest of wild cards—R. J. Romero. But how could R.J. have snuck his way downstairs to the dressing rooms and murdered Greg without any of us seeing him? And why would he want to after all of these years? Then again, if R.J. was desperate enough that he'd taken to blackmailing Merilee, was it possible that he was blackmailing Greg, too?

As I stood there, my mind racing, Marty came slowly and

heavily up the spiral staircase, puffing on a Lucky Strike. He'd changed into a rumpled polo shirt, shorts and his cheese-scented flip-flops. His shoulders were slumped, his eyes vacant.

And Mimi returned from her office, her eyes red and swollen. As she dabbed at them with a tissue I noticed that the knuckles of her right hand were scraped raw. The scrapes looked to be fresh. "Doctor Orr lives right around the corner," she said in a calm voice, mindful of the twins. "He'll be right over."

Two Sherbourne police cars pulled up outside the stage door. The wind-driven rain had begun to let up. The thunder was moving off into the distance, growing steadily more muted.

Mimi turned to Merilee and said, "I hate to say these words out loud but the curtain for act two should have gone up seven minutes ago. Our house is getting restless. Someone's got to tell them that there will *be* no act two. We have to send them home."

"I'll do it," Merilee said unhesitatingly. "Just let me change out of these pajamas."

"Nobody will notice or care." I led her by the hand out onto the stage and left her there facing the curtain while Lulu and I made our way into the wings.

She stood there collecting herself for a moment, then instructed a stagehand to raise the curtain. Everyone in the audience automatically started to applaud until they realized that Merilee was standing alone there onstage with her arms raised in the air, pleading for silence. "I'm sorry to have to tell you that the show cannot go on," she informed them in a strong, clear voice. "Greg Farber is . . . Greg is dead."

Screams and gasps of horror showered down upon her. Again she held her arms up, pleading for silence.

"Our prayers go out to Dini and their girls." The twins still hadn't been told. They were currently being distracted backstage by Dini and Glenda. "I want to thank each and every one of you for coming. But now I'm afraid I have to say good night. Have a safe trip home."

"*Isn't there anything we can do?*" someone called out.

"No, there isn't. Thank you. Please, just go home. Allow me to assure you that we'll refund your donations."

"*You . . . will . . . not!*" thundered the unmistakable voice of Katharine the Great, which pretty much put the kibosh on that idea. "*We're saving this place no matter what!*"

"*Kate's right!*"

"*We don't want our money back!*"

"*But what happened?*"

"*Did he have a heart attack?*"

"It was very unexpected," Merilee said. "I'm afraid that's all I can tell you right now. Thank you and good night."

She gestured for the stagehand to lower the curtain, then rejoined Lulu and me in the wings as we listened to the grief-stricken voices on the other side of the curtain. The excited ones, too, because the playhouse was full of media people, and while the theatrical legends would eventually stream home in their limos and town cars, the assembled reporters, photographers and TV camera crews would mob the stage door demanding answers. After all, Greg Farber, a major Hollywood movie star, had just died backstage in the middle of a gala stage benefit. Cause of death: unknown.

And until they did know they weren't going anywhere.

We weren't going anywhere either. Not until the Sherbourne Police had sent for a homicide team from the Connecticut State

Police's Major Crime Squad. Not until the investigators had arrived, been thoroughly briefed and written down the names and contact information of every performer, stagehand, usher, family member and ex-husband who'd been in the theater at the time of Greg's death. Criminal background checks would have to be run on everyone. Preliminary questioning would have to be conducted. Hours. We'd be there for hours.

Meanwhile, there was Dini to attend to. Doctor Orr turned out to be young and sunburned, as if he spent a lot of time out on the water in a sailboat. When he arrived he carried Dini down the service runway into Mimi's office and stretched her out on the sofa. It was a narrow, cluttered office with room enough for the sofa, a desk, a couple of chairs and not much else.

Dini was not doing real well. In fact, she was on the verge of hysterics. Doctor Orr rummaged around in his black bag and injected her with a sedative. Mimi fought back more tears as she stood there watching him. Marty was slumped in her desk chair dragging on a Lucky Strike and blowing the smoke out of an open window. Glenda was crowded in there with the twins, trying—and failing—to keep them distracted. The girls were alarmed by their mother's condition.

"Is Mommy okay?" Durango wanted to know.

"She's just a little bit upset right now," Glenda assured her.

"Why?" Cheyenne demanded.

"She'll be fine. Isn't that right, Doctor?"

"Absolutely fine," he said.

"What about Daddy? Where's Daddy?"

No one in the office responded. No one knew what to say.

I nudged Lulu with my sodden patent leather shoe. She glowered at me. I glowered back. I'm bigger. She went over to the twins and rolled over on her back so they could pat her belly.

"Hey, Lulu!" exclaimed Cheyenne.

Both girls fell to their knees and began petting her and tugging at her ears.

Glenda nodded to me gratefully.

"The sedative I've given her should relax her for a good eight hours." Doctor Orr snapped his bag shut. "I'll be in touch in the morning."

"Doctor, did you get the results back from Dini's blood work?" I asked.

He studied me cooly. "I'm sorry, you are . . . ?"

"Stewart Hoag, the author," Mimi said. "Merilee's ex-husband."

"Why, yes, of course. I'm a huge fan of your work, Mr. Hoag. Absolutely loved *The World According to Garp*."

"Thank you. I'm sure John Irving will be pleased to hear that."

"My mistake, sorry. Yes, I did get the results, but I don't believe in discussing such matters with anyone but my patient." He turned to Glenda and said, "Best thing right now is to get her into bed. She's not flying to Savannah tonight."

"I've just phoned her agent," Mimi said. "The business end of things is being seen to. I also spoke to the housekeeper at the beach house. She said the owners won't be back until next week. Dini and the girls are welcome to stay on for a few more days."

"Good." Doctor Orr looked at Glenda. "Are you okay to drive?"

"I'm perfectly fine. And the car's parked not twenty feet from the stage door."

"Mimi, do you think you can snag a burly stagehand to carry Dini out to their car? She's gone to sleep."

"Hell, I can do that," Marty said, stirring from the desk chair.

"If the Sherbourne police at the stage door give you any trouble just tell them that I said she's in no condition to answer questions until tomorrow morning."

I said, "Doctor, if the media scene out back is anything like I'm imagining—and I'm guessing it's ten times worse—Marty's going to need a police escort to and from the car. And Glenda will need one to the beach house."

He peered at me, his eyes narrowing fractionally. "Why do I get the feeling you've been through this sort of thing before, Mr. Hoag?"

"Only because I have."

"In that case, I'll accompany Mr. Miller and speak to the chief of police."

"Thank you, Doctor," Glenda said.

Marty gently picked slender little Dini up off of the sofa and said, "Okay, girls, we're heading out to the car with your mom and your grandma. You ready to rumble?"

"Can we take Lulu with us?" Durango wanted to know.

"I'm afraid not," Merilee said. "But she'll come visit you to-morrow."

"You promise?" Cheyenne pleaded.

"I promise," Merilee said.

I opened the door and Marty carried Dini up the corridor toward the stage entrance with Glenda and the girls following close behind. After the doctor had murmured a sympathetic good night to Mimi he hurried after them.

I caught up with him, matching him stride for stride. "Is it Lyme disease, Doctor?"

He let out a weary sigh. "Mr. Hoag, like I said . . ."

"Let me put it another way. When you initially examined Dini Hawes for her flu-like symptoms and took blood samples did she request that you test her for a certain medical condition that you were a bit surprised to hear her mention?"

He glanced at me sidelong. "I won't discuss that with you either."

"So she did, didn't she?"

"I didn't say that."

"You didn't have to. Your eyes just said it for you."

Those eyes glared at me disapprovingly. "You're a bit of a sneaky customer, aren't you?"

"I don't mean to be. It's just that I've spent the past several years hanging around with the wrong sort of people."

"What sort of people would that be?"

"Famous people."

BY THE TIME Marty carried Dini out to the car and a young Sherbourne cop had escorted him back, a half-dozen uniformed Connecticut State troopers from Troop F in Westbrook had arrived on the scene in their silver Ford Crown Vics to establish a perimeter around the playhouse. Politely but firmly, they muscled the mob of media people and celebrity gawkers behind it.

Meanwhile, we sat around on folding chairs on the wet stage waiting for the homicide investigators from the Major Crime Squad, who had to come from their headquarters in Meriden. A lieutenant and his sergeant pulled up twenty minutes later, followed closely by a pair of blue and white cube vans packed full of crime scene technicians wearing navy blue Windbreakers.

The lieutenant was a chesty fireplug with dark, hooded eyes and a head of mountainous, elaborately layered black hair that was reminiscent of John Travolta from his *Saturday Night Fever* disco heyday. He wore a cheap, shiny black suit that bore a striking resemblance to the cheap, shiny black suit that Pete Tedone, the fixer, had worn. In fact, *he* bore a striking resemblance to Pete Tedone, possibly because he was Pete's younger brother, Carmine.

This was made clear to me when Carmine Tedone pulled me aside for a private word after he'd been brought up to speed on who everyone was—not that he had the slightest trouble recognizing Merilee or Marty.

I tugged at my ear. "So that would make Frank Tedone of the Organized Crime Task Force . . ."

"My cousin, same as he is Pete's."

"Just out of curiosity, Lieutenant, is there anyone in the Connecticut State Police who isn't named Tedone?"

"Oh, sure. There's Bartuccas by the dozen, although we're all related by marriage a couple of generations back. You see my sergeant over there?"

I followed his gaze to the tall, gangly young plainclothesman who was giving instructions to a pair of troopers in uniform. He, too, wore a cheap, shiny black suit. Possibly they bought them in bulk—like rolls of paper towels.

"He's a Bartucca. My wife's cousin's boy, Angelo." Tedone called him over and said, "Sergeant, there's a tavern across the street from the stage door. Find out who went in and out during the time frame of the murder. The bartender will remember if anyone he didn't know stopped in. Or if he saw a car idling by the stage door that took off lickety split."

"Right, Loo," Sergeant Bartucca said.

"Oh, hey, and ask him . . ." Tedone opened a file folder so that I could see it was his brother Pete's file on R. J. Romero, complete with mug shots. "Ask him if this guy looks familiar."

"You got it, Loo." He went loping off with the file.

Lieutenant Tedone approached Mimi now and said, "Mrs. Whitfield, do you generally have someone guarding the stage door during performances?"

"This is a summer playhouse, Lieutenant. Not the Belasco Theater."

"So someone could have wandered in and out unnoticed while the first act was under way?"

"Yes, they could have."

"I'm told that you've let the audience go home."

"I couldn't exactly ask the likes of Governor Weicker and Jacqueline Kennedy Onassis to remain in their seats for half the night, could I?"

"Still, there's a chance that one of them saw or heard something. Have you got a complete list of their names?"

"Of course."

"Were there any no-shows?"

"Not one. The house was packed."

"Did anyone leave their seat while act one was in progress and not come back?"

"No one," I said. "I was standing in the back of the house. If anyone had left I'd have seen him. And if anyone had tried to slip backstage Sabrina would have seen him from her perch in the wings. Lieutenant, you don't honestly think that Greg was done in by Hume Cronyn, do you?"

"There's no call to take that attitude with me. I'm just covering my bases." He glanced down at a small notepad in his hand. "That would be Sabrina Meyer?"

Sabrina still had on her frumpy maid's costume and gray wig. The police hadn't let her go downstairs to change. She looked at him warily. "Yes . . . ?"

"You were seated in that chair over there during act one?"

"Yes, I was."

"Did you see *anyone* go downstairs to the dressing rooms during the first act? Think hard. It could be important."

"No, I didn't," Sabrina said without hesitation.

"I'm afraid I'll have to ask you to stay over tonight, Miss Meyer. We'll need your formal witness statement in the morning. And maybe you'll remember something when you've had a chance to sleep on it. A trooper will escort you back to the Sherbourne Inn."

"Can I go downstairs and change first? I don't usually look like this, you know. And my shoulder bag's down there."

"Of course." He gestured for a trooper to go with her. "Do you mind if my man searches your bag?"

"For what?"

"The weapon that was used."

"Do you classify a tampon as a weapon?" On Tedone's stone-faced reaction Sabrina said, "No, I don't mind."

She and the trooper left the stage together.

Tedone consulted his notepad again. "Martin Jacob Miller . . ."

Marty gulped nervously. "Jeez, you sound like Darth Vader. Call me Marty, will you?"

Tedone smiled faintly. "I understand it was you who found Mr. Farber's body in the men's dressing room. And that you immediately called out to Mr. Hoag, who joined you in there."

"Along with Lulu," I added.

Tedone frowned at me. "Lulu . . . ?"

She let out a low whoop at my feet.

"Oh, right. Your pooch. How about the three of us . . . ?"

"Four of us."

"*Four* of us go down to the dressing rooms and you show me how it all happened?"

Marty climbed to his feet. "Whatever you say."

"Would you like me to join you, Lieutenant?" Merilee asked. "I was right next-door with Dini."

"Not necessary, Miss Nash. I understand she's not feeling very well."

"Not at all well," Merilee said with a sad shake of her head. "Doctor Orr sedated her and sent her home to the beach house they've been renting on Point O'Woods."

"I'll keep a couple of cars parked outside of her house tonight. Make sure none of those tabloid creeps bother her."

"That's very considerate of you."

"Just doing my job," he said, coloring slightly.

As we made our way toward the spiral staircase we ran into Sabrina, who'd ditched her costume and wig for a tank top and linen shorts, brushed out her gorgeous golden ringlets and reclaimed her shoulder bag. She waved goodbye to us as she started for the stage door with her uniformed escort, who'd been rendered gaga by her transformation.

The sump pumps were going full blast down in the dimly lit corridor. The water level had gone down by two or three inches now that the rain had let up. Two crime scene technicians were taking Polaroid shots of the murder scene in the men's dressing room. One of the technicians was photographing Greg, who remained draped facedown over the plank just as we'd left him. The other was photographing the numerous sets of wet, dirty shoe prints that were all over the other planks.

Tedone asked the technicians to excuse us for a moment. They squeezed their way past us out into the corridor, leaving us crowded in there with Greg's body, Lulu's mackerel breath and Marty's curried mutton scent.

If Tedone was bothered by any of it he didn't let on. Just stood there staring down at Greg. "I was told you found him between the planks."

"We did," I said. "He was lying facedown in six inches of water with the back of his head bashed in. He wasn't moving. We were afraid he'd drown."

"So we lifted him up onto that plank," Marty said, nodding.

"Talk me through the moments leading up to that."

"It was the intermission between acts one and two," I said. "Everyone was in high gear. Stagehands were changing the set. Actors were changing their costumes. Meanwhile, the rain was coming down in torrents. I came down here to check on the flooding situation with Mimi, who was getting concerned."

"Did you see or speak to the victim?"

I nodded. "When Mimi and I were out in the corridor. The dressing room door was open and he—"

"Why wasn't it closed?"

"Because it was hot as hell in here," Marty said. "And Greg was changing into that heavy tweed suit."

"How did he seem to you?" Tedone asked me.

"Raring to go. He really aced act one. Or at least I thought he did."

"He totally did," Marty agreed. "Impressed the hell out of me."

"Were you in here changing your costume, too?" Tedone asked him.

"Briefly, until I had to use the men's john right across the hall. I get an uncontrollable case of the shits before and after act one of every performance I ever give. I'm somewhat legendary for it, kind of like the way Bill Russell used to throw up before every Celtics game."

Tedone looked at him with his mouth open for a moment before he turned back to me and said, "So the victim was alone in here when you and Mrs. Whitfield spoke to him from the corridor?"

"I assumed he was, but I can't say for sure. Someone else could have been in here. Don't ask me who. I wouldn't know. I also looked in on Merilee. She was afraid the show wasn't going well, what with the rain pouring down onto the stage and all. She was also concerned about Dini, who's been quite ill. In fact, Dini went into the ladies' room and threw up while I was there. Her mother, Glenda, didn't want her to go back out there for act two. Glenda's a retired school nurse. But Dini was determined to keep going."

"Dini's a trouper," Marty said admiringly. "She'd go out there with a broken bone sticking out of her leg."

"Merilee and Dini needed to change costumes, so Glenda started back upstairs. Mimi had already gone back up. I was just about to go up myself when Marty called out to me that he'd found Greg."

"I'd just returned from the men's john," Marty explained.

"About how long were you in the john?" Tedone asked him.

"Five minutes, maybe. Long enough to smoke my way through a cigarette. I found Greg just like Hoagy said—lying facedown between the boards in all of that water with his head bleeding. I took a lifeguard course once. After we pulled him up onto that plank I did what I was taught to do. The water came pouring out of his lungs, but he didn't cough or show any response at all. And his eyes . . ." Marty trailed off, shaking his head. "The dude was dead."

Tedone studied Greg's head wounds more closely. "Those are some nasty blows. Three, maybe four. Wonder what we're looking at in terms of a weapon."

Lulu let out a whoop from under one of the dressing tables.

"Why is she doing that?" Tedone asked me.

"Because she thinks she's found the weapon."

"How would she know that?"

"I can't help you there. She doesn't always tell me everything."

He let out a sigh. "Yeah, right. Pete warned me that you were an *uno*."

"Meaning . . . ?"

"One of a kind."

"He said that? I'm flattered."

"Being candid, I don't think he meant it as a form of flattery." Tedone moved over toward Lulu, who was sniffing delicately at a red brick on the floor that had been submerged in the floodwaters and was only now becoming visible. It was a brick stamped TUTTLE 1924, which indicated who'd made it and when. They used to do that with bricks. "We'll bag and tag it. Check it for blood, hair, fingerprints . . ."

"Lieutenant, let's say someone did smash Greg over the head with that brick," I said. "Assuming he was alive but unconscious when he pitched over, facedown, into the floodwaters . . ."

"He *was* still alive. Marty just said that he had water in his lungs."

"How many minutes would it take for someone in his condition to drown?"

"That's a question for the medical examiner, not me. I'd strictly be speculating."

"So speculate."

"We're talking multiple subdermal hematomas, possible skull fractures . . ." Tedone shoved his lower lip in and out. "I'd guess maybe three minutes. Why are you asking?"

"Just curious."

"Curious," he repeated, raising his chin at me doubtfully.

Marty let out a sudden sob, his eyes filling with tears. "Poor son of a bitch. He had it all going on. Dini, the twins, his career. Who'd want to do this to him?"

"That's what I'm here to find out," Tedone responded.

Marty glanced at him sharply. "Are you good at your job?"

"I'm good at my job," he assured him with quiet confidence. "And I'm sorry for your loss. Thanks for your help. You can get dressed now if you want."

Marty frowned at him. "I *am* dressed."

"Then in that case let's go back upstairs." Tedone started out of the dressing room into the corridor, pausing to look inside of the men's room. "How come you didn't flush the toilet?"

"I was afraid the septic tank would be flooded and it would overflow into the corridor. Do you think it would have?"

"Could be, but I'm a homicide investigator, not a plumber, remember?" Next he had a look in the ladies' room, where there were traces of vomit on the floor next to the toilet. His jaw muscles tightened. "Marty, I have to ask you to stay over tonight same as Miss Meyer."

"Absolutely, Lieutenant. Whatever you say."

After we'd made our way back up the spiral staircase Tedone grabbed one of the troopers who was on the stage door and told him to escort Marty past the horde of media people and on-lookers to the Sherbourne Inn. Off they went.

Another trooper came in clutching several Styrofoam take-out cups of hot coffee from the Backstage Tavern. "Lieutenant, Sergeant Bartucca told me to tell you the bartender didn't see anybody other than his regulars tonight," he reported as Tedone took a coffee container from him. "And no one was idling outside of the stage door."

"Got it, thanks." Tedone removed the plastic lid and took a grateful gulp, smacking his lips loudly, which immediately prompted Lulu to let out a sour grunt of disapproval. Merilee has an intense aversion to lip smackers that Lulu picked up from her. She's picked up a lot of her mommy's little aversions. People who pop their gum. People who click their forks against their teeth. People who say the word *snot*.

Another Crown Vic pulled up outside of the stage door now tailed closely by a low-profile ambulance, as in no siren, no blinking lights, no prominent markings. A jowly, middle-aged man in surgical scrubs got out of the Crown Vic, pausing to grab a doctor's bag from the backseat.

"This would be the chief medical examiner of the state of Connecticut," Tedone informed me. "Ordinarily, he sends his deputy to crime scenes. He only comes himself when it's a big one—which this is, in case you had any doubts."

"I didn't."

"The guy driving the ambulance is one of his assistants. Actually, we call them 'deaners' out here. Don't ask me why."

"Wasn't planning to."

The deaner, a tall, powerfully built young man who was also in scrubs, got out of the ambulance and joined his boss. Tedone went out and spoke to both men for a moment, paying no heed to the TV news cameras and lights and the reporters who were shouting questions at him from behind the perimeter. After they'd finished speaking, the deaner fetched a pair of oversize aluminum briefcases from the passenger seat of the ambulance. A trooper led the two men inside and downstairs to the dressing room.

Tedone returned to me and took a gulp of his coffee before he looked me up and down as if he were studying me for the first time. "I was hoping we'd get a chance to talk privately for a moment about R. J. Romero. Pete's brought me up to speed on his blackmail scheme. Also what he did to that poor rooster. Guy sounds like a real lowlife."

"Only because he is one."

"I understand he shares a history with the victim. The entire cast, for that matter. Could we be looking at one and the same case?"

"You're asking me my opinion?"

"If you don't mind," he replied, turning a bit testy.

"It did occur to me. R.J. resented the hell out of Greg's success. Thought he was a total stiff and that it should be *him* up there on the big screen, making all of those millions and living the sweet life. And here Greg was, smack dab in Sherbourne starring in a huge benefit performance in front of all of these theatrical legends. That had to piss R.J. off. But did it piss him off enough to kill Greg in cold blood without making so much as a sound? Because none of us heard an argument of any kind coming out of that dressing room."

"The sump pumps were running," Tedone pointed out.

"True enough. Maybe they could have masked the sound. But they couldn't have made him invisible. How did he kill Greg without *someone* seeing him slip in and out? It would involve split-second timing and an incredible amount of luck. And we're talking about a man whose luck has run out. He's a drugged-out mess."

"He's also an actor, isn't he?"

"And your point is . . . ?"

"Maybe he was wearing a disguise. It's a possibility, isn't it?"

"It is and it isn't. Let's say R.J. hatched a clever scheme to disguise himself as, say, Louise the frumpy maid, wig and all. You're right, he would have been totally unrecognizable. But he still couldn't have pulled it off."

"Why not?"

"Because Lulu would have been on him in a flash. She was up close and personal with Romero at the brass mill last night and in the parking lot at Walmart today. The sleazy bastard also paid a visit to Merilee's farm last night and beheaded the aforementioned Old Saxophone Joe. Trust me, if he had shown up anywhere near those dressing rooms tonight Lulu would have started barking her head off as soon as she got one whiff of him."

"You have a lot of faith in your dog's nose."

"Everyone has to believe in something, Lieutenant. I believe in Lulu's nose. Romero wasn't here tonight. In fact, I'll bet he's been hiding out from the rain somewhere and doesn't know a thing about this."

He glanced at his watch. It was nearly ten o'clock. "So you think he'll be waiting for you at that gate at eleven o'clock?"

"Absolutely. He's still on the run and he still needs that money."

"And are you still planning to pay him off?"

"I'm planning to show up."

"That's a big no. I want you to steer clear of that scene, understand?"

"Not even a little."

"We're reeling him in. I intend to question him about Farber's murder, then hand him over to my cousin Frank for the B & B Building Supply robbery."

"You can't do that, Lieutenant."

He raised an eyebrow at me. "And why not?"

"Because if you take him in for questioning he'll lawyer up and claim that Merilee was driving the car that night. He'll destroy her career. Your brother Pete did explain all of this, didn't he?"

"Relax. You got nothing to worry about."

"I have everything to worry about. The media will absolutely feast on this story."

"And I said relax. Romero won't be talking to anybody."

"Not acceptable. I told Pete I won't stand for anything 'unfortunate' happening to him while he's in police custody."

"And nothing will. The man's a junkie. That means we can tuck him away in isolation for at least twenty-four hours.

Maybe even forty-eight. He won't be talking to a lawyer. He won't be talking to anyone. He'll just disappear while we try to sort this mess out. Can you deal with that?"

I considered it for a moment. "Yes, I can deal with that."

"Good." Tedone gulped down some more of his coffee. "There's still one more suspect who we haven't talked about."

"And who would that be?"

He looked at me with those dark, hooded eyes of his. "You."

"Why on earth would *I* want to kill Greg?"

"Maybe he'd taken up on the sly with your wife."

"Ex-wife. And he hadn't."

"How do you know that?"

"Because Merilee and I don't keep things like that from one another. It's the secret to a happy former marriage. Besides, Greg would never do something like that to Dini. Or me, for that matter. We were friends. If he'd fallen madly in love with Merilee he would have told me."

"You make him sound like a stand-up guy."

"Only because he was one."

"How about the guy he was sharing the dressing room with?"

"Marty? What about him?"

"How'd the two of them get along?"

"They were never tight. Greg was the steady, buttoned-down type. Marty's a total wild man. But they were cordial, and respected each other's work. If you're asking me why Marty would want him dead I haven't got a reason for you. Besides, Marty was in the john when it happened, remember?"

"How could I forget? I'm still smelling it."

"May I ask you a procedural question, Lieutenant?"

"What is it?"

"When the M.E. performs the autopsy on Greg, will he do a workup of his blood?"

"Sure. Standard procedure."

"What will he test him for?"

"Alcohol and drugs, typically. Also any prescription meds that might point to an ongoing medical condition of some kind. Why are you asking?"

"Can you request that he run a specific test that may not be part of his standard autopsy procedure?"

"And why would I want to do that?"

"Because it might be the key to this entire case."

Lieutenant Carmine Tedone glared at me impatiently. "Are you going to tell me what it is or do I have to beg you?"

He didn't have to beg me.

IT WAS AFTER midnight by the time I followed Merilee's Jag home to the farm, both of us taking Joshua Town Road slowly and carefully so as to steer around the small branches and other bits of windblown debris that had come down during the storm. When we arrived I went directly to the chapel, opened the windows and got out of my sodden shoes, socks and tuxedo pants. Stripped off my tuxedo shirt, put on a T-shirt and jeans, then went inside the house and opened every window and screen door. We did not appear to have suffered a power outage. The VCR under the TV in the parlor wasn't blinking *12:00 12:00 12:00*, and the electric clocks were keeping the same time as Grandfather's Benrus.

I grabbed a flashlight, went back outside and took a quick tour of the property. The chickens had tucked themselves safely inside the barn during the storm and were just now starting to venture back out into their wire coop. I saw no major tree limbs down anywhere. No damage to any of the structures. I went back into the house and found Merilee seated at the kitchen table in an old flannel shirt, staring off into space, blown away. Lulu was seated in front of the refrigerator staring at it intently. I gave her an anchovy, then got the Macallan out of the cupboard and poured two generous jolts into a couple of vintage bar glasses, placing one in front of Merilee. It took her a moment to notice it there. When she did she reached for it and took a sip. My glass was already empty by then. I was refilling it when the business line rang. I'd made sure I gave the number to Lieutenant Tedone before we left.

"Wanted to let you know that we picked up that human scum Romero," he informed me in a tired-sounding voice. "He was waiting there for you at eleven o'clock just like you said he'd be. For what it's worth, he seemed genuinely shocked to hear that Greg Farber had been murdered. Unless, that is, he's one hell of an actor."

"I understand he was once considered one."

"We've arrested him on the grand theft charge and stuck him in isolation. We'll keep him tucked away there for as long as we can."

"And I have your word that no harm will come to him?"

"You have my word. But whatever happens after he makes bail is on you, understand? You can pay him off and pray he'll go away, but he won't. Not with this Farber murder on every front page across America. As soon as he lawyers up he'll start blabbing about Miss Nash and won't stop for as long as he has an audience. It's not too late to wise up and take my brother

Pete's advice. It's what I'd do if I were in your shoes. I'm talking to you man to man." He waited for me to respond. When I didn't he said, "But you're not going to, are you? Suit yourself. Good night."

I hung up the phone, got a slab of bacon out of the refrigerator and cut several thick slices. Placed them on the stove in the large Lodge cast iron skillet. Got some fresh eggs out. Dug a loaf of crusty French bread from the bread box. Also my manuscript, which I returned to its designated safe haven in the freezer chest in the mudroom with the venison leg.

"What did you mean?" Merilee asked me quietly.

"When?"

"When you said, 'And I have your word that no harm will come to him?' Come to whom?"

"They picked up R.J. tonight. He's a lowlife addict on the run. He and Greg were classmates who never liked each other. You know how the police like to wrap everything into a nice, neat package. I was concerned they might try to beat a confession out of him."

Merilee let out a snort. "What a great, big bucket of apple-sauce."

"I've missed your quaint little expressions."

"You, sir, are not telling me the real story."

"You're right, I'm not. But I will."

"When?"

"When this is over."

"This will never be over," she said miserably.

"Yes, it will."

"Hoagy, Greg was *murdered* tonight."

"Trust me, I haven't forgotten. But R.J. didn't do it."

When the bacon slices were ready I laid them on paper towels and cracked the eggs into the pan. There was a full glass bottle of Salem Valley Farms whole milk in the refrigerator. I poured us each a glass. Tore off two hunks from the baguette. Slid the eggs onto two plates sunny-side up along with the bacon and the bread and set one plate in front of her. She immediately began to eat. That's one thing I've always loved about my ex-wife. No matter how upset she is, she never loses her appetite. I ate mine standing at the sink. Certain meals taste better standing up. Bacon and eggs in the middle of the night happens to be one of them.

"The media will show up here tomorrow by the carload," I said as I munched on a mouthful of bread. "We ought to call the resident trooper in the morning and ask him to station a man at the foot of the driveway."

"Agreed."

She also agreed that our dirty dishes could wait until morning. That's another thing I've always loved about my ex-wife.

"Lulu and I will be heading out to the chapel now," I said. "Get yourself some sleep, okay?"

"I don't think I can." She glanced at me uneasily. "Darling, would you consider . . . ?"

"Would I consider what?"

"Would you stretch out with me for a little while and hold me?"

I didn't go in her bedroom very often. Had no reason to. I'd never slept in there. Didn't know if any other man had either. It was none of my business. Now that the tropical storm had passed the air had started to cool in the predawn hours. Her room had cross-ventilation. With the windows open wide there was a welcome, freshening breeze.

Merilee slid under the sheet and cotton blanket, still wearing her flannel shirt, and stretched out on her back, exhausted. I stretched out on top of the covers next to her. She rolled onto her hip and rested her head on my chest as Lulu curled up at our feet, her tail thumping.

"I keep thinking I should be crying for Greg and Dini and those sweet little girls who just lost their father," she confessed. "But I can't seem to muster any tears."

"They'll come."

"When?"

"When we figure out why it happened."

"How are *you* holding up?"

"This won't come as news to you but I don't like very many people. I liked Greg. He was one of the good guys."

"I'm sorry that you lost him, darling. The older we get the harder it is to find real friends. People whom we can really open up to, be ourselves . . ." She lay there quietly for a moment. "Poor Dini."

"What'll happen to her Julia Roberts project in Savannah?"

"They'll either wait a few weeks for her or they'll recast the part first thing tomorrow morning. It'll depend."

"On what?"

"On whether someone else is available first thing tomorrow morning."

"Yours is a cold business, Merilee."

"Yours isn't much warmer."

"No, it's not," I acknowledged, stroking her long, golden

hair. Remembering the feel and the scent of her. Beginning to ache inside. This was where I belonged every night, not out in the chapel. We belonged together. But it wasn't to be. Or at least it wasn't until she decided it was.

And so I lay there, listening to the wheels spin inside of my head. How had Greg's killer managed to pull it off in the crowded confines of those basement dressing rooms without being seen? I lay there, wondering, as a gentle breeze rustled the leaves of the apple trees. I was still wondering when I heard the first of the predawn birds start to warble and chirp. And then . . . then I heard a rooster crow. Quasimodo. God bless Mr. MacGowan. Good friends are hard to find. So are good neighbors.

Merilee cocked her head slightly on my chest, the better to hear him. "Is it my imagination or does Old Saxophone Joe sound different this morning?"

"Different as in . . . ?"

"Hoarse. Do roosters get laryngitis?"

Quasimodo crowed again. No getting around it. He definitely had a hoarse crow.

"He does sound a bit like Tom Waits today, now that you mention it. Maybe it was the storm last night."

"What would the storm have to do with it?"

"Merilee, I'm a city slicker, remember? I don't know from roosters."

She let out a yawn. "I think I might sleep now," she said before she proceeded to fall into a deep, peaceful slumber.

Me, I didn't sleep.

Chapter Seven

Merilee was up early, her face creased with fatigue as she stood there in a tank top and cutoffs sipping her coffee and watching Quasimodo strut around with the hens inside of the coop as if he owned the place. Her head, I observed, tilted ever so slightly every time she heard him crow. She *had* to know he wasn't Old Saxophone Joe, what with his pronounced hunchback—hence the name—plus he was bigger than Joe and his coloring was considerably redder. Clearly, he *wasn't* Joe. But, just as clearly, she'd decided she didn't want to deal with it right now. So the presence of this new rooster in our midst went entirely unspoken as we stood there together, drinking our coffee.

The morning air was deliciously fresh and clean after last night's storm, and scented with the lavender that was growing in profusion in the herb garden. The dew on the meadow grass glistened in the sunlight. The ducks were quacking in the pond. It was so goddamned beautiful it seemed impossible to believe that less than twelve hours earlier I'd been sloshing around in that flooded dressing room in the basement of the Sherbourne

Playhouse. That Greg Farber, one of America's most beloved movie stars, was dead. That any of it had happened.

Yet it had.

When I went back inside the house to refill my cup I flicked on the television in the parlor. *Good Morning America* had given over its entire show to memorializing Greg and his storybook Hollywood marriage to Dini. There were snippets of a *GMA* interview he'd given just last year about how much she and their twins meant to him. There were highlights from his films. Heartfelt video testimonials that were pouring in from Harrison Ford, Annette Bening, Jack Nicholson, Danny DeVito and many other actors with whom he'd worked.

Which isn't to say that the program was all hugs and kisses. Greg's "savage" murder was already being hyped as one of the most "explosive" crimes in showbiz history, which afforded them the opportunity to fling open the vault and pull out such grisly chestnuts as the fatal 1958 stabbing of Lana Turner's mobster boyfriend, Johnny Stompanato, by her fourteen-year-old daughter, Cheryl. Face it, Greg's slaying was prime crime. It had occurred in a dressing room of the historic Sherbourne Playhouse during a gala charity performance, while Jackie O and every heavy hitter in the New York theatrical world, up to and including Kate the Great, had been right there in the building.

I'm sure it was front-page news, but I didn't go out to the general store for a newspaper. When I strolled down to the foot of the drive with Lulu I discovered two Connecticut State Police Crown Vics stationed outside of the paddock gate, which the troopers had closed and latched shut. At least thirty reporters, paparazzi and TV news cameramen were crowded out there, their cars and vans lining the narrow country road. As soon as they caught sight of me they made with the shouting:

"Who killed him, Hoagy?"

"Was it Dini?"

"Had to be Dini, right?"

"Why'd she do it?"

"Was he cheating on her?"

"Who's the other woman?"

I ignored them. It's not easy but it can be done if you've had enough practice. Somebody ought to write a book about it someday. Not me, but somebody.

Merilee was in the shower when I got back to the house. I was putting down Lulu's 9Lives mackerel when the business line rang. Lieutenant Tedone again. He wanted me to meet him at the playhouse "at or around ten o'clock." There were "certain things" he wished to discuss with me. The noticeable chill in his voice indicated that he didn't wish to discuss these "certain things" on the phone, so I didn't press him. Just told him I'd be there.

By the time I rang off, Merilee had emerged, freshly scented with the fragrance of Crabtree & Evelyn avocado oil soap. She was wearing one of my old white sea island cotton dress shirts, striped linen shorts and sandals.

"Lieutenant Tedone wants to see me at the playhouse this morning," I said as Lulu, the noted Nose Bowl champ, worked away steadily on her breakfast.

"I'm going to spend some time with Dini at Point O'Woods," Merilee said. "She's going to need her friends right now. I'm sure she'd appreciate a visit from you, too. She knows how fond Greg was of you. Maybe you could join me there after you see the lieutenant?"

"Happy to. Unless he's decided to throw me in jail."

Merilee's green eyes widened. "Why on earth would he do that?"

"Justice moves in mysterious ways, Merilee. Do you want to come to the theater with me? Then we can go on to Dini's together."

"Hoagy, I don't ever want to go back there," she said in a somber voice.

"I don't blame you."

"How are things down at the foot of the driveway?"

"Crowded."

"In that case I'd like to take the Woody. I hate driving the Jag through the press hordes. I feel so exposed. Do you mind?"

"Not a bit. Keys are hanging in the mudroom."

"As are the keys to the Jag."

She'd already left by the time I'd showered, stropped grandfather's razor, shaved and doused myself in Floris. I dressed casually in a persimmon linen blazer, vanilla pleated cotton slacks, a pink shirt, blue-and-yellow-striped bow tie, white bucks and my handmade Panama fedora.

There was no way I was driving the Jag with the top up on such a bright, beautiful summer day. After I'd put it down I rolled down the windows and got in. Lulu hopped in eagerly. She loves to ride in the Jag.

I eased it slowly down the drive, its engine burbling. The troopers opened the gate and cleared a path for me. Once again I ignored the crush of media people who called out my name and shouted questions at me. Simply floored it the hell out of there, the Jag hugging the curves on Joshua Town Road. Lulu sat up with her large black nose stuck out the open window, enchanted by the breeze.

There was no shortage of activity on Sherbourne's town green that morning. And I don't just mean the media mob and celebrity gawkers who were crowded behind the barricade that the police had set up to keep the playhouse's stage entrance clear. Or the collection of Major Crime Squad cube vans that were on the scene as technicians continued to process the dressing room and corridor for evidence. A crew from Sherbourne Roofing was removing the blue tarps that they'd stretched across the roof yesterday. Or at least some of the tarps. Several of them had blown halfway across the green into the decorative yews that surrounded the gazebo. The crew that had installed the big wedding tent was packing it up and stowing it away in a pair of trucks. The caterer was taking away the folding tables and chairs.

I stashed the Jag in the parking lot of the Sherbourne Inn and strode across the green. Told the trooper who was stationed on the playhouse's front steps that Lieutenant Tedone was expecting me and went inside.

I found Mimi in her office, standing at the window behind her desk in a cream silk camisole and jeans watching the workmen on the green. Her shoulders were shaking. It wasn't until she heard me and turned around that I realized she was crying.

"It's *you*." Mimi came out from behind the desk and started toward me. "I'm so glad. I was hoping we'd get a chance to . . . to . . ." She broke off and threw herself into my arms, the tears streaming from her sky blue eyes down her perfectly sculpted cheekbones. I put my arms around her and held her as she sobbed and sobbed.

Until, that is, Lulu started to sneeze violently.

Mimi pulled away from me, arching an eyebrow at her curiously. "Why is she doing that?"

"Must be your perfume. Are you wearing Calvin Klein's Obsession?"

"Why, yes."

"She's allergic to it," I said as Lulu escaped into the lobby, sniffling and sneezing. "That's odd. She was in here with us last evening after Dini collapsed. She didn't sneeze one bit. Were you wearing it then?"

"No, I was wearing l'Occitane, a scent that I discovered when I was modeling in Provence years ago. But when I woke up this morning I wanted to smell younger. A bit trashy even. Does that make any sense to you?"

"No, but that's okay. It doesn't have to," I said, because I knew she was being straight with me. After all, she'd been downstairs in and around the dressing rooms last night shortly before Greg was murdered. If she'd been wearing Obsession at the time Lulu would have been sneezing her head off. But Lulu hadn't sneezed last night.

Still, when Mimi sat down at her desk, folding her slender hands in front of her, I noticed that nasty scrape on her knuckles again.

"What did you do to your hand?" I asked, taking a seat on the sofa.

She made a face. "I stupidly tried to help the caterer open a crate of champagne. After I immediately managed to make myself bleed he tactfully suggested I find something else to . . . to . . ." She began to cry again. I gave her my linen handkerchief. She dabbed at her eyes and nose. "Sorry, I can't seem to stop. I was counting on last night's performance to save this sweet old place."

"It did. No one has asked for their money back, have they?"

"Well, no," she admitted.

"If anything, the Sherbourne Playhouse is even more famous now than it was before," I said, studying her. "You shed a lot of tears last night, too."

"Of course I did. I was upset." Her swollen red eyes met mine. "Are you going somewhere with this?"

"You were a very successful young model in New York City right around the same time that Greg was a rising young stage star. You traveled in the same circles, hung out at the same bars and restaurants."

Her gaze hardened. "You don't miss much, do you?"

"I try not to."

"It happened before he married Dini. He wasn't sneaking out on her to be with me. He wasn't that sort of man. So get that thought out of your head."

"Wasn't in it."

Mimi sat back in her chair, sighing mournfully. "He was starring in a revival of *Picnic*. I was on the cover of that month's *Cosmo*. We met at P.J. Clarke's one night and I swear we were in bed together less than two hours later. I fell incredibly hard for Greg. I loved him more than any man I'd ever met in my whole life, all twenty-three years of it. If he'd asked me to marry him I would have said yes on the spot. But he didn't feel that way about me. For him, it was strictly physical. After six weeks or so he stopped calling me. Oh, how I cried and cried. And I absolutely hated his guts." She gazed out the window at the roofers who were wrestling with a wet tarp, shouting and cursing at each other. "And then I ended up calling him. I had to."

"To tell him you absolutely hated his guts?"

"No, to tell him that I was pregnant. I thought he should know."

"And . . . ?"

"And nothing. I had an abortion. It was no big deal."

"It's a very big deal."

"I've had three. Believe me, it's nothing."

I stared at her, not buying what she was selling.

"He asked me if I wanted him to pay for it. I said we could go halves. So we split it, just like a dinner tab, and went our separate ways. End of fling. End of story. All except . . ." Her mouth tightened. "Except that for me it was one of those special moments that happen in your life. A critical moment, I guess you writers would call it."

"I'd probably go with pivotal, but that's just me. How so?"

"I decided that I'd never, ever put myself through that again. Greg was the third guy I'd fallen for since I'd moved to New York from Wisconsin, and all three relationships had ended up with me sobbing my heart out. Never again, I told myself. From now on any relationship that I have with a man will be strictly a business transaction. So I found myself a rich, boring real estate tycoon, got a wedding ring out of him, twelve rooms on Park Avenue and the beach house in Point O'Woods—followed by a handsome seven-figure divorce when he decided it was time to trade me in for a younger model. And so now here I am, free as a bird. If I feel like having a fling I have one. If not then I don't. No muss, no fuss and no more tears."

"You don't miss it?"

"Miss what, Hoagy?"

"Being madly in love."

She was silent a moment before she said, "Nothing good comes from it."

"You didn't answer my question, Mimi."

"I didn't bash Greg's brains in, if that's what you're wondering."

"I'm not."

"Yet you're looking at me very oddly right now."

"I don't mean to. It's just that you're a very attractive woman, free as a bird and I haven't had sex with anyone during this particular calendar year." One of the most valuable lessons I've learned in the ghosting business is that if you want to get something then you have to give something.

"My, my. You're full of candid personal details, aren't you?" She studied me with newfound curiosity. "How are things between you and Merilee?" she asked in a manner that was meant to sound offhanded but wasn't.

"I'd like to say they're looking up, but I don't know."

"You two still love each other, don't you?"

"I can't speak for her, but in my case the answer is yes."

"You're a funny specimen, Stewart Hoag."

"How so?"

"You try to act all hard and cynical except you're not. Would you like to know what you are?"

"I'm dying to know."

"You're a romantic fool."

"Do me a huge favor and keep that to yourself, will you? You'll wreck my image."

Lulu let out a warning bark from the lobby. Someone was there.

"Easy there, pooch . . ." It was Lieutenant Carmine Tedone. "Is your tall friend around here someplace?"

I told Mimi I'd catch up with her later and joined him. Tedone had on another one of his cheap, shiny black suits. I figured he owned at least five, possibly seven, and rotated them daily. He wore a white shirt and a dark, muted tie. I figured he owned at least ten of each of those.

"How may I help you, Lieutenant?"

He eyed my persimmon blazer up and down rather coldly. He didn't seem to care for my summer ensemble at all. In fact, he looked as if he wanted to take a big bite out of my Panama hat. "Walk with me," he answered gruffly, starting backstage down the service corridor. "We found a stack of those 1924 Tuttle bricks out in the courtyard," he informed me over his shoulder as I followed him. "We also found out that the crew chief, Cyril Cooper, aka Coop, served time for dealing kilos of pot in Binghamton, New York, back in the late '60s."

"That's not saying a whole lot."

"Also one of the stage crew, Nona Peachy, who's a junior at Brown, was busted for coke possession when she was a sophomore at Sherbourne High."

"Again, not saying a whole lot."

"Hang on, will you? Just clearing my throat. My sergeant, Angelo Bartucca, spent some quality time with two members of the Sherbourne PD last night. It seems they've got themselves quite a little heroin problem in this picture postcard village. They took him to an abandoned farmhouse on the outskirts of town that's a known shooting gallery. Ang found three scuzzy smack freaks who swear that R. J. Romero was shooting up

with them there last night right around the time when somebody was beating Greg Farber's brains in."

"And you believe them?"

"Why not? Just because they're scuzzy smack freaks doesn't
mean they're liars."

"But it does mean they don't have a keen sense of the con-
cept of time. They're a lot like the French in that regard." We
strode past the aged lighting and sound consoles and arrived
backstage. The back door was open to let in the fresh air. The
crime scene techies were still coming in and out. "And that's
still not saying a whole lot because R.J. didn't do it. I already
told you that."

"So you did," he growled at me.

"You seem a tad grouchy this morning, Lieutenant, if you
don't mind me saying so."

"I got two hours of sleep last night. I got bosses breathing
down my neck. I got journalists everywhere . . ."

"These aren't journalists. These are celebrity crime lem-
mings. Different breed entirely."

"Well, you'd know a lot more about that than I would."

"Was that supposed to be some kind of a dig?"

He studied me dubiously with his hooded dark eyes. "My
brother Pete says you've been around the block more than a
few times with this sort of business. That it's almost a specialty
of yours."

"I don't seek it out, Lieutenant, if that's where your mind is
going."

"So it just sort of finds you? Is that how you'd put it?"

"I'd put it that celebrities are very proud, insecure people who have a lot of secrets. I'd put it that they and the people close to them will go to any length to keep those secrets from the public. They also hold grudges."

"That what you think happened here? Somebody was settling a grudge?"

"I really don't know."

We went down the spiral staircase to the basement dressing rooms. The sump pumps had taken care of the floodwaters. Portable box fans had been set up to air the space out. But it still smelled damp and moldy down there, possibly because it *was* still damp and moldy.

We stood in the doorway of the men's dressing room watching Tedone's crime scene people work. "Have they found anything useful yet?" I asked him.

"So far they've isolated eight different sets of shoe prints on the floor planks in here. When they're sure that they've got them all they'll try to match them to the individuals who had reason to be in here. It's tedious work, and there's no telling if it'll lead us anywhere, but that's what they do."

"How about the medical examiner? Was he able to determine anything from the blows to the back of Greg's head? How tall the killer was, whether he or she was right-handed or left-handed . . ."

"You watched too much TV when you were a kid. The M.E. is rarely able to determine any of those things. Would you like me to tell you why?"

"Yes, I would."

"Because the victim is tumbling to the floor as he's being hit. That makes it nearly impossible to determine the height of the assailant or whether said assailant was right- or left-handed. We do know that the victim was hit numerous times with considerable force."

"What does that suggest?"

"That someone was really pissed off at him. We also know that he was alive when he went facedown into that water. He drowned."

"We knew that last night."

"We didn't *know* it," Tedone shot back irritably. "We assumed it."

"Lieutenant, what am I doing here? Why did you call me?"

He raised his chin at me. "Let's continue this conversation elsewhere."

We went upstairs and out the stage door to the courtyard, where the crew members were coming and going from the adjoining barn as they stored the furniture and props from last night's one and only abbreviated production of *Private Lives*. Nona Peachy waved at me. I waved back.

Tedone stood there in the sunlight glaring at me. "Okay, let's have it. Tell me how you knew."

"How I knew what?"

"You were right about Greg Farber's blood work. He *was* HIV-positive. How did you know?"

"And what about Dini?"

"What *about* her?"

"Did you speak to Doctor Orr? Is she HIV-positive as well?"

"I'm not discussing any details about her medical condition. Whatever Orr has told me is strictly confidential."

"I'm going to take that as a yes."

"Take it any way you want, but I am not, repeat not, confirming that Dini Hawes is HIV-positive. That's beyond the scope of what I can share with you."

"Yet you want me to share everything that I know with you. Hardly seems fair."

"This isn't about what's fair or unfair. And you still haven't answered my question. How the fuck did you know?"

"Call it an educated guess."

"Based upon what?"

I didn't respond. Just waited him out. Took my hat off, adjusted the brim ever so slightly. Settled it back on my head. Watched Lulu mosey over to a pile of bricks—vintage Tuttles just like the murder weapon—and begin sniffing at them delicately.

Finally, Tedone said, "We've reached out to Farber's personal physician in New York City, but he's on vacation in Crete. Until we can talk to him we have no idea when Farber contracted the AIDs virus. Or if he even knew that he *had* contracted it, for that matter." He glared at me some more. "Now talk to me about this educated guess of yours. You have any idea how he picked it up?"

"How would I know that?"

"You two were friends, weren't you?"

"Yes, we were. Which is why I'm not going to speculate."

"Was he stepping out on his wife?"

"If he was, he didn't say anything to me about it."

"Must have been," Tedone mused aloud. "Picked it up from having unprotected sex with some bimbo."

"That's certainly one possibility."

He peered at me intently. "What's another?"

"I just told you, Lieutenant. I'm not going to speculate."

"If that *is* how he picked it up, then he sure was behaving recklessly in this day and age." Tedone ran a meaty hand over his face. "You think it's possible he didn't know that he had it?"

"I do, actually. He was scheduled to fly out to L.A. last night to begin shooting the new Clint Eastwood western. When stars of Greg's stature sign on to do a picture the studio makes them take a preproduction physical for insurance purposes. I have no doubt they'd have given him a blood test in L.A. before he left for Death Valley. If Greg knew that he was HIV-positive, then there was no way he would have passed that test. Maybe he'd schemed a way of getting around it, like bribing the medical technician to substitute someone else's blood. I've heard of it being done. But he wasn't like that."

"Like what?"

"He was a straight shooter. A decent, honest guy."

"Really? Because he sure doesn't come off like one."

I let that particular dig slide on by. "Lieutenant, has Dini been officially notified that Greg was HIV-positive?"

"I'm on my way over to Point O'Woods to tell her right now," he said unhappily.

"Is Marty Miller still around or has he gone back to New York City?"

"He's still at the inn. So is Sabrina Meyer."

"Do you consider them suspects?"

"I consider them persons of interest. I want to have another conversation with each of them before I let them go."

"Same as you're having another conversation with me?"

"Well, yeah, if you want to look at it that way."

"I'm curious about something, Lieutenant."

He sighed irritably. "Yeah, what is it?"

"Why have you shared this with me before you've informed Dini?"

Tedone wouldn't tell me. Just glanced down at Lulu, who

was stretched out at my feet having a little snooze, before he said, "For your information, I'm not buying that 'educated guess' line of BS you gave me when I asked you how you knew he was HIV-positive. You're holding out on me. What's the deal? Are you protecting somebody?"

"I could be."

"Who?"

"If I told you then I wouldn't be protecting them, would I?"

"Meaning you don't trust me, is that it?"

"Meaning I've learned the hard way that law enforcement agencies are incapable of keeping anything under wraps. It always leaks out. Always. Nothing personal, Lieutenant."

Tedone shoved his lower lip in and out. "I got to say, I'm still not entirely sold on you, despite your advance billing."

"What advance billing? To whom have you been speaking about me?"

"For my money, you strike me as just a little bit too slippery."

That was enough to wake up Lulu, who let out a low growl. I told her to let me handle it.

"Why do you say that, Lieutenant?"

"Because I get the feeling you're working me."

"Are you trying to tell me that you're not working me?"

"I'm doing my job. What are *you* doing?"

"Trying to find out who killed my friend," I said. "And I will."

"HUH ... WHA?"

When I phoned up to Marty's room from the lobby of the Sherbourne Inn I'd apparently awakened him from a heavy slumber, even though it was nearly noon. "I thought we should have a talk. Shall I come up or would you rather come down?"

"No, no. You can . . . wait, who is this?"

"It's Hoagy."

"*Hoagy . . .*" Marty's voice filled with sadness. "Come on up, man. By all means."

Lulu and I took our time going up the steps to the third floor, which almost gave Millie, Marty's sturdily built young waitress, enough time to get dressed and sneak out of his utter mess of a room, which reeked of sex, Southern Comfort and Marty's own rich, personal aroma. Just not quite. She was still scrambling around on her hands and knees in search of her left sandal when Marty let me in. He wore a pair of boxer shorts and nothing else. She wore a Red Sox T-shirt, cutoffs and a pronounced hickey on her neck. Her hair was a mess. Her face was puffy. She looked hungover and hugely ill at ease.

Lulu gave her an assist by nosing her sandal out from under the bed.

She grabbed it and put it on, smiling uncertainly at Marty. "Will I see you later?"

"Absolutely," Marty said with such conviction that even I believed him.

She hurried out, closing the door softly behind her.

"She's seventeen." He flopped down on the four-poster bed, blubbery, unshaven and dissolute. "The age of consent in Connecticut is sixteen. And no, I'm not proud of myself." He rubbed his sleep-heavy eyes and lit a Lucky Strike, dragging on it. "But I was depressed and lonely and that cop made me stay over."

"You don't owe me an explanation, Marty."

"I know, but I owe myself one."

When I was fourteen I once drank an entire quart of South-

ern Comfort with my best friend, Cecil Nelson Widdifield—
that's right, U.S. Congressman Cecil Nelson Widdifield—and
to this day even the faintest whiff of it makes me queasy. I
went to the windows and opened them wide. Directly across
the street on the town green a half-dozen photographers were
snapping photos of the inn.

Marty used the bedside phone to order a pot of coffee. "I
may jump in the shower while I'm waiting for it," he said to me
after he'd hung up.

"Don't let me stop you. Please."

He went in the bathroom, closed the door and I heard the
shower running. His third-floor room was smaller than the
one they'd given Merilee one floor below but still loaded with
Victorian charm. I threw the patterned quilt over the unmade
bed so I wouldn't have to look at or smell anything that I didn't
want to look at or smell. Marty was still in the shower when
there was a knock at the door. I opened it. A different sturdily
built young milkmaid bustled in toting a tray with a pot of
coffee, cup and saucer, cream, sugar and a cute little basket of
miniature muffins of some kind. My guess would be cranberry.
She put it on the ornate writing table, smiled at me politely and
let herself out.

Marty emerged from the bathroom a moment later in a
terry cloth bathrobe, poured himself some coffee and set it on
the nightstand. Then he flopped down on the bed, propping
himself up with several pillows, reached for his coffee and took
a huge, grateful gulp.

I sat in the ornate chair that went with the ornate writing
table. Lulu stretched out at my feet.

"Lieutenant Tedone wants to talk to me sometime today,"

Marty said. "Strictly informally, he assured me. At least he's not dragging me to headquarters in handcuffs."

"Why would he want to do that?"

"Because I'm his prime suspect or main suspect or whatever the fuck they call it. That's pretty damned obvious, isn't it? I shared that dressing room with Greg. I should have been in there changing for act two when it happened. Except I wasn't, I swear. I was in the john across the hall. Tedone *knows* that. He saw the evidence for himself. But he keeps giving me the feeling that he doesn't believe me."

"He's just doing his job. That's how those guys operate. Don't let him mess with your head. *I* believe you. Besides, why on earth would you want to beat Greg's brains in with a brick?"

"That part's easy. Dini used to be my girlfriend. I still care about her."

"Still not getting the easy part."

"Because Greg gave her the AIDS virus. Dini's HIV-positive." I kept my face blank. "And you know this how?"

"She told me last night just before we went onstage. Doctor Orr had just called to give her the news. She asked me not to tell anyone."

"And yet she told you."

"We share a history together. We're still close."

"Did she know that Greg was cheating on her?"

Marty eyed me over the rim of his cup. "She didn't say. And I haven't heard any rumors. I've been in Vancouver for the past two months shooting the new Bruce Willis, and before that I was in London doing my twelve-week run of *Salesman*. Besides, maybe he wasn't. Cheating on her, that is."

"Meaning . . . ?"

"Maybe *she's* seeing someone else and she gave it to Greg."

"You don't believe that for one second."

"You're right, I don't." Marty let out a gloomy sigh. "It was damned stupid of him, that's all I know. You've got to be so careful these days. I always wear a condom. Look in that wastebasket over there if you don't believe me."

"Not necessary," I assured him. Lulu echoed the sentiment by making a low, unhappy noise at my feet.

"I always liked the guy, Hoagy. He was a decent person. This whole thing's a shame. A damned shame." Marty drained his coffee cup, got up and poured himself some more. "What about that lowlife shithead Romero?"

"What about him?"

"He couldn't stand Greg. He shows up in town and, wham, Greg is suddenly facedown dead in six inches of water. Kind of fits together, doesn't it?"

"It does, except Romero has an alibi of sorts. Three different smack freaks saw him shooting up at an abandoned farmhouse on the outskirts of town at the time of the murder."

He shook his head at me. "*That's* an alibi?"

"Of sorts, like I said."

He sat back down heavily on the edge of the bed and lit another Lucky Strike, sighing gloomily once again. "Know what, Hoagy? This totally sucks."

"You're right, Marty. It totally does."

I FOUND SABRINA seated on a tree-shaded bench in the inn's showy rose garden writing a postcard to someone. Two of the gardeners were ogling her from twenty feet away as they trimmed a boxwood hedge. Sabrina was ignoring them. She was accustomed to being ogled. She wore a sleeveless linen summer dress that was artfully unbuttoned so as to show off her long, bare legs. Sabrina had great legs. Great everything. Flawless skin. Slanted, smoldering eyes. Those gorgeous, cascading ringlets of golden hair. She had talent, too, according to Merilee. Emotionally fragile, yes, but that's hardly uncommon among performers. In fact, it's pretty much the norm.

She looked up at me as I approached her. "I'm sending a postcard to my mom," she confessed, smiling faintly. "She likes it when I send her postcards. Plasters them all over her refrigerator with Snoopy magnets."

"Where does she live?"

"Hackensack. Just like in the Billy Joel song."

"Is that where you're from?"

"Yup."

"Are you a fan of the Piano Man?"

Sabrina eyed me with suspicion. "Why?"

"Because it would mean the end of our relationship before it's even had a chance to start."

"Can't stand him. My taste tends more toward Erroll Garner. I get goose bumps whenever I hear him play 'Misty.'"

"Meyer, have you been reading up on me?"

She frowned. "I don't know what you mean."

"I mean that my fondness for the Little Elf is somewhat legendary. *Esquire* once wrote an entire article about it."

"Is that right? I had no idea. Seriously."

"May I join you for a few minutes?"

"Please do. I'm bored out of my skull. Did you know that there's absolutely nothing to do in Sherbourne?"

I sat on the bench. Lulu climbed up onto it and squeezed

herself in between us. Subtle, Lulu is not. She knows a threat to her happy home when she sees one.

Sabrina patted her on the head. "But I'm stuck here because Lieutenant Tedone wants to talk to me again, which is a total bummer because I was supposed to read for a part in Sydney Pollack's new film today. It's just a bit role, but it's *Sydney Pollack*."

"Maybe they'll let you read for it tomorrow."

"No chance. They won't hold it open for me. I'm a nobody." She shifted around on the bench, recrossing her legs. "I start to get jittery if I sit around and think too much, and for me it's just a quick bunny hop from jittery to the panic express. My world can turn into a really dark place *so* fast. You have no idea."

"Yes, I do. I happen to be a resident of the same world."

Her eyes studied my face searchingly. "Smack?"

"Coke."

"For real?"

"Do you think I'd make something like that up?"

She lowered her gaze. "I've been clean for fifteen months."

"And you're going to stay clean. And I wouldn't fret about missing that audition. Your career is about to take off like a Titan missile. You'll be getting a huge amount of attention because of Greg's death. The casting agents will know who you are. Everyone will know who you are. In fact, you'll look back on this someday and realize that Greg Farber's murder was your big break."

Sabrina looked at me in horror. "You make it sound like *I* killed him to boost my career."

"Did you?"

"You're serious, aren't you? You're genuinely asking me that."

"Actually, I'm trying to prep you for the scene that you'll be playing later today with Lieutenant Tedone."

"Meaning you think he's going to talk to me like that?"

"Meaning I *know* he's going to talk to you like that."

She shook her blond ringlets at me, dumbfounded. "Why on earth would I want to kill Greg?"

"You tell me. Were you two romantically involved?"

"I hardly knew him. Or any of these people. I just met them two weeks ago after Merilee took me on as a favor to the drama school. They've been super nice to me, but it's not as if we hung out together or anything. Marty did try to hit on me . . ."

"Now there's a surprise."

"And he's a genius but he's, I mean, totally gross. Ugh."

"You were seated in the wings during act one last night, weren't you?"

"That's right. I wanted to get a feel for the energy, like I told you."

"Since you were already in full costume and makeup you had no reason to go down to the dressing rooms during the act break. What *did* you do?"

"Stayed right where I was and watched the stagehands rushing around setting up for act two while the rain was pouring down on them. It was total mayhem, like watching a Buster Keaton movie. Do you like Keaton?"

"Love Keaton."

She smiled. "For real?"

"Absolutely. I never kid around about Buster Keaton. You saw your fellow cast members go downstairs to change, I'm guessing."

She nodded those golden ringlets. "Sure."

"But, just to be clear, you didn't go down there yourself, correct?"

Sabrina hesitated. "Actually, I did try to, sort of. Mimi had asked me to keep an eye on Cheyenne and Durango for a minute while she went down there, remember? And while I was sitting there with them I suddenly got it into my head that Louise would look even frumpier wearing a garish smear of bright red lipstick. So I went down the spiral staircase to ask Merilee what she thought but it was so flooded down there and so many other people were crowding the ladies' dressing room—you, Glenda, Mimi—that I just skipped the idea and went back upstairs."

"So you didn't go in the dressing room?"

"No."

"Who watched the twins while you were down there?"

"Nobody. They're not babies. I told them to stay put. They stayed put. Besides, I was only gone for a second."

"While you were down there did you see anyone go in or out of Greg and Marty's dressing room? Anyone or anything that you weren't expecting to see?"

Sabrina's eyes flickered, her gaze suddenly avoiding mine. "No, nothing."

I studied her, positive she was holding out on me. "Sure about that?"

"Yes, I'm sure."

"Okay. And then what happened?"

"I went back upstairs, like I said. Glenda and Mimi came back up not long after I did and then—"

"Which one of them came up first?"

"Sorry?"

"Which one of them came back upstairs first?"

"Mimi, then Glenda maybe a minute later. And then I heard Marty holler out your name. I guess that's when he'd found Greg. After that all hell broke loose."

We fell silent for a moment, seated there in that too-perfect rose garden, the air heavy with the scent of fresh flowers and the not-so-fresh scent of 9Lives canned mackerel courtesy of Lulu, who remained parked between us, mouth-breathing in the summer warmth.

"Is this the sort of stuff that the lieutenant will be asking me?"

I nodded. "Pretty much."

"Thanks for the prep."

"My pleasure."

Sabrina glanced at me uneasily. "Do you mind if I ask you a nosy question?"

"Not at all."

"What's it like? Merilee's life, I mean."

"Success doesn't make your problems go away, if that's what you're wondering. In fact, it can make them a lot worse because you're still *you* except now everyone in the world thinks they know you. And own you."

Sabrina swallowed, her face darkening. "Did she tell you that I had to check myself into McLean last year?"

"She did."

"My older brother turned me on to smack. He was totally into it."

"Is he still?"

"No, he's dead."

"I'm sorry."

"Don't be. He was a messed-up person who wrecked the lives of everyone around him."

"Merilee also told me you've got it together now. She thinks you're the total package, you know."

"Are you just saying that to cheer me up?"

"Do you need cheering up?"

"No, I'm good. Really, I am. Just antsy to get back to the city, that's all. I'd give anything to have what Merilee has. A career that allows her to pick and choose her projects. And a man like you who's smart, talented and kind to share my life with."

"I'm not exactly sharing her life. She's just letting me work on my new book in her guest cottage because it's currently a hundred and seventeen degrees in my apartment."

She eyed me curiously. "You mean you two aren't together?"

"That's correct."

Which prompted Lulu to let out a low, unhappy grumble.

Sabrina looked at me with those slanted dark eyes. "So you're available?"

"By most people's definition of the term. But I'm not unattached."

"Are you saying you still love her?"

"That pretty much covers it."

She sighed regretfully. "Me, I can't seem to meet anyone who's worth knowing. I love spending time with writers. You're such interesting people to talk to."

"Really? That hasn't been my experience."

"You're toying with me. Please don't. I'm being serious here." She found a scrap of paper in her shoulder bag, scribbled her phone number on it and handed it to me. "Call me when you get back to the city, okay? We can meet for coffee or go to a museum or something, can't we?"

"I don't see why not."

"Call me," she repeated. "I mean it."

POINT O'WOODS WAS one of those ritzy old-money private beach colonies like Fenwick in Old Saybrook, the one where Katharine Hepburn lived. To get there I first had to navigate my way around the Guilfoyle town green, then dip under the Amtrak railroad bridge and drive out onto a promontory that jutted out into Long Island Sound—although very, very few people ever made it that far because as soon as you dipped under the railroad bridge you ran smack dab into a kiosk manned by a full-time guard who wouldn't permit you to proceed any farther unless you were (a) a Point O'Woods resident, (b) on his official guest list or (c) there to repair someone's washer-dryer.

The colony consisted of about three-dozen mammoth natural-shingle turn-of-the-century bungalows with turrets, sleeping porches and wraparound balconies. All of them shared access to a private beach, tennis court and nine-hole pitch and putt golf course. Most of the bungalows had been in the same families for generations. They rarely became available for sale on the open market. Mimi had come into hers strictly because her divorce lawyer had been a world-class shark. Her next-door neighbors, who were currently vacationing in France, had been nice enough to let Greg, Dini, the twins and Glenda use their house while they were rehearsing *Private Lives*. Their only stipulation had been that the golden retrievers, Steve and Eydie, had to stay behind in New York City.

Dozens of paparazzi, to my total lack of surprise, were crowded just outside the dip under the railroad bridge waiting for a money shot of Dini when she emerged from seclusion. Two Guilfoyle police cars were there to keep them from blocking the road. I pulled the Jag up at the kiosk, gave the guard my name and told him that I was expected. He phoned the house and spoke very deferentially with someone there, rather like a white-gloved doorman on Fifth Avenue does when he's phoning the penthouse. After he'd hung up he nodded his head at me and told me to head for the last house on the right.

A dirt road took me past one giant bungalow after another. Some had privet hedges around them. Others simply had open acres of lawn. I saw no people anywhere. When I arrived at the last house on the right I spotted Merilee's Woody parked outside a four-car garage. I also saw Glenda getting out of a rental Ford Taurus with a couple of shopping bags. Evidently she'd arrived just a moment before I had. I pulled up next to her and waved.

"Oh, hello," she said in a voice that was decidedly less than warm. "I've been in the village picking up a few things."

"A prescription for Dini?" I asked as Lulu and I got out of the Jag.

"I don't see how that's any of your business," she responded sharply.

"You're absolutely right. It's not."

I followed her down a brick path to a bluestone terrace that faced the Sound. It was a rare gem of a summer day. No milky haze. No humidity. Just a deep blue sky with puffy white clouds and a bright golden sun. The water was sparkling and beautiful. I counted four, five, six sailboats out there picking up the fresh breeze that last night's storm had left behind.

Merilee was seated with Dini at a teak table shaded by an umbrella. There was a pitcher of iced tea and glasses on the table. The twins were out on the lawn rather listlessly tossing a Frisbee back and forth—until they spotted my short-legged partner.

"Come play with us, Lulu!" Cheyenne called to her.

"Come on, Lulu!" Durango chimed in.

Lulu stayed put next to me, grunting sourly. She hates playing Frisbee. Hates it.

"Lovely spot, isn't it?" Merilee said with forced good cheer as I joined them at the table.

"It is. I've never been out here."

"That's the whole point of these private colonies. They don't want to mix with us common folk." Merilee glanced over at Dini before she turned back to me, lowering her voice. "Lieutenant Tedone stopped by with some rather devastating news from the medical examiner."

"How are you doing, Dini?" I asked, studying her across the table. She looked as if she were in a trance, positively goggle-eyed by shock and grief.

"Did I just hear my mother come home?" she asked in a timid voice.

"You did. She went in the house."

"Come play with us, Lulu!" Cheyenne called out once again. *"Please!"*

I looked down at Lulu. Lulu looked up at me. I suggested she take one for the team and pretend to have fun chasing the stupid Frisbee back and forth. She dutifully went ahead and did just that, barking playfully as she ran back and forth from one twin to the other, making them giggle.

"The girls seem to be holding up well," I observed as Glenda came outside and joined us at the table.

"It hasn't sunk in yet," Glenda said. "That their daddy is dead, I mean. Greg was away on location an awful lot and they've gotten accustomed to his long absences. They're still convinced that he'll be coming home one of these days, despite what we've told them." She let out a regretful sigh. "They'll face up to it soon enough, but for now they're just children being children."

Dini continued to sit there in silence.

"How are you doing, Dini?" I asked again.

"Do you mean how do I feel about Greg being dead or how do I feel about finding out that he infected me with the AIDS virus?" Dini gazed at me across the table, her pale blue eyes puddling with tears. "I feel like a victim. I also feel like the world's biggest idiot."

"You've been through a lot, dear," Glenda said to her. "And you still have a slight fever, you know."

"When did you find out that you're HIV-positive?" I asked her.

"Doctor Orr dropped the news on me yesterday afternoon. I phoned him from my room at the inn while I was trying to rest up after our dress rehearsal. I immediately called my own doctor in New York, who's making an appointment for me to see the top AIDS specialist in the city as soon as we get back. My doctor swore to me that being HIV-positive is no longer a death sentence. They're having excellent results with AZT along with a cocktail of other drugs, vitamins, minerals and a special diet. He promised me that I can still lead a long, productive life."

"He's right," Merilee said, taking Dini's small hand.

"Did you know that he was cheating on me?" Dini asked me point-blank.

I shook my head. "Hadn't a clue. And, for what it's worth, I'm not convinced that Greg knew."

Dini looked at me with desperate hope in her eyes. "You mean . . . you think it's possible he wasn't aware that he had it?"

"I do. Greg loved you. He loved your girls. I refuse to believe he'd knowingly give you the virus."

Dini considered that for a moment. "Well, *he* didn't get it from *me* if that's where you're going with this. I never cheated on him. Not once."

"He wasn't thinking that, Dini," Merilee assured her. "Were you, Hoagy?"

"Of course not," I said, which wasn't exactly true. It was entirely possible that Dini was seeing another man. It was clear during rehearsals that she and Greg hadn't been getting along. There was tension in their marriage.

Dini reached for her iced tea and took a sip, her hand trembling slightly. "I've pulled out of the Julia Roberts movie. They're talking to Sissy Spacek."

"She's a wonderful actress," Merilee said. "But she's not you."

Dini's eyes welled up as she gulped back tears. "Thank you, but I-I just don't know if I have it in me to keep going. Or if I even want to."

"You must," Merilee insisted. "Your girls need you. I won't insult your intelligence by trying to put a smiley face on this. Your life as you knew it has been nuked. And it'll only be a matter of a few more hours before the press gets hold of this and the whole world finds out—which will make it a hundred times more awful. But you *will* get through this. You're a fighter, Dini. You've always been a fighter. And we'll be by your side every step of the way, I swear."

The girls were still throwing the Frisbee. Lulu chased it a couple of more times before she decided she'd had enough and flopped down under the table at my feet, panting. I patted her and told her she was a good girl. She assured me she expected an anchovy reward.

The phone rang inside the house.

"A housekeeper came with the place," Dini said. "She'll answer it."

A moment later a tall, gaunt lady who had to be in her eighties came out of the house and said, "The fella at the gate said there's a man hee-yah in a station wagon." She had one of those salty Rhode Island accents that you still heard occasionally in southeastern Connecticut among working-class people of a certain age, which is to say old. "Says he works for your family. Has himself two golden retrievers with him. You know we can't have those dogs hee-yah in the house. The missus is allergic."

Dini's eyes widened. "My god, what is *Eugene* doing here?"

"Wants to help out, I imagine," Glenda said with an absence of enthusiasm.

"But what are we going to do with Steve and Eydie?" Dini wondered.

"Would it be okay if the dogs slept in the garage?" I asked the housekeeper.

"Don't see why not," she responded. "As long as they don't howl."

"They won't," Dini assured her. "They'll be good and quiet. Please tell the guard to let him in."

"Yes, ma'am."

A black Volvo station wagon rolled in soon after that and parked next to the Jag. Eugene got out and raised the tailgate. Steve and Eydie leaped out of the back of the car and came bounding across the lawn toward the twins, barking excitedly. The twins greeted them with tremendous glee as Lulu crouched under the table at my feet, eyeing them with silent disdain. She can be a bit of a snob when it comes to big, dumb slobberers.

Greg's twenty-six-year-old personal assistant, Eugene Inagaki, strode toward us, his face a mask of grief. Eugene, a third-generation Japanese-American from Fresno, was no taller than five feet eight but extremely well put together and nimble on his feet, as one would expect from the man who'd been the number one ranked intercollegiate squash player in America his junior and senior years at Yale. He had on a Yale T-shirt, baggy shorts and Topsiders. Wore his black hair a bit on the shaggy side and was unshaven.

"Don't hate me, Dini," he pleaded as he crossed the terrace toward her, blinking back tears. "I had to come. I just had to."

"Of course you did," she said soothingly. "I'm glad you came, Eugene." Dini got up from the table and gave him a warm hug. "Besides, the girls have been missing Steve and Eydie. But the dogs will have to sleep out in the garage."

"I'll put down the backseat of the Volvo and sleep with them," he said.

"So will we!" Durango exclaimed as Steve and Eydie licked her face.

"Absotootly!" Cheyenne chimed in.

"You girls are *not* sleeping in the garage. And neither are you, Eugene. We'll find you a bedroom. There must be at least eleven of them."

"That's real kind of you," he said. "I figured I could find a motel or something, but I wanted to be here for you to help run interference with the press. I mean, you're all alone out here."

"She's not all alone," Glenda said to him curtly. "She has me."

"Of course she does," Eugene said, backpedaling quickly. Me, I sensed no great love between the two of them. "I just wanted to make myself available is all I meant." He heaved a sigh of grief, his muscular chest rising and falling. "I can't believe Greg's gone. He was such a good man."

"Yes, he was," Dini said softly.

Eugene got around to exchanging somber greetings with Merilee and me before he turned back to Dini and said, "Tell me, what can I do first?"

"You can get those dogs some exercise," Glenda ordered him. "They're barking their fool heads off."

"Sure thing. They've been cooped up in the car for hours." He clapped his hands and started toward the beach, the retrievers dashing along after him.

"I could use some exercise myself." I got up from the table, glancing down at Lulu. She wasn't budging. She'd played Frisbee. She wanted nothing more to do with further physical activity.

"Can we come, too?" Cheyenne pleaded.

"It's time for your lunch," Glenda replied. "Come inside and eat."

"But we can eat when we come back," Durango protested.

"Do what Grandma says," Dini told them.

"Okay, Mommy," they responded in glum unison, starting toward the house with their grandmother.

I caught up with Eugene on the beach as the dogs romped in and out of the surf. I found a discarded tennis ball on the sand and tossed it high and far into the water. The dogs dove in eagerly and swam to get it. I watched them, waiting patiently for the stabbing pain in my old javelin shoulder to subside.

I still maintain Grandfather's membership in the Racquet and Tennis Club, and had invited Eugene to play squash there one afternoon last fall. Or rather I should say he'd played squash and I'd stood nailed to the floor watching him like a sweat-soaked statue. After he graduated from Yale he attended the film school at NYU for a semester before he changed direction and got an MBA from Columbia. He wanted to be a producer someday, and I had no doubt that he would be one. He was highly competitive and whip smart. Greg had met Eugene a year ago when he'd been Greg's gofer on a movie Greg had shot in Seattle for Rob Reiner with Michelle Pfeiffer. Eugene had impressed him so much that he'd offered him a job as his personal assistant. Eugene had jumped at the chance. If you lack social contacts in the movie business, there are two paths to becoming a producer—either you claw your way out of a studio mail room or you become a star's personal assistant.

"How are you holding up, Eugene?"

"Not real well." Eugene gazed out at the sailboats on the water, swiping at his eyes with the back of his hand. "Do they have any idea who killed him?"

"Not yet. But they will."

Steve swam back to us with the ball in his mouth, dropped it proudly at my feet and shook himself, treating both Eugene and me to bracing saltwater showers. Eydie was still out there swimming around, hoping for another chance. I threw the ball in her general direction. Steve dove in and swam after it, but Eydie beat him to it this time.

"Glenda wasn't real thrilled to see me," Eugene said. "Did you notice?"

"She wasn't happy to see me either. I don't think it's personal."

"No, it totally is. She thinks I'm a parasite. She doesn't understand that it takes someone with my skill set to watch out for creative people and protect your interests. Because, let's face it, when it comes to the fine print you're all a bunch of helpless children." He glanced over at me. "No offense."

"None taken."

Eydie swam back with the ball in her mouth and went running down the beach with it. Steve chased after her. In and out of the water they went, bounding joyfully. I watched them, filled with envy. Dogs live happier lives than we do. Somebody ought to write a book about that someday. Not me, but somebody.

"Tell me, Eugene, how long had it been going on?"

"How long had what been going on?"

"You and Greg."

"I don't know what you mean."

"Yes, you do. You know perfectly well what I mean."

Eugene's eyes widened in fright. "He *told* you?"

"Inadvertently. And I didn't let on that I knew."

"I don't understand. What did he . . . ?"

"Greg said to me that the two of us should go out for beers when he got back to New York from shooting the Eastwood picture."

Eugene shook his head at me, bewildered. "So . . . ?"

"So using the English language is how I make my living, Eugene. I'm making no judgments here but there isn't a straight guy in America who refers to beer in the plural. Straight guys drink beer together. Gay guys go out for beers."

"This is a real thing that you're saying to me. You're serious?"

"Do I look as if I'm kidding?"

"No," he conceded as we walked along the water's edge, the dogs romping way ahead of us. "No, you don't."

"So let's try a do-over. How long had it been going on?"

Eugene lowered his eyes, swallowing. "Three months."

"Not that it's any of my business but had Greg always been bisexual?"

"He said no. He swore to me that I was his first male lover."

"Did you believe him?"

"I did. He was very nervous our-our first time. But he told me that he'd loved me from the moment he first set eyes on me. And I knew that I loved him, too. Don't ask me why. There's no explaining such things." He glanced at me curiously. "You were aware that I'm gay, weren't you?"

"Never gave it much thought, to tell you the truth. I don't consider someone else's sexuality to be any of my business— unless it does become my business."

"I came out when I was sixteen. Got the crap beat out of me a couple of times in high school for my trouble. Being a little Asian fag boy isn't exactly the road to popularity in Fresno. But I am who I am. And I'm not ashamed."

"Nor should you be. Did Dini know about the two of you?"

"Not a chance. She has the twins and her work and her bitch of a mom."

"Do you think *she* knew?"

"Glenda? Wouldn't shock me. She has a very suspicious nature."

"Eugene, I know how upset you are right now, but I have some more bad news for you. Or at least I believe it will come as news."

"What is it?" he asked, his voice turning heavy with dread.

"Greg's autopsy revealed that he was HIV-positive. This information hasn't been made public yet. Nobody knows. But I thought *you* should know. Dini hasn't been feeling well lately. Some bug that's been going around, they thought. Anyway, she got a blood test and it turns out she's HIV-positive, too. We're assuming she got it from having unprotected sex with Greg, since she swears she hasn't slept with anyone else." I looked over at him. "Which brings us to the question of how Greg contracted it."

"Are you . . . ?" Eugene slowed to a halt, stunned, and wavered there for a moment before he sank slowly to his knees in the wet sand. "You're telling me I have AIDS?"

"I'm telling you that if Greg wasn't seeing anyone else . . ."

"He wasn't."

"You're sure about that?"

"I've never been more sure of anything in my life."

"Then you should get a blood test as soon as you get back to New York."

Eugene remained there on his knees in disbelief. "So Dini got the virus from Greg," he said slowly.

"Unless she gave it to Greg. Is there another man in her life?"

"There's no one, Hoagy. I'm around her all of the time. She's as faithful as they come." Eugene gazed up at me. "I feel perfectly healthy. But if what you say is true then I must have the virus, too. It doesn't add up any other way."

"Eugene, I don't mean to get personal . . ."

"*Personal?* Dude, we passed that signpost ten miles back."

"Have you been seeing anyone else?"

"No way. Not since I broke it off with Marc four months before I met Greg, and we'd been in a monogamous relationship for almost two years."

"What happened between you and Marc?"

"It just wasn't working anymore. Marc's an angry person, especially when he drinks. I didn't want that kind of anger in my life, so I ended it. He lives in Miami now. South Beach."

"Any chance Marc was seeing someone else while you two were still together?"

"He swore to me that there wasn't but he must have lied to me, the reckless, drunken bastard. That's the only way it . . ." Eugene fell into brittle silence. "Marc's the last person in the world who I want to talk to right now, but I ought to call him and tell him. It would be the responsible thing to do, right?"

"I'm afraid so."

"I never, ever did the bar scene, Hoagy. I'm a moral, religious person. I'm not some sleazeball home-wrecker. Greg and I genuinely loved each other." He gazed up at me beseechingly, still kneeling there in the sand. "You believe me, don't you?"

"Yes, I do. But where was this going, Eugene?"

"What do you mean?"

"We live in a puritanical society. An actor can't be one of the top three leading men in Hollywood if he's openly gay."

"Don't you think I know that?"

"So where was it going? Say you brought Steve and Eydie out to the Eastwood shoot in Death Valley. Were you planning to stay there with them for the entire six weeks?"

"Greg wanted me to."

"There are no secrets on a location shoot. You know that. If you and Greg were bunking together everyone would have found out."

Steve and Eydie came sprinting back up the beach to us and flopped down next to Eugene on the wet sand, panting.

"We had a serious conversation about that," he said, patting the wet dogs.

"And . . . ?"

"He still wanted me to come. Told me that he couldn't stand to be away from me for that long." Tears began to stream down Eugene's face. "I told him, I said, 'Greg, Dini will find out. The whole world will. You'll ruin your career.' He told me he d-didn't care because we were soul mates and were meant to be together."

"You're *sure* that Dini didn't know?"

"Hoagy, I'm not *sure* of anything," he confessed, climbing slowly back up onto his feet. We started walking our way back toward the house. The dogs ran back into the surf, barking gleefully.

"A Connecticut State Police homicide investigator named Tedone is going to interview you. I'd advise you to be candid with him. If he senses that you're withholding anything he'll latch on and won't let go."

"Are you telling me I need a lawyer?"

"Can you account for your whereabouts last evening?"

"I was in the apartment on Riverside Drive. The doorman can vouch for me. I went downstairs to sign for a script from a messenger service at around eight. The limo driver was supposed to pick it up on his way out to Sherbourne to get Greg and Dini. It was the latest draft of Dini's film. I hear she's dropped out."

"She has."

"That's too bad. It's a good script. And Jonathan Demme's a master. It would have been great for her to have a chance to work with him. Do you think anyone but Demme could have gotten that performance out of Jodie Foster in *The Silence of the Lambs*?"

"That whole Anthony Hopkins Hannibal Lecter thing wasn't too shabby either," I said, because it seemed to comfort Eugene to talk about work.

"I hear you. Scariest performance *ever*."

As we walked along the water's edge I noticed Merilee striding briskly toward us from the house. She had a strange, frightened look on her face.

"What is it?" I asked her when she reached us.

"Lieutenant Tedone just phoned," she said to me, her voice cracking. "It's Sabrina Meyer. She was just found in her room at the Sherbourne Inn with a needle in her arm. A heroin overdose, he thinks. She's dead, Hoagy. That gifted, beautiful girl is dead."

Chapter Eight

Sabrina Meyer, Hack-Hack-Hackensack native and highly promising young graduate of the Yale School of Drama, was stretched out on top of the bed in her second-floor room of the Sherbourne Inn with her head propped up against a couple of pillows. She was wearing the same linen dress she'd had on when we'd been chatting in the rose garden a couple of hours earlier, though her sandals were off now and she was sporting a fresh accessory in the crease of her left forearm—a disposable syringe that was stuck in a vein there. She'd tied off with a leather belt. The state's jowly chief M.E. was hovering over her in his scrubs and murmuring instructions at his powerfully built young deaner. Tedone stood there watching them and looking extremely miserable.

"I'm here at Lieutenant Tedone's request," I said to the uniformed Connecticut state trooper who was blocking the doorway.

Tedone turned at the sound of my voice. "You squeamish?"

"Not generally."

"Then come on in."

The trooper stepped aside and I went on in, my stomach

muscles tightening. The smell of vomit was overpowering even though the windows were wide open. A coagulating stream of it ran from the side of Sabrina's mouth and down her lovely, swan-like neck before it puddled in the indentation above her collarbone, drenching her golden ringlets. Her unseeing dark eyes were wide open, their pupils contracted to tiny pin dots.

Lulu, who does happen to be squeamish, did one lap around the room, her nose to the rug, before she went back out into the hallway to wait for me.

"Reads heroin O.D. all of the way," Tedone said to me grimly. "Her lips are already starting to develop a bluish tinge, see? Choked on her own vomit."

"Better her own than someone else's."

"Was that supposed to be some kind of a joke?"

"Forgive me, Lieutenant. I'm just trying to hold on to what's left of my sanity."

"Damned shame. Such a pretty girl. Wouldn't surprise me one bit if this turns out to be some of that 'Tango and Cash' that was floating around last year. Nasty, nasty stuff—smack laced with fentanyl, a surgical tranquilizer that's something like fifty times stronger than heroin. Addicts were dropping like flies from it all over New York City before it made its way out here by way of Bridgeport, where it killed dozens more before we finally got it off of the street. But you never get all of it."

I said nothing. Just stood there thinking about how beautiful and alive Sabrina had been two hours ago, how full of talent and dreams.

"It got its name from that piece-of-shit Stallone movie," he added.

"You say that as if there's any other kind of Stallone movie."

He looked at me in amazement. "Are you trying to tell me you didn't love *Rocky*? Everybody loves *Rocky*."

"I'm not everybody. And do we really need to have a conversation about Sly Stallone right now?"

Tedone narrowed his eyes at me. "Let's step out into the hallway. I don't like the way you look."

"How do I look?"

"Shook up."

"Really? I can't imagine why."

We went out into the wide, carpeted second-floor hallway with its Victorian urns and potted plants. Tall front windows looked out over the village green and the famous Sherbourne Playhouse.

"Chambermaid found her," Tedone informed me quietly. "She'd asked for some fresh towels earlier today. When the girl brought them up and knocked there was no answer, so she used her passkey, went in and there she was." He thumbed his jaw thoughtfully. "There's no sign of a struggle. No bruising around her upper arms or throat. Bedcovers aren't rumpled. Room's neat as a pin. It plays accidental overdose. Unless, that is, it wasn't accidental."

"Are you suggesting she committed suicide, Lieutenant?"

"I have to consider all of the possibilities."

Lulu was busy sniffing the hallway rug outside of the door to Sabrina's room. She'd gotten a whiff of something. Followed it toward the third-floor stairs, then slowly up the stairs, snuffling and snorting all of the way. At the top of the stairs she made a right turn and I lost sight of her for a while. Then I heard her start barking.

"Good girl, Lulu. You can come back now."

She came slowly back down the stairs *kerplunk-kerplunk* on her short legs, returned to me and sat on my foot, gazing up at me adoringly. "You're right, I owe you another anchovy," I promised her.

"What was that all about?" Tedone demanded.

"Basset hounds were originally bred to scent rabbits, did you know that? The only scent hound that's superior to a basset is a bloodhound."

He shook his head at me, bewildered. "They have rabbits in here?"

"Not that I'm aware of."

"Then why are we talking about rabbits?"

"I'm still thinking about it."

"About *what*?"

"If Stallone has ever made a movie that I liked. I suppose *Nighthawks* wasn't awful."

He let out an exasperated sigh. "No offense, Hoagy, but you're starting to get on my nerves."

"What, just now? It usually happens much faster. I have no idea why. I try to be helpful and cooperative. Maybe I should start bringing doughnuts to the crime scene. Do you think that would help?"

Tedone glowered at me in baleful silence.

"No one saw anybody come in or out of her room?"

"Not a soul. Nobody heard any raised voices coming out of there either. Why, do you have reason to believe someone was in the room with her?" On my silence Tedone tried a different approach. "How well did you know her?"

"Well enough to know she had a problem with heroin. She

told me she'd been clean for fifteen months, but you and I both know that a drug problem never goes away. Ever."

"That sounds an awful lot like the voice of experience."

"Only because it is."

"You think she brought the stuff with her from New York City?"

"How would I know? Did you search her bags?"

He nodded. "We didn't find anything. And the M.E. didn't find any other needle marks on her arms. He can't do a thorough search of her body until he gets her back to the morgue, but he did check the usual nooks and crannies, like in between her toes. She looks clean." He thumbed his jaw. "Any chance she was having an affair with Greg Farber?"

"Do you mean was she so despondent over his death that she freaked out and shot up for the first time in more than a year? Is that what you mean?"

"There's no need to get testy with me," Tedone fired back.

"You're right. Forgive me. It's a plausible scenario, except for two things. One, she wasn't having an affair with Greg. Two, I had a lengthy chat with her downstairs in the rose garden before I went to Point O'Woods and she wasn't the least bit upset. Just eager to get home to New York. She was hoping that the two of us could get together there sometime. Even gave me her phone number."

He raised a thick black eyebrow at me. "You mean she hit on you?"

"I don't know if I'd call it that, but she was definitely trolling."

"Trolling? I don't know what that is."

"You've never heard of trolling?"

"What I'm saying—"

"It's a bit like hitting on someone but more goal oriented. She thought that I might prove to be a useful contact."

"Because of your connection to Merilee Nash?"

"Exactly."

"So it wasn't about the two of you having sex?"

"No, it was definitely about the two of us having sex. But it's primarily transactional. That's show business, Lieutenant. All relationships are transactional in one way or another."

Tedone tilted his head at me curiously, crossing his arms before him. "Refresh my memory, will you? Where was she when Farber was getting himself murdered in his dressing room?"

"Sabrina didn't appear in act one. She watched it seated on a folding chair in the wings in full makeup and costume. She did tell me that she started downstairs during the intermission to try out some red lipstick, but that the ladies' dressing room was such a mob scene that she abandoned the idea and came right back up." I paused, recalling the way her eyes had flickered at me. "But she seemed evasive when she told me about it. As if she were holding out on me."

"Why would she do that?"

"Because she thought it would be smarter to keep her mouth shut. Obviously, she was mistaken."

"Are you telling me you think she was murdered?"

"No, I don't think she was murdered. I know she was. Sabrina must have seen Greg's killer. The killer knew it and had to take care of her. So he, or she, visited Sabrina in her room this afternoon and persuaded her to shoot up."

"How do you 'persuade' someone to shoot up?"

"Easy. By holding a loaded handgun to their head."

"Yeah, that would work pretty good," Tedone conceded. He looked down at Lulu, then back up at me. "You sound awful damned sure about this."

"Like I told you, I was with her in the rose garden before I went out to Point O'Woods. She was focused, together and clean. She wasn't shooting smack. And while we're on the subject of smack, is Romero still on ice?"

Tedone nodded. "No way he could have pulled this. Mind you, by tomorrow afternoon he'll be back out on the street. Those lowlifes always manage to scrounge bail. My sergeant's convinced that Romero is somehow the key to this whole case. Me, I don't see it. What do *you* think?"

"I think that every time I turn around, I run into him—or a headless rooster. By the way, you'll want to talk to Eugene Inagaki, who was Greg's personal assistant. He's out at the beach house with Dini. Drove out today from New York with their dogs."

"And why will I want to do that?"

"Because Eugene was Greg's lover. I'm certain he's the one who gave Greg the AIDs virus, which Greg then passed on to Dini."

Carmine Tedone stared at me with his mouth open for a long moment before he said, "Did she know that her husband's lover was another man?"

"Eugene says she didn't. And she certainly gave no indication that she did. Me, I don't know. I didn't think it was my business to ask, what with her being a grieving widow and all. That's your job."

"What about Dini's mother, Glenda?"

"As . . . ?"

"As Farber's killer. If Farber gave her daughter the AIDS virus because he was two-timing her with his gay assistant, that sure sounds like a motive to me."

I considered this for a moment. Wondered if Dini had shared the results of her blood test with Glenda before the curtain went up. Wondered if it could have been Glenda who'd killed Greg. She'd been alone in the corridor outside of the ladies' room when Dini was in there throwing up. Marty was in the men's room dealing with his own issues. Greg was all by himself in their dressing room. For a precious few seconds no one had eyes on Glenda. She definitely could have rushed in there and bashed him in the head with that brick. A few seconds were all she'd have needed.

"Plus Glenda's a retired nurse," Tedone added. "That puts her in play if Sabrina's overdose was no accident." His face dropped. "Wait, what am I saying? Glenda was at the beach house when Sabrina's O.D. went down."

"Actually, she wasn't, as a matter of fact. Glenda didn't get there until a few seconds before I did. Told me she'd been running errands in Guilfoyle."

"You're saying she could have murdered Sabrina and beaten you to Point O'Woods from here?"

"Conceivably. I wasn't in any hurry. And the guard at the kiosk had to call the house before he'd let me in. She's been living there for two weeks and would have slipped right on through."

"So the old lady's unaccounted for and therefore a suspect."

"Glenda's also fierce when it comes to protecting her daughter. Fierce, period. If it was she whom Sabrina spotted coming out of the men's dressing room then I'd totally buy her making sure Sabrina wouldn't live to tell about it." I paused, mulling it over. "Mimi Whitfield was down there during intermission, too, don't forget."

"Did she have a grudge against Farber?"

"Of a sort. She and Greg had a wild affair back in the Gerald Ford years. She was madly in love with him. Greg, not Gerald Ford—as far as I know."

"Was it mutual?"

"She told me it wasn't. That for Greg it was strictly a fling. But he did get Mimi pregnant."

Tedone's eyes widened. "Did she have the baby?"

I shook my head.

"Did he pay for the abortion?"

"They went Dutch."

"*How* many years ago was this?"

"Fifteen, maybe."

He shrugged his shoulders. "Ancient history."

"There is no such thing when it comes to love, Lieutenant. Especially if there was a baby involved."

He stood there scowling at me. "Kindly explain something to me, will you? How are you finding all of this stuff out? I'm starting to feel like you're the one who's running the case and I'm the one who's taking notes and making coffee runs. I guess he wasn't kidding."

"Who wasn't kidding?"

"Friend of mine on the job in New York City. Extremely sharp homicide detective. Very."

"'Very' as in he's extremely sharp or 'Very' as in his name is Romaine Very?"

"That's his name. Romaine Very."

"What a small, strange world we inhabit. He happens to be a friend of mine, too. Well, not exactly a friend. But our paths have crossed several times."

"That's what Ro said. He phoned me first thing this morning when the story broke. Wanted to be sure to give me some advice about you."

"Which was . . . ?"

"He said you're an annoying pain in the keester—to which I said tell me something I don't already know—but that your mind works in ways that ours don't. And by 'ours' he meant professionally trained investigators who actually know what we're doing. But he told me to do whatever you suggest, no matter how nutso it sounds, because you have freakish insights into human behavior. He figures you must have been exposed to a massive dose of radiation as a child. Some kind of cold war medical experiment or something."

"Very said that?"

"He did."

"Lulu contributes quite a bit, you know."

"Whatever. All I know is this case seemed pretty straightforward to me twenty minutes ago and now I'm so mixed up that I'm getting my first migraine headache in eleven years. So have you got any advice for me?"

"Take a couple of aspirin and stretch out for a few minutes with a damp washcloth over your eyes. The symptoms should pass pretty quickly."

"I meant about this case," he said between gritted teeth.

"Lieutenant, are you asking me what I would do if I were you?"

He sighed irritably. "I guess I am."

"Well, okay. But you won't like it."

"Now there's a huge surprise. What would you do?"

"You're serious about this?"

"Totally serious. Lay it on me."

So I laid it on him.

THE BACKSTAGE TAVERN had been situated directly across the street from the stage door to the Sherbourne Playhouse for as long as the Sherbourne Playhouse had been the Sherbourne Playhouse. It was a hybrid townie/summer theater haunt, which meant that hanging from the wall behind the battered hardwood bar, you could find anything from a vintage Carl Yastrzemski jersey to a yellowing lobby poster from an early-1930s production of *Forsaking All Others*. The Backstage was popular with local landscaping and tree crews, which explained why the sound system immediately assaulted my ears with Van Halen's "Jump" when I strolled in the door. Van Halen ranked as the preeminent rock band among local workmen who spent significant hours per day in close proximity to leaf blowers and wood chippers. I'm guessing there's a connection to be found there, but I don't really feel like committing a lot of time to thinking about it.

The Backstage's old plank floorboards smelled like beer. Its illuminated brewery signs advertised lagers that had passed out of existence decades ago. The menu was limited to burgers, chili, fried clams . . . Actually, it was kind of a dump. But it was an authentic dump. Such places are getting harder and harder to find as our world is taken over by the sterile sameness of fast-food franchises. Therefore, I cherish them.

Marty and Mimi were seated together in a booth looking

downcast. She was sipping from a mug of coffee. He was scarfing up a basketful of fragrant onion rings and washing it down with a bottle of Rolling Rock. Otherwise, it was empty in the Backstage at 3:00 P.M.

I sat down next to Mimi. Lulu started to curl up at my feet but immediately started sneezing again from Mimi's Obsession and moved across the aisle, settling under another booth.

Our waitress, a haggard type in her forties with frizzy black hair and a hostile expression on her face, sashayed over to ask me what I wanted. I ordered a Rolling Rock and three anchovies.

She glared at me. "You just say *anchovies*?"

"I did."

"How you want them?"

"On a plate. Cold, if possible. They're for my short-legged friend over there," I explained, steering her gaze across the aisle at Lulu.

"Theater people," she muttered under her breath as she headed for the kitchen.

"I don't think our waitress likes me," I said.

"Hoagy, I've been coming here for seven years," Mimi said. "She doesn't like anyone."

"Sabrina was a talented girl," Marty said mournfully. "She had a real future. This shouldn't have happened. It shouldn't have fucking happened."

"You're right, Marty, it shouldn't have," Mimi said consolingly, her long, slender fingers stroking his chubby hand.

The cynic in me wondered if Marty was playing the sympathy card to try to maneuver his way into Mimi's fancy Park Avenue panties. She was way out of his league, society wise, not to mention six inches taller than he was. But nothing deterred Marty.

"*Why* did it happen?" he demanded, his eyes tearing up. "I know she had a history with drugs, but I can't believe she'd let this thing with Greg hit her that hard unless . . . was she shtupping him?"

Mimi's face tightened ever so slightly. "I wouldn't know."

Our waitress brought me my Rolling Rock and Lulu's anchovies on a small plate, which she set before me with great disdain. I thanked her and slid the plate under the table across the aisle in front of Lulu, who promptly wolfed them down. The waitress watched, shaking her head, before she walked away, muttering some more.

"I spoke to Sabrina in the rose garden right after I talked to you," I said to Marty. "She seemed to be doing fine, but smack never lets go. One minute you're okay, the next minute you're not."

"Hoagy's right," Mimi said. "Back when I was modeling I knew three different girls who used heroin to keep their weight down. They thought they could just dabble at it. Chipping, they called it. They were fooling themselves, but they couldn't fool the camera. Their looks went just like that," she said with a snap of her fingers. "And then all three of them ended up hopelessly addicted."

I sipped my beer. "Do you think she brought it with her from New York or scored it out here?"

Marty looked at me in disbelief. "In *Sherbourne*?"

"There's heroin in all of these little towns out here."

"What's with this bullshit, Hoagy?" Marty demanded with a sudden burst of anger.

Lulu let out a low growl from across the aisle.

I told her to let me handle it. "Bullshit as in . . . ?"

"You and I both know that R. J. Romero has been circling around us for days. So do the police. Why are they even bothering to talk to anyone else? It's R.J. who killed Greg. That smug son of a bitch always had it in for him. Thought Greg was a total stiff. Yet it was Greg who got the career, the fame, the Oscar—everything that R.J. thought *he* deserved. I guarantee you he did it. And I'll bet you he shot up Sabrina, too. She must have seen him slipping out of our dressing room. So he snuck into the inn and shot her up. Or held a knife to her throat and made her shoot herself up. Whatever it took. He wouldn't care. The bastard has no conscience. Why aren't the police going after *him*, huh?"

"He has an alibi for last evening when Greg was murdered. He was getting loaded at a shooting gallery in an abandoned farmhouse on the outskirts of town. Three different people saw him there."

"You mean three different *junkies* saw him there. That's no alibi."

"He's also on ice."

"What does that mean?" Mimi asked me.

"It means that the state police arrested him late last night for stealing a truckload of Marvin windows and he's currently in their custody. He couldn't have killed Sabrina."

Marty looked across the table at me in surprise. "I didn't know that."

"Lieutenant Tedone is trying to keep it under wraps."

"Why?"

"For a reason that has nothing to do with Greg, Sabrina or any of this."

"Yet *you* know about it. How come?"

"See above, re: for a reason that has nothing to do with Greg, Sabrina or any of this."

"In other words you're not going to tell us. Whatever." Marty popped the last of the onion rings in his mouth and took a swallow of Rolling Rock, belching loudly. "All I know is that this whole thing sucks. We cleared our schedules and came out here to give a little something back. Everyone in the theater world was behind us. They all showed up. Mimi, you did an amazing job of putting it together. And look what happens. We end up with two cast members dead."

"You know what I feel like doing?" Mimi fumed. "Telling the town of Sherbourne to just go ahead and tear the damned playhouse down. I don't care anymore. For me, that dear, sweet little place will never be the same. I'm quitting as director, that's for damned sure."

"You can't quit," I said. "You just staged a major fund-raiser. What will happen to all of the money you raked in last night?"

"Someone else can take over," she said brusquely. "I'm done."

Marty lit a Lucky Strike, dragging on it deeply. "I'm done, too. I want to go home. When will they let us leave?"

"As soon as they figure out what happened."

"But that could take weeks," he protested.

"Nope, don't think so. Mimi, you got Dini a room at the Sherbourne Inn yesterday afternoon so that she could take a nap before the performance. Would you happen to remember what floor it was on?"

"The third floor, I think. I'm not positive."

"I am," Marty said. "She was right across the hall from me on the third floor. So what?"

"Does she still have her room key?"

"I have no idea," Mimi said. "They'd know at the front desk."

The tavern's door opened now and in walked Merilee with Dini, who looked ashen-faced and devastated.

Marty's face immediately crumpled at the sight of her, his eyes moistening. He went to Dini and gave her a bear hug. "How are you holding up?"

"I'm hanging in," she answered softly.

"What are you doing here? Why aren't you at the beach with the kids?"

"Lieutenant Tedone asked me to come. He wants to see me at the theater."

"All of us," Merilee said. "Cast, crew, everyone."

"What for?"

"He wants to conduct a reenactment of the intermission," she explained. "Nail down exactly where everyone was when Greg was murdered, what they were doing and who they were doing it with."

"Whose dumb-ass idea is this?" Marty wondered.

"Probably some crazy fool who was exposed to too much radiation as a child," I said.

"Eugene's walking the dogs on the green," Dini said. "My mother and the girls are there, too. Do we have time for a cup of tea?"

"Of course," Merilee said.

"Have a seat right here," Mimi said, sliding out of the booth. "I have to go back to my office."

"And I have to head back to the inn to take a humongous dump," Marty said. "Those onion rings went right through me."

"Thank you for sharing that with us, Marty," I said.

"Yes, thank you, Marty," Merilee said. "You're a dear."

He took Dini's hands in his and squeezed them, gazing at her with deep concern. "Will you be okay?"

"I'll be fine," Dini assured him. "See you in a little while."

Marty and Mimi paid their checks at the cash register and took off. Merilee and Dini sat in the booth with me. Lulu joined us now that Mimi and her Obsession were gone, curling up at Merilee's feet.

The frizzy-haired waitress bustled over, her sour face filling with sorrow. "What can I get you, hon?" she asked Dini in a kindly voice. "On the house."

Dini smiled faintly. "Could I have a cup of hot tea, please?"

"You got it. How about you, Miss Nash?"

"An iced tea, please."

"Another Rolling Rock?" she asked, glaring at me.

"You talked me into it."

"And how about your little friend? Three more anchovies?"

Lulu let out a whimper from under the table.

"That would be a yes. And also a bowl of water, please."

"The anchovies aren't on the menu. I don't know what to charge you."

"Why don't you just charge me for two extra Rolling Rocks?"

She mulled this over before she said, "I can live with that." Then she went off to fill our orders.

"I still say she doesn't like me."

"What have they found out about Sabrina?" Merilee asked me.

"Lieutenant Tedone is trying to convince himself that she was so distraught over Greg's death that she injected herself with a fatal dose of 'Tango and Cash.'"

"I take it you're not buying that."

"Sabrina was clean and together. She had everything to live for."

"Everything," Merilee acknowledged. "What do *you* think happened?"

"I think she accidentally saw what happened and that Greg's murderer wasn't taking any chances. So he—or she—visited Sabrina in her room at the inn and took care of her. That's how I see it, and Lulu's backing me up."

Dini frowned at me. "How is she doing that?"

"We have our methods."

Merilee smiled. "Hence the anchovies?"

"Hence the anchovies."

The waitress brought us our orders, plopping Lulu's plate and water bowl in front of me. I slid them under the table.

"You want anything else just say so, hon," she told Dini in a kindly voice before she walked away.

I watched Dini sip her tea. "Seriously, how are you?"

She shrugged her narrow shoulders. "Busy. There's a lot to take care of. I spoke to our lawyer about Greg's financial affairs, his estate, all those sorts of things, cold as it sounds. And I've asked Eugene to look for another job. The girls will miss him. They adore Eugene. Hell, even *I* like the two-timing gay bastard."

I exchanged a look with Merilee before I said, "You knew about the two of them?"

Dini nodded glumly. "But only after being completely in the dark for months. God, I'm such a clueless idiot. And now . . . now I've got a great big *HIV-positive* stamp on my forehead. No one will ever hire me again."

"That's not true," Merilee said.

"And no man will ever want to make love to me."

"Also not true."

"Get real, Merilee," she said heatedly. "I'm about to become America's most famous leper. I may as well go home to Siler City with Mom and raise the girls there, assuming they don't set up a roadblock at the Chatham County line to keep us out."

"I can't even imagine how devastated you must be feeling right now," Merilee conceded gently. "But it's not 1983 anymore. They've made amazing strides in treating HIV patients. And everything's changed since Magic Johnson went public two years ago. What he did was huge. People are so much more educated and aware now."

"Did your mom know about Greg and Eugene?" I asked Dini.

Dini's pale blue eyes studied me. "Why are you asking me that?"

"Because she shot some pretty chilly looks at Eugene when he showed up with the dogs today. She's also no fool, I've noticed."

Dini didn't give me an answer. Just sat there in tight-lipped silence.

I tried a different approach. "There was tension between you and Greg during rehearsals. Was that because you'd found out about Eugene?"

She nodded her head ever so slightly. "A few days before we came out here to start rehearsals a friend of ours called me one afternoon and mentioned that she'd just seen Greg and Eugene coming out of Eugene's apartment on Bank Street in the West Village, which I thought was kind of strange because Greg was supposed to be at his dermatologist on Madison Avenue in midtown. I called the dermatologist's office. The receptionist said that Greg had called that morning to reschedule the appointment. When he got home later that afternoon I asked him how his appointment had gone. He said it went fine. He flat out lied to me, Hoagy. That was something he'd never, ever done before," Dini recalled, her eyes flashing with anger. "And I didn't let him get away with it. I told him that he and Eugene had been seen together coming out of Eugene's apartment. I demanded to know what was going on."

I leaned forward slightly. "And . . . ?"

"He came clean. Said that he'd never loved a man before but that he loved Eugene 'body, mind and soul' and that Eugene loved him, too. I was so-so *flattened* that I seriously considered pulling us out of *Private Lives*. But we'd made a commitment to Merilee. We couldn't bail on her at the last minute. Who would she get to replace us, Farrah Fawcett and Ryan O'Neal?" Dini paused to sip her tea. "And my mother *did* know, in answer to your question. She caught them hugging in the den one morning a couple of months ago. They weren't aware that she saw them, and she didn't tell me about it. Not until today."

Merilee frowned at Dini. "Why didn't she tell you at the time?"

"She didn't think I could handle it emotionally. That I'd shatter into a million pieces." Dini's voice was weary with resignation. "She thinks I'm a delicate porcelain child, as you may have noticed." She looked across the table at me. "Eugene told me that you and he had a serious talk on the beach. Tell me what you honestly think. Was he aware that he was carrying the virus?"

"I don't think so. He fell to his knees in genuine shock when
I told him about the M.E.'s findings. And swore to me up, down
and sideways that he'd never have had unprotected sex with
Greg if he'd known."

"And do you believe him?"

"I do."

"I feel the same way about Greg. He wouldn't have had unprotected sex with me if he'd known he was carrying it. He
wasn't capable of doing something that evil. He wasn't a bad
person. He was just . . ." She broke off into hopeless silence
for a moment. "Greg was a mess. He thought of himself as a
good husband, which he wasn't. He was a cheat, and all torn
up inside about it. He also knew perfectly well that he and
Eugene could never come out as a couple. So, for the sake of
his career, and for the twins, he told me he thought we should
stay together. And he actually expected me to go along with the
idea. He even said that I could see someone else if I wanted to.
'How big of you, you piece of shit!' I screamed at him. I told
him I wanted a divorce right away. I promised him I'd keep
quiet about why we were splitting up. And I would have, too.
As far as I was concerned it was nobody else's business that I'd
lost him to *Eugene*."

"You couldn't have kept a lid on it," I told her. "The instant
you filed for a divorce the tabloids would have dug and dug
until they found Eugene's ex-lover, Marc, down in Miami and
dumped a pile of cash in his lap."

"I know," Dini acknowledged bitterly.

"And now every dirty detail is guaranteed to come out. Face
it, Dini, this is going to be even bigger than Magic Johnson.

After all, no one on the Lakers ever drowned in the basement of the Fabulous Forum. Or at least not that we're aware of."

"I know that, too. Same as I know that being HIV-positive isn't a death sentence. I can continue to work. I can even be in a loving relationship with another man. My life isn't over."

"That's all true," Merilee said to her encouragingly.

"So why does it feel like it is?" Dini wondered, choking back tears.

Merilee took her hand and gripped it, her own eyes brimming with tears.

The tavern door opened now and Glenda came bustling in with Durango and Cheyenne.

"Ah, *here's* Mommy," she exclaimed with forced gaiety. "I told you we'd find her."

The girls ran to her. Dini put her arms around them and hugged them tightly.

"Eugene has driven back to the beach house with the dogs to wait for us," Glenda informed Dini in a cool voice.

"Thank you, Mother. Would you like to sit down?"

Glenda didn't budge. Just stood there staring at me with an extremely guarded expression on her jowly face. "Lieutenant Tedone asked me to deliver a message to you."

"He did? What is it?"

"I'm supposed to tell you that it's showtime."

Chapter Nine

He'd brought back everyone to the Sherbourne Playhouse who'd been there last night. Mind you, when I say everyone I don't mean the likes of Jackie O or Gentleman Gerry Cooney. The celebrities who'd packed the house weren't summoned back. By everyone I mean Mimi, who looked extremely tense. Her jaw was clenched, her sky blue eyes narrow slits. I mean Cyril Cooper, aka Coop, the ponytailed crew chief, and the volunteers who'd been helping him ready the stage for act two while Greg Farber was busy drowning to death downstairs in the men's dressing room. Corralling all of them had taken some doing. Nona Peachy, for example, had already split town. Tedone had to put out an APB on the Brown drama student. A Rhode Island state policemen pulled her over on I-95 near Watch Hill.

"I was on my way to visit a friend whose family has a beach house there," she told me, wide-eyed, as we all stood clustered on the stage. "Never been so scared in my life."

"You have no reason to be. The lieutenant is just being thorough."

"That's easy for you to say. You didn't have a cop chase you down on the highway with his siren blaring."

By everyone I mean Dini, who looked frightfully pale under the stage lights as Glenda stood watch over her, acting highly indignant. Cheyenne and Durango stood very quietly together near Dini, holding hands. By everyone I mean Merilee, who was calm and unruffled in that way she has of being calm and unruffled at uncommonly tense moments. My ex-wife would have made an excellent NFL quarterback or astronaut, I've always felt. By everyone I mean Marty, who wasn't calm at all. He was chain-smoking Lucky Strikes, his left knee jiggling, jiggling.

Lieutenant Tedone slurped from a carton of coffee and paced the stage, shooting baleful looks at me. "We've put a lot of people to a lot of trouble. I sure hope you know what you're doing."

"That makes two of us, Lieutenant."

"Okay, that right there—what you just said—that didn't fill me with a ton of confidence."

"I apologize. There's absolutely nothing to worry about. Actually, that's not true. There's quite a bit to worry about. But before this hour is over I assure you that you'll have your killer in custody."

The stage set from act one—the French hotel terrace—had been resurrected. The backdrop was in place. Coop's stagehands had fetched the furniture and props from the warehouse and positioned them just as they'd been last night. Everything was exactly as it had been, minus the rain pouring down. Also minus Sabrina, who was no longer seated in the wings on a folding chair in her frumpy Louise costume, due to her presently being on an autopsy table in the M.E.'s lab. Nona Peachy had been immediately recruited to take her place, maid's costume, frumpy wig, the works.

The dressing rooms downstairs were all prepared. The makeup tables were fully stocked. The act two costumes were hanging in readiness—minus Greg's tweed suit, which, like Sabrina, was presently at the M.E.'s office. As was Greg.

"Darling, is this absolutely necessary?" Merilee wondered when I asked her, Dini and Marty to change back into their act one costumes.

"I'm afraid so. We need to reenact what happened down to the tiniest detail. I'll stand in for Greg." Although I refused to put on makeup. I also couldn't wear Greg's act one costume, which didn't come close to fitting me. Instead, I wore the ensemble that I was already wearing—my persimmon linen blazer, vanilla pleated slacks, pink shirt, striped bow tie and white bucks. This is why it's important to dress appropriately for any occasion that might arise, no matter how unexpected or bizarre.

The curtain was up. Mimi sat in the same front row seat she'd been in last night, as did Glenda and the twins.

"Are we ready?" asked Tedone, who stood in the wings with Sergeant Angelo Bartucca and a half-dozen troopers in uniform.

"I believe we are," I said.

"Then let's do this, okay?"

By "this" he meant run the final lines of dialogue from the end of act one between Sybil (Merilee) and Victor (me). Victor says, "To absent friends" and raises his champagne glass. Sybil raises her glass and says, "To absent friends." They both laugh rather mirthlessly, then sit down on the balustrade with an incredibly stubborn ham of a basset hound parked between them. There was no denying her so I didn't even bother to try. "It's awfully pretty, isn't it?" Sybil says, gazing out at the view. "The moonlight, and the lights of that yacht reflected in the water—" And Victor says, "I wonder who it belongs to."

And then the curtain slowly fell, just as it had last night, minus the roar of applause.

"Okay, let's everyone stay put for a moment, please!" Tedone called out before the crew sprang into action to clear the stage for act two. "Just to be perfectly clear, Miss Hawes, where were you and Mr. Miller while Miss Nash and Mr. Farber were saying those final lines?"

"Right here in the wings next to Sabrina," Dini recalled.

"That's right." Marty nodded his balding head. "Right here next to . . . sorry, hon, what's your name?"

"Nona."

"Is that short for Winona?"

"It's not short for anything. It's my name, Mr. Miller."

"Call me Marty," he said, grinning at her.

"You don't mind if I continue, do you, Marty?" Tedone asked him.

"Not a bit, Lieutenant. Go right ahead."

"So you two were still here. You hadn't gone downstairs yet." Dini nodded. "That's right."

Now Tedone turned to the show's director. "What happened next?"

"Coop and his crew had fifteen minutes to transform this stage from a rain-soaked balcony in the south of France to Amanda's flat in Paris," Merilee replied. "They also rigged up a rain canopy over the sofa so that we could sit on it without getting soaked. A brilliant bit of improvising, Coop. I meant to tell you last night and didn't get the chance."

"Weren't no big thing," Coop said modestly.

"Do it now," Tedone told him.

"Do what, boss?" Coop asked him.

"The set change. Same way you did it last night, canopy and all. On the clock. Can you spare Nona?"

"If you're telling me she needs to stand in for Sabrina then so be it. Okay, gang!" Coop called out. "Let's get it on!"

And with that his crew immediately sprang into action. One team of stagehands hoisted the backdrop of the harbor and lowered the back wall of Amanda's Paris flat into its place, complete with windows overlooking the city. One team hustled the balustrade and terrace furniture offstage while another came in with the sofa and end tables, setting them on their marks on the floor. As they worked, swiftly and silently, the Sherbourne Playhouse's lighting man, an old pro, shifted the moonlit terrace into the interior of an apartment at 10:00 A.M.

Meanwhile, the play's three surviving stars, Greg's stand-in and Lulu hustled down the spiral staircase to the dressing rooms. Mimi and Glenda followed, as did Lieutenant Carmine Tedone and Sergeant Angelo Bartucca. Even though the dimly lit basement corridor was no longer flooded, Tedone asked Mimi to turn the sump pumps on.

She frowned at him. "Whatever for?"

"I want the noise level down here to be the same as it was last night."

"Of course." Mimi flicked them on, one by one.

"I'm not comfortable doing this," Glenda complained, raising her voice over the rumble of the pumps.

"Doing what, Mrs. Hawes?" Tedone asked.

"Leaving the twins upstairs without someone to look after them. Sabrina I knew. I don't know this Nona person. And that stage crew is a motley group. Some of the language I've been hearing . . ."

"A trooper will watch over them, okay? Sergeant, have a man sit with the twins."

Bartucca squeezed past Glenda and darted up the stairs to take care of it.

Reluctantly, Glenda stayed put, glancing around warily.

"We're just trying to be accurate, Mrs. Hawes," Tedone explained. "You folks encountered major pandemonium down here. The flooding. The racket that those pumps were making . . ."

"And everyone was concerned about Dini," I said. "That's why *you* came down here, wasn't it, Glenda?"

"Well, yes," she acknowledged. "My girl was running a fever of a hundred and two point eight that afternoon, and even though she'd gotten some rest at the inn before the show I thought she still seemed unsteady on her feet during act one."

"How are you feeling now?" Tedone asked Dini.

"How do you *think* I feel?" Dini demanded.

He reddened. "Sorry, I just meant . . ."

"No, *I'm* sorry, Lieutenant. I didn't mean to bite your head off. I feel better, thank you. My fever seems to have broken."

"Well, that's good." Tedone turned to me and said, "And you came down here to . . . ?"

"Check on the flood conditions with Mimi. We got down here just in time to see Marty come sloshing out of the men's dressing room in his boxer shorts and charge straight across the hall into the men's john to attend to his roiling innards.

The men's dressing room door was open. Greg was changing into his tweed suit. I waved to him and called out that the show was going great."

"As did I," Mimi said.

"And how did Mr. Farber seem?"

"Excited."

"Very much so," Mimi agreed.

Tedone ran a hand over his face, mulling it over. "So he was changing costumes while Mr. Miller was experiencing his, um, intestinal difficulties. Meanwhile, in the ladies' dressing room . . ."

"We were changing for act two," Merilee said. "Or trying to. It wasn't easy. It's a tiny space. Hoagy and Mimi had stopped by. And so had Glenda, who insisted upon checking on Dini."

"She was very shaky," Glenda said defensively. "You weren't feeling well, were you, dear?"

"No, I wasn't, Mother," Dini allowed. "I felt weak and nauseated. In fact, I had to dash across the hall to the ladies' room to throw up."

Glenda nodded. "I went with her and waited right outside of the bathroom door. I could hear her in there, even over the racket of those sump pumps."

Tedone turned to Mimi. "What did you do next?"

"Started back upstairs. I was hoping our plumber would show up with more sump pumps."

"And how about you?" he asked me.

"I chatted briefly with Merilee in the ladies' dressing room while she was changing. Then Dini returned from the bathroom, which was my cue to leave. Glenda's as well."

Tedone turned his attention to Glenda. "Mrs. Hawes, were

you outside of the ladies' room the entire time your daughter was in there?"

"Yes, I was."

"So you can vouch for the fact that she didn't leave the ladies' room."

Glenda looked at him in confusion. "And go where?"

"Say, into the men's dressing room to kill her husband."

Glenda's eyes flashed at him angrily. "She went from her dressing room to the ladies' room and then back to her dressing room. She didn't visit Greg. And she for darned sure didn't kill him."

"Even though he'd been cheating on Dini with another man?" I pressed her. "Even though he'd given her the AIDS virus?"

Now it was my turn to get a nasty look from Glenda. "I don't know if you're trying to bait me, young man, but I don't appreciate your insinuations."

"Duly noted. And thank you for calling me 'young man.' That doesn't happen very often anymore unless I visit my parents at Essex Meadows. Lieutenant, if I may . . ."

"Go ahead," Tedone grunted.

"It seems to me that we have a generous choice of plausible scenarios here," I said over the rumble of the sump pumps. "But, first, may I ask you to turn those damned things off? I'm getting this weird grinding sound inside of my head and I'd swear I'm starting to hear '*Paul is dead, Paul is dead, Paul is dead* . . .'"

"You're hearing *what*? Wait, never mind. I don't even want to know." Tedone went around and flicked them off.

Blessed silence.

"Thank you, Lieutenant," I said. "Dini came out of the ladies' room after being sick and went into the dressing room with Merilee to change, which meant it was time for me to leave. Mimi had already gone back upstairs. Glenda was heading up the staircase herself. I was just about to join them when Marty came out of the john and asked me if I thought it was safe to flush the toilet. We talked briefly about septic overflow— although not briefly enough to suit me—before he returned to the men's dressing room from the john. That's when he called out to me. When I went in there I discovered Greg lying face-down on the floor in the floodwaters with the back of his head bashed in. Now let's examine the players here . . ." I looked from Merilee to Dini to Marty, then at Glenda before I settled on Mimi. "We know, for instance, that you're an excellent candidate. You were down here at the time of Greg's murder and you've been harboring a deep hatred for Greg for years. The man broke your heart into a million pieces when he didn't say, 'I love you, Mimi. Let's have our baby together. Marry me.'"

"*What?*" Dini shrieked. "Hoagy, what in the hell are you—?"

"Sorry, Dini. I assumed you knew. I guess he kept that particular nugget to himself. It so happens that Greg and Mimi were a sizzling hot item back when Greg was starring in a revival of *Picnic* and she was at the height of her cover girl fame. It also happens that he got her pregnant."

Dini looked at Mimi coldly. "So I gather."

"It was before you two got married," Mimi said defensively. "He told me you split up after you left Yale."

"We went our separate ways for a while," Dini conceded.

"All I'm saying is he was flying solo when it happened. He

wasn't cheating on you with me. Not like he was cheating on you with *Eugene*."

"Okay, that's not helping, Mimi," I said.

"Well, *excuse me*," she shot back. "But this is your doing, not mine. Why did you even have to bring it up?"

"Because it speaks to motive. You loved him."

"I did. But he didn't love me. When I told him I was pregnant the thought never occurred to him to do anything other than get rid of it."

Glenda bristled. "It's not an 'it.' A fetus is a human life, and abortion is murder."

Mimi rolled her eyes at her. "Glenda, I've had a hard couple of days, and I already can't stand you, so kindly spare me the pro-life diatribe or I swear I'll smack you right in your fat face."

"All right, let's settle down, ladies," Tedone growled. "Go on, Hoagy."

"My point, Mimi, is that last night was finally your chance to get even with him. But after talking to you in your office this morning I don't believe that you killed him."

She tilted her head at me curiously. "And why is that?"

"Because it was you who brought up that Greg got you pregnant. I didn't know a thing about it. What killer goes out of her way to drop a motive on herself? Have you ever heard of a killer doing that, Lieutenant?"

"Can't say as I have," he replied, thumbing his jaw.

"Besides, Mimi, you couldn't possibly have gone to Sabrina's room at the inn this afternoon and forced her to shoot up that fatal dose of heroin."

Tedone frowned at me. "Why not?"

"Because if she'd been in Sabrina's room today Lulu would

have smelled her Obsession and started sneezing her head off. She's highly allergic to it."

Merilee nodded. "That's true, Lieutenant, she is. And she's very, very reliable when it comes to her allergies, aren't you, sweetness?" She bent down and gave Lulu a pat. Got a tail thump and low whoop for her trouble.

"Therefore, Mimi's in the clear," I said. "Which brings us to Dini and Glenda—either acting alone or together. Personally, I've been leaning toward the idea of together. Let's set the scene again. I was in the ladies' dressing room with Merilee. We'd closed the door. Mimi had gone upstairs. Marty was in the john. Greg was alone in the men's dressing room. The only person who can vouch for Dini actually being in the ladies' room at that particular moment is Glenda, who was standing right outside of the ladies' room door. What mother wouldn't lie to protect her daughter if that daughter, say, went flying out of the ladies' room and whacked her cheating, bisexual husband in the head with a brick?"

"And then what about Sabrina?" Tedone asked. "Who killed her?"

"Glenda, of course. Dini was at the beach with the twins. That left it up to Mommy. Don't forget she arrived at the beach house at virtually the same time I did, which leaves her unaccounted for at the time of Sabrina's death. And she's a retired nurse who knows her way around a hypodermic needle."

Glenda glared at me with total contempt. "You have all of the answers, don't you? And just exactly where did I get the heroin that I used to kill that unfortunate young woman?"

"That's a very good question. Where did you?"

"Young man, I didn't like you when I first met you. And now I'm liking you even less."

"I'm sorry to hear that. But thank you again for calling me 'young man.'"

"And I *don't* care for the way your little dog is staring at me."

"That's because you're behaving toward me in a hostile manner. She's very protective of me. And she's not little. She's just short." I turned back to Tedone. "Sabrina told me she got an idea during the act break that a slash of bright red lipstick would make Louise, the frumpy maid, look even frumpier. She started down the spiral staircase to the ladies' dressing room to test it out on Merilee, but encountered such a crowd of people that she turned right around and went back upstairs. But I'm positive she saw something while she was down there. She wouldn't tell me what, but she was afraid. I could see it in her eyes. My guess? She saw Dini coming out of the men's dressing room after Dini had just brained Greg. And Dini saw her. Dini's a big star. She could have derailed Sabrina's career with one snap of her fingers. So Sabrina kept her mouth shut. Sabrina would have kept it shut, too. But you couldn't take that chance, could you, Dini? So you had your mom go to the inn and inject her with that 'Tango and Cash.' Glenda, how did you manage to shoot her up without a struggle?"

"I do not know what you are talking about," Glenda said to me in a slow, clear voice, as if she were addressing a recalcitrant child. "I did not purchase any heroin. I did not go to the inn. I was shopping in Sherbourne. There are shopkeepers who can vouch for me."

"Perhaps they can," I conceded. "But they can't vouch for

where you were ten minutes before you got there. It all adds up, Lieutenant. After all, Dini *had* been wronged by Greg in the worst way imaginable." I looked over at Dini. "Are you going to come clean or are you going to stand there and tell us that you *didn't* duck into the men's dressing room and smash Greg in the head with that brick again and again and—"

"Hoagy . . . ?" Merilee's hand was on my arm. "She's been through a lot. Must you be so harsh?"

"We're not playing beanbag, Merilee. And Greg was my friend. I liked the guy. He messed up big-time, but he didn't deserve to drown facedown in that filthy water."

"Well, I don't feel a drop of sympathy for him," Glenda said heatedly. "And I resent you suggesting that he deserves any."

Tedone ran a hand over his layered mountain of black hair. "We know where that 1924 Tuttle brick came from. There's a pile of them out in the courtyard. But what was it doing in the men's dressing room?"

"Propping up one of the dressing table legs, Loo," his young sergeant replied. "The table's all rickety now."

"That's a good catch, Ang."

"Plain as day," he said modestly.

"Seems like an open-and-shut case to me, Lieutenant," I concluded. "Dini smashed Greg in the head with that brick until he toppled over facedown in the floodwaters. No one heard it happen because the sump pumps covered the sound of the attack. By the time Marty found him and called out to me, the poor guy was already dead. We were too late to save him."

Marty nodded gravely. "Too late."

"And then Glenda coldly eliminated Sabrina, who had witnessed Dini leaving the dressing room."

Tedone considered this a moment before he turned and looked at Lulu. "Your dog . . ."

"What about her, Lieutenant?"

"This afternoon, she went up the stairway to the third floor of the inn from Sabrina's room and started barking. How come?"

"Because she smelled the traces of gunk that were still on Glenda's shoes from the flooded dressing rooms last night. I've no doubt that Glenda cleaned them thoroughly. Just not thoroughly enough to deceive a top-shelf scent hound like a basset. You should have worn a different pair of shoes today, Glenda."

"These are my only comfortable pair," she said defensively. "My feet bother me. Besides, I already told you. I never went near that girl's room."

"And yet Lulu followed your scent up the staircase from Sabrina's room to the room that Dini used to grab a nap, the one right across the hall from Marty's room. You went up there to retrieve something that Dini had left behind."

"It didn't happen that way," Glenda maintained, shaking her head. "Dini didn't kill Greg. I didn't kill Sabrina. You're wrong about *all* of this."

"I was figuring a new guest would have moved into the room, but the manager informed me that you folks still had the key. So you went up there after you killed Sabrina to fetch whatever it was that Dini had forgotten to take with her. What was it, Glenda? What did she forget?"

"I didn't kill that girl!" Glenda's face was getting tomato red. "I was never there at all, I swear!"

"That's the only thing I still can't figure out, Lieutenant. What it was that Dini left behind," I said as Dini gaped at me in fright. "I'd suggest your men search every inch of that room, because aside from that one nagging detail this case is as tight as a drum."

"It is not!" Marty spoke up angrily. "It's total bullshit! Dini would *never* kill Greg. She couldn't. It's not possible."

Tedone raised an eyebrow at him. "Do you know something more than you've told us, Mr. Miller? Did you see or hear anything?"

Marty shook his head. "No, nothing. Just what I've already told you."

"Then you can't help her, Marty," I said. "No one can. Here are your killers, Lieutenant. Glenda committed an act of premeditated murder, so she'll never see the outside of a prison again. Dini is another story. What do you think, will she be tried for manslaughter?"

"That'll be up to the district prosecutor," Tedone replied. "I wouldn't rule out second-degree murder."

"Whatever she's charged with, she's a beloved movie star and will doubtless become a figure of great sympathy, what with the extenuating circumstances and all. Greg having a gay lover and giving her the AIDs virus. Her being a single mother who has to raise the twins on her own now. Hell, a slick criminal defense attorney might even convince a jury that it was *Greg* who committed the crime against *her*."

"I doubt that," Tedone said. "It's manslaughter at the very least."

"How many years behind bars will she be looking at?" I asked him.

"Somewhere in the neighborhood of eight. Maybe five if she's lucky enough to get a sympathetic parole board."

"*And* lucky enough to get her proper dosage of HIV meds while she's in prison," I pointed out. "Penitentiaries are hotbeds of theft and black marketeering when it comes to AZT. Not exactly the healthiest environment either. There's the starchy, greasy food, lack of fresh fruit and vegetables. Plus those places are petri dishes for germs. Bronchitis and pneumonia always going around. I'd have major, major health concerns if I were you, Dini. And with your mother in prison God knows who'll end up looking after the twins. I imagine they'll be placed in foster homes. Maybe the same foster home if they're lucky. It sure would be a shame to separate them. But, hey, Greg got what he deserved for what he did to you. I can see your side of it. Truly, I can."

"But, Hoagy, I didn't kill him!" Dini cried out helplessly. "I *swear!*"

"Ladies, I'm afraid we have to continue this conversation at the Major Crime Squad headquarters in Meriden," Tedone said.

Dini blinked at him, aghast. "I'm under arrest?"

"No, but I am bringing you and your mother in for official questioning. If I were you I'd contact your lawyer. I'd also suggest that you say nothing further."

"B-But she didn't do it!" Glenda sputtered. "*I* didn't do it!"

"Please follow me," Tedone said, starting for the spiral staircase.

"Hoagy, this can't be happening!" Merilee protested, utterly distraught.

"I'm afraid it is, Merilee. I'm sorry."

"The twins," Dini said to Merilee pleadingly. "Would you . . . ?"

"We'll bring them home to the farm with us," Merilee promised her. "We have plenty of room, and they'll be fine there until this horrible mistake gets straightened out."

"I *didn't* kill him!" Dini sobbed. "Hoagy, I'm telling you the truth. You've *got* to believe me!"

"I wish I did believe you, Dini. I've always liked you. And you've been a good friend to Merilee. But you have to admit how painfully obvious it is that you're the one who grabbed that brick and smashed Greg over the head again and again and—"

"Stop this, damn it!" Marty erupted furiously. "Don't you talk to her that way! *She's* the victim here, you coldhearted prick. Don't you see that? Don't you possess so much as one single fucking ounce of human decency?"

I gazed at him sympathetically. "I'm sorry, Marty. Truly, I am. I should have taken into account how hard this must be for you. I completely forgot."

"Wait, forgot what?" Tedone asked me.

"That he and Dini were romantically involved back when they were in drama school together."

"We lived together for an entire semester." Marty smiled at Dini fondly. "I still think that's the happiest I've ever been in my life."

Tedone peered at him. "You two lived together? I didn't know that."

"She took up with Greg after me," Marty said. "Before me she'd had a fling with that lowlife greaseball Romero. Dini and every other girl in our class, including Merilee."

Merilee's jaw tightened, but she remained silent.

Marty pulled a Lucky Strike from the breast pocket of his

mothball-scented vintage checked sports jacket and lit it with a butane lighter, dragging on it deeply as he continued to look fondly at Dini. "I thought we were for keeps, you and me. But it was rock-solid Greg who was right for you. Not someone who's as screwed up as I am."

"Your personal hygiene may have had something to do with it, too," I suggested. "Have you considered that?"

Marty looked at me, bewildered. "My what?"

"Did I just say that out loud? I do that sometimes. Sorry. I took a lot of psychedelics in my youth."

Marty turned back to Dini. "It's funny how wrong you were about him. Greg *was* just as screwed up as I am. The only difference between us was that I was the better actor. *Am* the better actor. Audiences really, really liked him. He was very good at convincing them that he was a decent guy. He genuinely believed he was a decent guy. But that's not acting." He looked over at Merilee, his eyes coldly serious. "Tell me the God's honest truth. Do you think Greg could have played Willie Loman?"

Merilee said, "I really don't see how that has anything to do with—"

"*Could* he?" Marty demanded.

"No, I don't," she replied, uneasiness creeping into her voice. "I don't think he was capable of understanding Willie's despair."

"*I* understand it." Marty stabbed himself in the chest with a stubby thumb. "I live with it *every day of my life*."

"You've never had a long-term relationship with anyone else after Dini left you for Greg, have you, Marty?" I said.

"They don't seem to work out," he said with a shrug. "So?"

"So maybe that's because you've never stopped loving her.

You have your little flings with bovine teenaged waitresses but the only woman who you've ever loved, and still love, is this one standing right here." I looked over at Dini, who was staring at Marty wide-eyed, not blinking, like a terrified bunny. "You'd do anything for her, wouldn't you?"

Marty stubbed out his cigarette on the basement floor with his shoe. "If I could. So?"

"So let's climb out on a shaky limb for a second and say that Dini and Glenda *are* actually telling the truth—that after Dini threw up in the ladies' room she returned directly to her dressing room. At that particular moment, Marty, you were . . . where were you?"

"Parked in the men's room. I had the shits, remember?"

"Right. The Lieutenant and I even saw the evidence to prove it. But what we don't have is proof that you were in the men's room that entire time. Such as, say, *before* Dini got sick, when Glenda had barged into the dressing room to check on her. Mimi and I had stopped by, too, which means there was a brief window of time when there was no one in the corridor. You could have raced across the hall from the john into the men's dressing room—unseen—bashed Greg's head in, dumped him facedown in the floodwaters, raced back into the john—unseen—closed the door and stayed in there while Dini was throwing up in the ladies' room and Glenda was hovering outside of the ladies' room door. Then Dini returned to the dressing room and Mimi and Glenda headed back upstairs. I was just about to follow them when you emerged from the men's room a second time and engaged me in that stimulating conversation about septic overflow. Then you returned to the men's dressing room, pretended you'd just discovered Greg and called out my name. I came running. We tried to save him but we were too late. Very clever on your part, Marty, except for one small, unforeseen circumstance."

"What circumstance would that be?" Tedone asked me.

"Sabrina had decided to experiment with that slash of bright red lipstick. On her way down the stairs to the ladies' dressing room she saw you, didn't she, Marty? Saw you darting back into the john in your billowy boxer shorts after you'd killed Greg."

"You tell me, Hoagy," he responded. "You're the one who's spinning this fable. I don't have the slightest idea what you're talking about."

"You're a huge star. Sabrina didn't want to make any trouble. Didn't want to get involved, period. So when I asked her if she saw anything she kept her mouth shut. But you couldn't count on her keeping it shut, could you? Eventually, under repeated questioning, she was going to contradict your version of the events and testify that you *weren't* in the john that whole time—which would have blown a great big hole in your story and ruined everything."

Marty said nothing in response. His face had gone blank.

"You've used drugs off and on for years. I have no problem believing that you scored some 'Tango and Cash' back when it was around. No problem believing you carry it with you wherever you go. It's your suicide kit, isn't it? In case you decide you can't cope with the total misery of your life for one minute longer. Like father, like son. I also have no problem believing you talked your way into Sabrina's room at the inn, sobbing about your good friend Greg. You sobbed and you sobbed. In fact, you were such an emotional wreck you told her that you'd decided to shoot up. You talked her into shooting up with you, didn't you? That was a genuinely cruel thing to do to her, Marty. She was fragile."

"We're all fragile," Marty said in a quiet, faraway voice. "Besides, she wasn't exactly that hard to convince."

The dimly lit corridor fell eerily silent now.

"Marty, *you* did this?" Dini's voice was barely more than a whisper. "How could you . . . ?"

"He took you away from me!" Marty cried out. "I wake up miserable every day. I stuff my face. I get drunk. I get high. I fuck stupid, doughy waitresses. But it doesn't help. Nothing helps. *Nothing.* The pain never goes away. *Never.* Sure, I've managed to keep going. And I've survived, in my own pathetic way. But when I found out that he'd cheated on you with *Eugene* and that you're now HIV-positive, there was *no fucking way* I was going to let him get away with that. He was rotten to the core, Dini. He didn't deserve you. He deserved to die."

Dini began to weep. "Oh, Marty, you fool . . ."

"Did you say anything to him?" I asked.

Marty looked at me curiously. "Did I what?"

"Did you say anything to Greg?"

"You mean did I deliver a soliloquy? What was there to say? It wasn't as if I planned it or anything. Sitting there on the hoop I suddenly realized that he had to die. The clarity was remarkable. So I poked my head out, saw that the coast was clear and ran across the hall. Grabbed that brick from under the table leg and bashed the hell out of him with it. After he fell facedown into the floodwaters I ran back across the hall into the men's room and closed the door, like you said." Marty looked at all of us as we stood there staring at him. "I *had* to do it, don't you understand?"

"I do understand, Marty," I said. "The same way I understand that his killer had to be you."

He frowned at me. "Why do you say that?"

"Because you were the only person down here who nobody had eyes on for those few precious seconds that you needed—aside from Glenda, that is, who was parked outside of the ladies' room all by herself listening to Dini vomit. But there's no way in the world that Glenda would have ever killed Greg."

Glenda looked at me in surprise. "Why not?"

"Greg was the father of your grandchildren. He was family."

She lowered her eyes. "It's true, he was."

"And then there's that footprint scent in the carpet from Sabrina's second-floor room to the third floor. Lulu wasn't following Glenda's shoe prints to Dini's room. She was following *your* highly scented flip-flops to your room across the hall from hers, which is where you went after you killed Sabrina." I paused, feeling a heaviness in my chest. "I blame myself for that. I should have kept an eye on her. Brought her to Point O'Woods with me. Only I didn't, and I'll never, ever forgive myself for that. For as long as I live, whenever I hear Erroll Garner or watch Buster Keaton, she'll be in my thoughts. And I have *you* to thank for that. But she seemed okay out there in the rose garden, writing her postcard to her mom. So I left her there. And while I was driving down to the beach she went back up to her room and you knocked on her door. Marty, you've just made it sound as if you didn't plan to kill Greg. That it was a sudden moment of . . . what did you call it, clarity? But not Sabrina. Killing Sabrina was cold, calculated, and incredibly cruel. You preyed on her weakness. You're a great actor, Marty. One of the best. But you're not one of the good guys. *This* is who you are."

Marty had started to breathe more heavily. Beads of perspiration were forming on his forehead. "My career is all I have," he said vehemently. "Without it I'm just another fat nobody. Sabrina would have taken it away from me if she'd talked."

"Don't ever do that around me again, Marty," I said.

"Don't do what?"

"Try to put the onus on Sabrina. She's not to blame. *You* are."

"Is that a fact?" he shot back at me, his voice suddenly turning cold as ice. He'd assumed a different role now. He was no longer a pathetic, heartbroken figure. He was a wily, cornered predator. The transformation was so swift it was breathtaking. "Prove it."

"What do you mean by that?" Tedone asked him.

"I mean there are no bruises on Sabrina's body. Prove it wasn't an accidental overdose. Prove that I was even there."

"They'll find your prints all over her room," Tedone pointed out.

"So what? I had a fling with her. We were getting it on."

"In your dreams." Mimi looked at Tedone. "I heard him try to hit on her the first night of rehearsals. Sabrina blew him off."

Tedone mulled this over. "Still, he does raise a reasonable point. She was a recovering addict, alone in a strange town. She'd just been through a heavy emotional experience. She was depressed."

"She wasn't depressed," I insisted. "She was in good spirits when I left her there in the rose garden. Her career was about to take off."

"*That's* what freaked her out." Marty nodded sagely. "I've met a ton of actors who are terrified of success. They're much more comfortable being failures."

"I've met writers like that, too. They feel much safer wallowing in a nice, soft cushion of self-pity. So what? We're overlooking what really matters here."

Marty peered at me. "Which is what?"

"The ripe scent of your flip-flops that Lulu followed from Sabrina's room up the stairs directly to your room on the third floor. The scent that meant Sabrina wasn't alone in her room. *You* were there. And you're not really going to do this, are you?"

"Do what?"

"Expose yourself as a no-good, lying weasel right here in front of Dini. You love her, or so you keep telling us. You love her so much that you killed Greg because of what he did to her. So now's the time to man up, Marty. Man up and tell us the truth."

"The truth?" Marty let out a huge sigh, his chest heaving as he breathed in and out. "I went down to Sabrina's room in tears. And I wasn't acting. I truly was a wreck. I *killed* Greg. I-I told her I wanted to shoot up. She tried to talk me out of it. Wanted to take me to the hospital. She was so sympathetic and caring. A real nice girl. And I was sorry I had to do what I did to her. You can choose to believe that or not. I'm guessing you won't."

"Good guess."

"I told her that the only way I'd make it through my grief over Greg's death was if she'd shoot up with me. I talked her into it. I'd brought my suicide kit with me from New York, just like you said. I bring it with me wherever I go, because I never know when I'm going to crash and burn. A couple of packets of 'Tango and Cash.' Disposable syringes. A spoon. A length of rubber tubing to tie off. I cooked it and filled two syringes. I tied off with the tubing. She tied off with a belt. We counted to three and then . . ."

"And then . . . ?"

"She shot up and I didn't. Just gathered up my kit and left. She was probably a goner by the time I was back upstairs in my room."

"What did you do with your kit?" Tedone asked him. "The other syringe, the spoon, the heroin . . . ?"

"It's in a suitcase in my room."

Tedone peered at him in surprise. "It's evidence. Why didn't you get rid of it?"

"Get rid of it?" Marty's eyes widened. "No way. I'd freak out if I didn't have it with me."

Tedone continued to peer at him, trying to understand this famous, gifted Oscar and Tony Award–winning actor Martin Jacob Miller. I could tell from the expression on his face that he wasn't having any luck. "After we found Miss Meyer's body we knocked on the door to your room. You weren't there. Where were you?"

"Taking a walk around the village." Marty shrugged his soft shoulders. "Contemplating what a miserable son of a bitch I am."

We all fell silent. Dini stood there grief-stricken. Both Merilee and Mimi had their arms around her.

"It's time to head upstairs, Mr. Miller," Tedone said finally.

Marty nodded defeatedly. "Sure, whatever you say. Am I under arrest?"

"When you're under arrest you'll know it."

"How?"

"Because I'll tell you. Right now, I'm taking you in for formal questioning."

"Wait, are all of those media people still out there?" The thought of this seemed to greatly distress Marty.

"I'm not going to put you in handcuffs," Tedone said to him in a calming voice. "We're just going to walk out to my car and go for a ride, okay?"

Marty lit another Lucky, his hand shaking, and dragged on it deeply before he said, "Sure, okay. But before we go upstairs is it okay if I use the john down here? My insides are about to explode. I should never eat onion rings."

"Not a problem," Tedone said. "Only, wait a sec . . ." He patted Marty down. The checked sports jacket, starched white shirt, pleated cream-colored slacks, even his argyle socks.

"You think I'm wearing an ankle holster or something?" Marty asked, watching him in amazement.

"Mr. Miller, I don't know what to think. I just do my job."

"I'll be right out."

"Take as long as you need."

Marty went in the men's room and closed the door.

The rest of us moved down the basement corridor toward the stairs.

"He's loved me all of these years?" Dini sounded dazed and forlorn. "*That's* why he killed Greg?"

"He was defending your honor," I said. "Rather chivalrous in a sick, twisted sort of way."

"Marty's always been partial to grand, Shakespearean gestures," Merilee recalled. "He's also a devotee of Dumas—*The Three Musketeers, The Count of Monte Cristo.* And he loves *The Prisoner of Zenda* with Ronald Colman. I swear he knows that movie line for line."

"Big Errol Flynn fan, too, or so he told me."

That was when we heard the thud.

It came from the men's room.

Tedone raced back there. "You okay, Mr. Miller?" he called to him through the door.

There was no response.

I joined Tedone. "Marty?" I hollered.

Still no response.

Tedone flung open the door and Marty came tumbling out headfirst onto the hallway floor. That thud we'd heard was the sound of his head thumping against the door when he'd passed out. His jacket was off, his shirtsleeve rolled up so that he could tie off with a length of rubber tubing. The needle was still in his arm, the vomit still spewing from his mouth as he gagged, shuddered and then went still. Dini and Mimi both screamed. Merilee just stood there and stared. She isn't given to screaming.

Cursing, Tedone hollered up the stairs for an EMT crew.

Glenda, the retired Chatham County school nurse, knelt with a grunt, feeling for Marty's vital signs. "They can't save him," she said heavily, her gaze fixed on the rubber tubing that was still knotted tightly around his arm. "He's gone. More of that same 'Tango and Cash,' I imagine."

Tedone peered in dismay at the kit on the men's room floor. "He didn't have that on him when I just patted him down. I'd stake my career on it."

"He planned ahead, Lieutenant," I said quietly. "Hid it in there when we were still upstairs. He knew."

"He knew *what*?" Tedone demanded angrily.

"That he wasn't going to get away with it."

Dini fell to her knees, resting her cheek on Marty's chest despite the stench of his vomit, and began to sob. They were painful, gut-wrenching sobs. I stood there looking at her and wondered how she was going to put her life back together. Her husband was gone. Her health was compromised. What would she do? Take the twins and flee home to Siler City with Glenda? Stay put in New York and slug it out? My guess was that she would stay put and fight to keep working. She came across as fragile, but she was a battler to her core. All great actresses are.

I knelt and put my hand on her shoulder. "Dini, I'm sorry I had to get a little rough with you and your mom, but I needed to piss him off. It was the only way."

Dini sniffled softly. "I understand."

Glenda didn't. Just glared at me with a Vulcan death stare. She wasn't the forgiving type.

I helped Dini to her feet.

She stood there, swiping at her eyes, then moved away from Marty toward the staircase. "Mother, shall we take the twins back to the beach house now?"

"Certainly," Glenda responded. "But Eugene has to leave."

"Absolutely. I'll tell him to go."

"We'll be needing statements from both of you," Tedone said to them. "Can you stick around for another day before you go back to New York?"

"Of course, Lieutenant."

"Thank you. I'll be in touch. And I'm sorry that it . . . that it came to this. I should have been able to stop it from happening."

"Don't blame yourself," Dini responded quietly. "There was no way you could have known he was planning to kill himself."

"I'm going to follow them down to the beach," Merilee said to me. "Do what I can to help out. I'll see you later at the farm, okay?"

"I'll be there. Wait, hang on, there's something on your cheek . . ." I leaned over and kissed it and gave her a hug.

She hugged me back, tightly, for so long that I thought she was never going to let me go. When she did her green eyes were shining at me. "Thank you, darling."

"For what?" I asked, getting lost in them.

"For being you."

Then she went up the spiral staircase behind Mimi, Dini and Glenda. I stayed down there with Tedone and the Oscar and Tony Award–winning actor Martin Jacob Miller, who none other than Kazan himself had said was the best Willy Loman ever.

Tedone looked at me, nodding his head. "Okay, I get it now."

"Get what, Lieutenant?"

"Very told me you'd irritate the hell out of me but that I'd end up thanking you."

Lulu let out a low moan of protest.

"You and your partner both, I should say." He bent down and patted her. She thumped her tail happily. Tedone watched her carefully, frowning. He seemed a bit disappointed. "That's it? There's nothing more?"

"Such as . . . ?"

"I thought maybe she'd bark three times or give me her paw or something."

"You watched too much TV when you were a kid, too, Lieutenant. Lulu's not Lassie or Rin Tin Tin. She's a real dog."

"Sure. Right. Don't know what I was thinking." But he still seemed disappointed.

"Besides, I'm the one who should be thanking you."

"For what?"

"You've kept us safe and relatively sane these past twenty-four hours by keeping Romero on ice."

His face fell. "Yeah, about that. I'm afraid he's been arraigned on the grand theft charge, which means he'll be out on the street as soon as he raises bail. Then it'll take him about a minute and a half to find a shyster lawyer who's dying to get his name in the tabloids. Your troubles with Romero are far from over."

"I know."

"What are you planning to do about it?"

"You're not hinting again at that arrangement your brother Pete and I discussed, are you?"

"Well, yeah."

"Tell me, Lieutenant. What would you do if you were me?"

Carmine Tedone suddenly looked very weary. "I can't answer that. Not officially. If it was my woman whose life and career were being threatened I'd do *something*, I'll tell you that much. I wouldn't just sit back and let that creep drag her through the mud. But you don't strike me as the type who'll let that happen. You know how the world works."

"You're right, I do. And I'm sorry that I do. I was a whole lot happier before I did."

"You and me both, brother."

Chapter Ten

It was late afternoon by the time Merilee joined up with me back at the farm. It seemed so deliciously tranquil there. The breeze off of Whalebone Cove was rustling the leaves of the apple trees. The ducks were quacking in the pond. The chickens were conversing in their coop. Merilee announced she was going to take a good, long walk in the woods. Lulu decided to keep her company. I decided to pull my manuscript from the deep freeze and sit down with it at the writing table in the chapel, fully intending to escape back into my fictional universe while the Ramones blasted from my turntable.

But it was no use. There was still too much ugly reality somersaulting around in my head.

When the business line rang I had no doubt who it would be. Same hoarse, phlegmy voice. Same mocking, insinuating tone. "That you, smart guy?"

"It's nice to hear from you again, Mr. Romero. I've missed our little chats. It's been a while."

"That's because I've been locked away in a padded cell. I'm guessing you already knew that, seeing as how it was the cops who showed up for our eleven o'clock meet, not you. You ratted me out, you flaming piece of shit."

"Consider yourself lucky that's all I did."

"What's *that* supposed to mean?"

"It means you're still alive. There was a very strong case being made by a lot of very influential people that you should be taken out. If it weren't for me you'd be dead right now."

He let out a laugh. "Like Greg and Marty are, you mean?"

"And don't forget Sabrina Meyer."

"Never heard of the bitch."

"How did it make you feel?"

"How did what make me feel?"

"When you heard that Greg and Marty were dead."

"I didn't *feel* anything. Why would I?"

"They were friends of yours."

"Bullshit. They were never my friends. When I needed their help, a good word whispered in the right director's ear, they both turned their backs on me. So I couldn't care less that they're dead. Fuck them." He fell silent on the other end of the line for a moment before he said, "Nothing's changed except for the price tag, smart guy. It's gone up to thirty-five thou. I'm giving you one more chance to make good on your word. Tonight, nine o'clock, same place. Show up with anything less than thirty-five thou and I go straight to the *Enquirer* and tell them the whole, sad story about the night when the great big movie star got high on coke, ran over a Yale professor and left him for dead. Is it a deal?"

"Fine," I said. "It's a deal."

With a click the line went dead.

I went inside the house, found a manila envelope and tucked the Lyme–Old Lyme phone book inside. It made for a good, snug fit.

That was when Merilee and Lulu came home from their walk. Merilee flopped down at the kitchen table, pooped. Lulu took a long drink from her water bowl before she flopped down, too.

"How was your walk?"

"Good. It gave me some time to think. Let's sit out on the deck. There's a nice, cool breeze."

"All right."

We sat on the Adirondack chairs overlooking the cove and watched the osprey circle overhead, floating on the breeze.

"Time to think about what?"

"Marty, mostly," she replied. "He always resented Greg's good looks, Greg's ease around other people and, more than anything else, that Greg took Dini away from him. Marty channeled his pain and his loneliness into amazing performances. Became one of our finest actors. Yet his resentment never, ever stopped eating away at him. How heartbreaking is that?"

"From where I sit? Pretty damned heartbreaking."

"Greg was a solid pro. He deserved his Oscar. But he rarely made a movie or play better simply by being in it. Marty did. Marty was a genius. But no one will think of him that way now. They'll remember him as the crazy man who murdered Greg Farber and then died of a drug overdose while he was sitting on the toilet, just like Lenny Bruce and Elvis." She let out a long sigh of regret. "Is it too early for a glass of chilled Sancerre?"

"It's never too early for a glass of chilled Sancerre. Stay put, I'll get it."

There was a half-empty bottle in the refrigerator. I grabbed it and two glasses. Dug the remains of several cheeses from the cheese drawer, Lulu's anchovy jar, a knife and a hunk of baguette. Set it all on a tray and carried it outside. Merilee got busy unwrapping the cheese. I poured the wine, handed her a glass and fed Lulu an anchovy.

"I ran into Mr. MacGowan when I was out walking," she said, sipping her wine. "He asked me how Quasimodo was fitting in."

"Damn. He promised me he'd keep his trap shut."

"What happened to Old Saxophone Joe, darling?"

"You don't want to know."

"Yes, I do."

"Well, okay. R.J. showed up here when we were away and beheaded him. I gave Joe a proper, respectful burial. I can show you where the marker is."

"Thank you, I'd appreciate it. I want to plant something there for him."

"And then I asked Mr. MacGowan if he could spare a rooster."

"Hence Quasimodo."

"Hence Quasimodo."

She smeared some Maytag blue on a piece of bread, nibbled on it and sipped her wine, eyeing me over the rim of the glass. "Is R.J. out on bail?"

I nodded.

"He's called again, hasn't he?"

"He has. And he still wants his hush money. I'm giving it to him tonight. He'll use it to pay off whomever it is he owes it to. It's my sincere hope that he will then go to jail for a solid decade for stealing that truckload of Marvin windows. It's also my sincere hope that this nostalgic Yale Drama School reunion of yours has run its course and that I can go back to work on my book."

"I'm coming with you tonight."

"Absolutely not. You can't."

"Why not?" she demanded indignantly.

"He could be setting a trap. Have a photographer with him. You can't be seen with him, Merilee. Can't be mixed up in any of this. Just leave it to me, okay? After tonight, this mess with R.J. will all be over."

OUR RENDEZVOUS SPOT by the old brass mill's front gate was no more picturesque or fragrant than I remembered it from last time. Again, I spotted him by the orange glow of his ciga-rette.

"Give it here," he said right away, meaning the money.

"I guess this means we're dispensing with pleasantries," I said, handing him the manila envelope.

He ripped it open greedily, shining his flashlight inside. "What the hell's this?"

"The current Lyme–Old Lyme phone directory. And they're damned hard to come by, so I want it back."

"Where's my fucking money?"

"There is no money, R.J."

R.J. gaped at me in disbelief. "What do you mean there's no money? What the fuck is this?"

"This is me doing something that absolutely no one else thinks I should do. I'm giving you one last chance to walk away. If you ever come near Merilee again, I'll kill you. If you try to peddle your version of that hit-and-run incident to the tabloids, I'll kill you. If you so much as *speak* to a tabloid reporter, I'll kill you. I'll get away with it, too. The police will even thank me. If you're too stoned or screwed up or just plain stupid to realize that I'm trying to do you a favor, then so be it. But I need to give you this chance. You see, I don't want you on my conscience. It's already plenty crowded, and getting more crowded each and every day," I said as my thoughts turned to Sabrina Meyer from Hack-Hack-Hackensack and her bright future that was never, ever to be.

R.J. was still gaping at me. "You're playing *head games* with me? I owe some very dangerous people that money. I promised I'd have it for 'em tonight. I *need* that money!"

"Too bad. You're not going to get any."

"You don't get to walk away from this, bro." His voice had turned menacing now. "For this, I have to mess you up."

In response, Lulu moved around behind him, a low growl coming from her throat. She has a very menacing growl for someone who once got beat up in Riverside Park by a Pomeranian named Mr. Puffball.

"Tell her to cut that out," R.J. warned me, his eyes widening.

Lulu moved in closer, baring her teeth at him, her growl now a full-throated snarl.

"I ain't kidding around. She comes any closer I'll blow her head off!"

Actually, what he did was kick her. Or I should say he tried to. Not a wise move. All he got for his trouble was Lulu's jaws clamped hard around his bare ankle.

Cursing angrily in pain, R.J. reached into his waistband for his Glock. That was when his nose collided with my right fist. He went straight down, blood gushing from his nose. The Glock clattered away on the pavement. He lunged for it.

He never made it.

Two shots rang out from the darkness. R.J. took the first one in the chest, the second in his throat. He let out a soft gurgle, shuddered and then he was gone.

I whirled—and my flashlight's beam found Merilee standing there behind me in a safari jacket with the farm's .38 clutched in her hand and a strangely calm expression on her face. Lulu ran to her and tried to climb up her leg, whooping and moaning. Me, I went and took the gun from her. Then I heard rapid footsteps on the pavement. Someone was running toward us. It seemed Merilee wasn't the only one who'd decided to tail me that evening.

Pete Tedone knelt beside the late R. J. Romero, then looked up at us inquiringly.

"Merilee Nash, say hello to Pete Tedone, Lieutenant Tedone's brother."

"Very pleased to meet you, Mr. Tedone," she said quietly.

"The pleasure is all mine, Miss Nash. Which one of you . . . ?"

"I did," I said quickly.

"He did not," Merilee insisted. "I'm the one who shot him."

"Well, you'd both better go right home and stay there. I'll take over from here." Tedone pocketed R.J.'s Glock. Then took the .38 from me and gripped it in each hand before he stuck it in R.J.'s dead hand and fired it once into the air. "Okay, here's what happened," he explained. "You hired me to make the payoff and it went sour. He pulled his .38, the two of us grappled for it and it went off."

"But that .38 is registered to Merilee," I pointed out.

"He stole it from the farm when he killed your rooster."

"We didn't report it stolen."

Tedone waved me off. "Don't worry about that. This is what you're paying me for." He pointed to the manila envelope tucked under my arm. "Is that the drop money?"

"No, it's the Lyme–Old Lyme phone book."

Pete Tedone frowned at me. "Where's the money?"

"There is no money."

"You showed up here without any money?"

"That's correct."

He took a deep breath, letting it out slowly. "I got to tell you, Hoagy. For a bright guy you sure know how to act stupid."

"So I've been told."

"And now I want you to beat it. Both of you. You two were never here tonight, understood?"

We understood. Started back toward the old stone bridge with Lulu trotting along ahead of us. Merilee had left her beat-up old Land Rover next to the Jag. Tedone's Chevy Tahoe was parked alongside. When I looked back at him, Tedone was crouched over R.J.'s body with his flashlight, going through his pockets. Merilee didn't look back. She never looked back.

"MERILEE, ARE YOU okay?"

"I'll be fine, darling. Although I do wish you'd stop asking me that."

It was two hours later and I was still waiting for an emotional response from her. Grief. Horror. Something, anything. So far, she'd just behaved as if it were any other night. Pronounced herself starved. Put away a late supper of Caesar salad and four-alarm chili washed down with two frosty bottles of

Bass Ale. Had herself a leisurely soak in the claw-footed tub. Now she was snuggled in bed in the moonlight with a cool breeze coming off of Whalebone Cove. The only indication that she was the least bit bothered about having pumped two shots into R. J. Romero earlier that evening was that she asked me if I'd mind keeping her company for a bit. I sat in the worn leather easy chair next to the bed sipping a Bass with Lulu snoring contentedly at my feet.

"Merilee, I still have one more thing I need to ask you."

"Fine. What is it?"

"Why did you do it?"

She gazed out the window for a long moment. "As an act of mercy," she replied softly. "You didn't know the young R.J. The wild and gifted and beautiful R.J. The man who couldn't miss. This R.J. was so strung out, desperate and sick that he'd become a menace to everyone, including himself. I did the humane thing by putting him down."

"You loved him, didn't you?"

"With all of my heart and soul," she acknowledged readily. "When he and I split up I didn't think I'd make it. It took months and months for the wounds to heal. And years before I believed it was even possible to love a man again."

"What changed your mind?"

"You did, silly."

"Good answer."

"Hoagy, would you do me a huge favor and get under the covers with me for a little while?"

I stripped to my boxers and slid under the covers with her. She rolled onto her hip, her head resting on my chest. I put my arm around her and held her.

"I still carry it around all of the time," she confessed. "Not a day goes by that I don't think about it. We *killed* that poor man."

"You weren't driving. He was."

"But I could have called the police. Given the family some comfort. I could have done *something*."

"You're absolutely right. And tonight, you did."

"I had to. He killed Old Saxophone Joe. You know who was next, don't you? Lulu. He would have killed Lulu, I swear. And then he'd have gone after you. Do you know what would happen to me if I lost you? I'd fall to pieces."

"Why, Merilee, you almost sound as if you're still a tiny bit fond of me."

"Oh, shut up. I had to do it, Hoagy. I had to protect my home. H-had to protect my-my . . ." And then they came. The tears. I held on to her tight as she cried. She cried for the Yale School of Architecture professor whom they'd left for dead that night so many years ago. She cried for the gifted but uncontrollable wild beast from Federal Hill whom she'd loved and lost and tonight had put down like the rabid animal he'd become. She cried for Greg. She cried for Dini, who'd lost her husband, and for Durango and Cheyenne, who'd lost their father. She cried for Marty, who couldn't cope with his broken heart and bitterness and, after years and years of trying to destroy himself, had finally succumbed to the darkness and destroyed Greg. And Sabrina. She cried for herself and for her fellow members of their uncommonly gifted class at the Yale School of Drama. There had never been a class nearly as talented before or since. And maybe that wasn't such a bad thing. I've begun to think that strange, horrible things can happen when there are too many talented people in the same place at the same time. Somebody ought to write a book about it someday. Not me, but somebody.

She was still crying when the early predawn birds began to chirp. Didn't cry herself out until Quasimodo let out his first hoarse crow of the morning, which was so pathetic that it made her laugh through her tears. "I just can't get used to him. I keep expecting to hear Old Saxophone Joe."

"That makes two of us." Lulu let out a low, unhappy grunt from the leather chair. "Correction, three of us."

Shortly after that, Merilee closed her eyes and fell into an exhausted sleep. As she lay there in my arms, it occurred to me that despite all of our ups and downs—the years of loving each other, hating each other—that I still didn't know Merilee Nash. None of us really know the person whom we love. That's nothing but a sweet illusion. Then I closed my own eyes and, smiling, fell asleep with the stranger in my arms.

About the author

About the book

Read on

Insights,
Interviews
& More . . .

Meet David Handler

About the author

D. L. Drake

DAVID HANDLER has written ten novels about the witty and dapper celebrity ghostwriter Stewart Hoag and his faithful, neurotic basset hound, Lulu, including the Edgar- and American Mystery Award–winning *The Man Who Would Be F. Scott Fitzgerald*. He has also written eleven novels in the bestselling Berger & Mitry series and two novels featuring private eye Benji Golden. David was a member of the original writing staff that created the Emmy Award–winning sitcom *Kate & Allie*, and has continued to write extensively for television and films on both coasts. He lives in a 200-year-old carriage house in Old Lyme, Connecticut. ∾

Meanwhile,
Twenty Years Later . . .

Truly, it never occurred to me when I retired the Stewart Hoag series in 1997 that twenty years later I would find myself returning to my witty, dapper celebrity ghostwriter and his faithful, neurotic basset hound Lulu. The advent of the Internet, cell phones and viral videos, not to mention the blood sport competition between twenty-four-hour cable news channels, had convinced me that the era of celebrity secrets was over and out. And so was Hoagy.

And yet here we are again.

Hoagy and Lulu returned from their two-decade hiatus last year in *The Girl with Kaleidoscope Eyes* and now you've been reading and, I hope, enjoying its sequel, *The Man Who Couldn't Miss*. Meanwhile, as I sit here writing these words, I'm busy plotting out yet another adventure.

How did this happen? Dan Mallory, who was then an executive editor at William Morrow, talked me into it by throwing a wicked curve ball at me: Reboot the Hoagy series as period novels that take place way back when I was originally writing them. As in, say, back in 1992, when I wrote on a Mac LC that was connected to a printer but not to my phone line. Why would it be? I had no dial-up connection to anything or anyone. E-mail wasn't yet a part of everybody's life. Neither were cell ▶

phones. The Internet, Google, Facebook, Twitter? All way off in the future. In 1992 I had a landline and an answering machine. Also a fax machine, churning, churning. God, I hated that damned fax machine.

I was instantly enthralled by Dan's idea. Couldn't resist the opportunity. And I can't begin to tell you how much fun I've had writing Hoagy and Lulu again. Especially Lulu. I really missed her.

Ever since I resumed the series, many readers and fellow authors have asked me whether it was hard to find Hoagy's voice again. After all, I'd written eleven Berger & Mitry Dorset novels since I'd said goodbye to Hoagy in *The Man Who Loved Women to Death*, as well as a pair of Benji Golden detective novels and a couple of thrillers. How did I pull it off?

Actually, it was no problem at all. I just sat down and started writing him again as if I'd never stopped. That's because Hoagy's voice is *my* voice. He is genuine, unfiltered me. Oh, sure, I do a huge amount of polishing and rewriting. Trust me, I'm not nearly as witty and perceptive as Hoagy is morning, noon and night. Sometimes I can be a droning bore. Ask anyone who knows me. They'll tell you: "Sometimes David can be a droning bore." But there was no groping around blindly in the darkness to find him again. He was right there. He's been there all along. Same Hoagy. Same me.

Actually, allow me to rephrase that. Same Hoagy. *Not* the same me, which is something I've found to be quite fascinating. I mentioned that I stopped writing Hoagy twenty years ago. What I didn't mention was that I *began* writing Hoagy long before that. I started my first draft of *The Man Who Died Laughing* way back in 1985 when I was still in my early thirties. It was only the second novel I'd ever written, and my first crime novel. I recall deciding that I would make Hoagy approximately my age. I also decided that as the series progressed I would obliquely reflect the passage of real time. Over the course of the eight original novels, Hoagy changes from someone who is beginning to notice that thirty is receding in his rearview mirror, to someone who sees forty getting closer and closer in the headlights up ahead. He definitely gets older.

Lulu? She never gets any older. Can't. I didn't want to deal with the reality that dogs age faster than people do and—if the series lasted for more than ten or twelve years—she'd, well, die. I remember asking my original editor, Kate Miciak, what the rules were about the aging of pet sidekicks. After an incredibly long silence she responded: "Um, David, there *are* no rules."

To me, Hoagy's voice seems exactly the same now as it did before. Nothing has changed. He's still staring at forty. Still wondering if he'll ever be able to rediscover the elusive writing talent that prompted the *New York Sunday Times Book Review* to label him "the first major new literary voice of ▶

the 1980s." Yet, as I was working away on *The Girl with Kaleidoscope Eyes*, I slowly became aware of a reality that should have been incredibly obvious to me from page one.

Hoagy's the same age, but I'm not.

I'm twenty years older. That's twenty years of wisdom and bewilderment— heavy on the bewilderment. Twenty years of successes and failures. Twenty years of joy and agony. Twenty years of friends and loved ones lost. I'd written fifteen books during those twenty years. Liked most of them. Some I didn't. It never occurred to me that any of this would make Hoagy's voice any richer or more insightful.

And yet it apparently has.

When I finished the first draft of *The Girl with Kaleidoscope Eyes*, I e-mailed the manuscript to my agent, Dominick Abel. When I got home from my Sunday evening yoga class a few days later, there was a voice mail on my cell phone from Dominick, a very proper Brit who *never* calls me on the weekend. When I played it back I heard him say, "H-Hello, David . . ." His voice was choking with emotion. I immediately panicked, thinking the next words I was about to hear were "grapefruit-sized tumor." But no, he was calling to tell me that he'd just finished reading the new Hoagy and that it was "just . . . just *wonderful*." When Dan Mallory finished reading this book, *The Man Who Couldn't Miss*, he wrote me to tell me how much the relationship between

Hoagy and his beloved ex-wife, Merilee Nash, has grown. He used words like *poignancy* and *maturity*.

"*Maturity?*" *Me*?

I'm beginning to realize that these new Hoagy novels have more going for them than they did before. More emotional weight. I know, I know—it came as a complete surprise to me, too. They're still funny. Or at least *I* think they're still funny. Hoagy is still Hoagy. Lulu is still Lulu. And I'm still the same smart aleck who was always getting sent to the principal's office for being "a disruptive influence" and constantly "sassing the teacher." I haven't changed a bit. Really, I haven't.

I'm just a teeny, tiny bit older, that's all.

David Handler
Old Lyme, Connecticut ∿

More from David Handler

THE GIRL WITH KALEIDOSCOPE EYES

Once upon a time, Hoagy had it all: a hugely successful debut novel, a gorgeous celebrity wife, the glamorous world of New York City at his feet. These days, he scrapes by as a celebrity ghostwriter. A celebrity ghostwriter who finds himself investigating murders more often than he'd like.

And once upon a time, Richard Aintree was the most famous writer in America—high school students across the country read his one and only novel, a modern classic on par with *The Catcher in the Rye*. But after his wife's suicide, Richard went into mourning . . . and then into hiding. No one has seen him or heard from him in twenty years.

Until now. Richard Aintree—or someone pretending to be Richard Aintree—has at long last reached out to his two estranged daughters. Monette is a Martha Stewart–style lifestyle queen whose empire is crumbling; and once upon a time, Reggie, a gifted poet, was the first great love of Hoagy's life. Both sisters have received mysterious typewritten letters from their father.

Hoagy is already on the case, having been hired to ghostwrite a tell-all book about the troubled Aintree family. But no sooner does he set up shop in the pool house of Monette's Los

Angeles mansion than murder strikes. With Lulu at his side—or more often cowering in his shadow—it's up to Hoagy to unravel the mystery, catch the killer, and pour himself that perfect single-malt Scotch . . . before it's too late.

"*The Girl with Kaleidoscope Eyes* is Handler at his best, drawing us close to his hero and the hero's beloved pooch, Lulu, while introducing us to some of the scuzziest Hollywood characters this side of James Ellroy."
—CTNews.com ∾

Discover great authors, exclusive offers, and more at hc.com.